Table of Contents

Chapter 1

It was a cold winter night in Brooklyn in the month of January when Cat was awakened from her sleep to the sound of her mother and aunt having a heated discussion. Cat was the complexion of a brown paper bag with long hair that touched her waist, and tight eyes that changed colors when the light hit them, much like a cat. This was, in fact, how she became nicknamed, Cat. Her mother always said her eyes reminded her of a cat.

Cat could hear her mother saying, "I am not like you! I am so tired of you guys always trying to put me down for having six kids by six different men! It is not my fault that all your men always wanted me." Cat was 16 years old, and she was old enough to know where this conversation was going. Cat wanted to get the gossip, and getting the gossip was what she was known for. She always pretended to be cleaning or doing something around the adults so she could hear their conversations. However, this particular night was not just a normal conversation. It was more like World War II, but only with two Black women. As Cat quietly tiptoed down the stairs and sat on the bottom stair, she could hear her mother's voice elevate as she enunciated every syllable.

Then, out of nowhere, her mother shouted, "If it wasn't for your father molesting me, I wouldn't have gotten pregnant at the age of 16— and your mother acted like she did not know by covering it up and making me get an abortion!"

Cat's aunt Sharon, who was the youngest of all her aunts and uncles, and was referred to as 'Ms. Got it Together,' was the one person Cat looked up to. The

1

Transition of a Butterfly

Transition of a Butterfly

Dr. Saniyyah Mayo

Published by Mayo Publishing
12223 Highland Ave. #106-580 Rancho Cucamonga, California 91739
saniyyahmayo.com

Cover and Interior Design by Dimitrius Mayo

Library of Congress Control Number: 2017906803

Published in the United States of America

ISBN- 978-0-9891580-1-5

family referring to Aunt Sharon as 'Ms. Got it Together' was their way of insulting her, but Cat saw it as a compliment. Cat watched her aunt Sharon struggle through law school while everyone in the family talked about how she thought she was better than them. Despite her family's jealousy and rude remarks toward her, she thrived. Sharon was exactly who Cat aspired to be like when she grew up. Cat had heard this conversation more than enough times to know there was no new gossip to be heard. Cat already knew that multiple family members molested her mother as a child and that she lashed out at anyone she came in contact with, despite the fact that it was her mother that she was really angry with.
Cat woke up the next day at 6 am sharp as she always did. Cat knew if she didn't wake up her younger brothers and sisters and feed and change the twins, who were only 6months old, there would be hell to pay. Cat was like the mother, the oldest of six. Her younger siblings came to her if they were hungry and needed something. Her mother did not mind Cat being the second mother because it allowed her to party and come and go as she pleased. Cat resented being the oldest. She always had to miss out on being a teenager due to having to take care of her five younger siblings. She did her morning job duties and off to school she went.
Cat arrived home after school to the worst news she thought she would ever hear. Her mother had been dating a guy for only three months and he wanted her to move to California with him. "This is typical," Cat thought. She was not fazed by the sudden transition. They moved five times a year due to her mother not being able to pay the rent or one of her male friend's

wives busting their windows out, among many other things. Cat was usually the one that kept it together and reassured her younger siblings that everything would be okay, but this time was different. They were moving across the country—all the way to California—and Cat felt unsure of the outcome. When they moved across town Cat never changed schools, so she never had to meet new friends. Even though Cat's mom was from California and that was where all their family lived, she was still reluctant to go. Cat's mother, Connie, barged her way into the room and before Cat could finish her thoughts, her mother started telling her to get up and start packing. Cat knew they were moving but she did not think it would be that day. Cat began to pack all their belongings and as she started to pack the kitchen, her mother informed her that they were leaving all the big stuff, dishes included.

Cat was very wise for her age, and when giving her mother wise counsel, she always phrased her sentence in a way that seemed like she was posing a question. Cat looked at her mother in disbelief and asked, "If we are leaving all the dishes, then how are we going to cook and eat?"

"Don't worry about all that! Just do what I told you to do. You're the child and I am the mother."

Cat was irate. Her mother always gave her adult responsibilities, but when she questioned the irresponsible decisions her mother made, she was always reminded that she was a child. Cat did what she always did and followed her mother's orders. A few hours had passed and Cat had packed the entire house by herself. As Cat was leaning against her bedroom window, she heard men talking. She looked

3

out her window and saw Connie's boyfriend, Chuck, and his friend, Ray, with a U-Haul. She knew that meant to start loading their things onto the truck. She grabbed a bag and headed outside. Connie, Chuck, and Ray watched her as she loaded bag by bag without offering any assistance. Chuck started huffing and puffing. Cat knew her mother so well that she knew what Chuck was trying to convey through his passive aggressive behavior. He wanted her to hurry up. Connie's men were always the same. She always had loser boyfriends that were not good for much of anything besides watching T.V. all day and spending hours with her in the bedroom. Sometimes, even their names were the same. Cat rolled her eyes when Connie was not watching and continued as though she did not know what Chuck was doing.

Chuck turned to Connie and whined, "When is she going to be finished so we can go?"

Cat started moving faster because she did not want to be drug by her hair and beaten, as that was normally what Connie would do when her boyfriends had complaints about Cat. The neighbor observing from the window sent her three boys downstairs to help Cat. She usually sent her sons to assist Cat with groceries and taking out the trash because she felt bad watching how Connie treated Cat. The neighbor also knew what would happen next if Cat did not load the truck in Chuck's timing. The neighbor had called Child Protective Services on Connie before but the agency sent a male employee out and Connie seduced the man with sexual favors, convincing him not to write a negative report, and he didn't. Connie had a way with the men to get just about whatever she wanted because she did not require much. Sex and what she wanted to hear men say were her only expectations.

The truck was finally loaded and Cat was tired and cold when her mother told her to get all her siblings and get into the back of the U-Haul. She did as she was told and loaded them up. She grabbed their pillows and covers and made it cozy and comfortable because she knew it would be a long ride. As the neighbor watched out her window in disbelief that Connie was making the children ride in the back of the U-Haul, she sent her sons out with snacks for the road trip. Connie closed down the load door and locked it, and off they went.

Two hours into the ride her siblings stopped complaining and fell asleep. Cat thought they would never be quiet. Cat took naps on and off but she could not get any rest because she watched over the twins to make sure they were okay through the night. Cat was dosing off as she felt the truck come to a complete stop. She was happy that they were stopping because she needed to go to the bathroom and so did her brother, Jeremiah. Cat heard two doors slam and then Connie at the back of the truck unlocking the roll up door. Before she could get it all the way up Cat hopped up and ran Jeremiah to the bathroom. Connie woke up the others and told them to go to the bathroom. Cat looked around the rest stop and saw a big sign that said: Welcome to Georgia. She was a little disappointed because she thought they were at least in Texas. She had never been out of the state before so she did not know how long it took to get to California. Plus, she knew not to ask any questions for fear of getting on Chuck's bad side. Too many questions meant that Chuck might get irritated and Cat would reap the consequences. So she smiled, and hopped back in the truck, after making sure all her little brothers and sisters went to the bathroom. She pulled hand sanitizer out of her purse and handed it out and gave them a snack that the neighbor had prepared for them. Connie pulled down the door and locked it and Cat could hear the truck starting back up. The kids kept complaining of the darkness inside the truck so Cat put her flashlight on her phone so they could see one another. They played and laughed as Cat dosed off and went to sleep. They stopped a few times to get gas and food before they reached their destination: California! For the last time Cat heard the truck come to a complete stop and like all the other times she was anxious to get out of the truck. She was dying of boredom. Her cell phone had died for constantly putting her flashlight on to sooth her siblings. So Cat could not wait to stretch her legs and get some of that California sunshine that beamed down in the winter that she had heard many stories about. Connie rolled the door up and Cat ran out of there like a racehorse. She was running so fast she did not realize she was running right into the lion's den, her grandmother's house.

As she reached the inside of the doorway she realized that people were sitting in the living room looking at her. Cat was embarrassed. She did not know what to say. She recognized the people from pictures and stories she heard told by her mother, but she did not know them personally. Connie came in right behind Cat and Cat was relieved. Cat could see the mixture of feelings in the room. Some people screamed, "Connie!" and hugged and kissed her, and others—all women- rolled their eyes and never moved from their seats. Cat looked at the women and thought to herself that these must be the women that Connie was referring to when she said their men all wanted her. Cat had a half smile on her face because she did not know if they were welcomed or being passive aggressively dismissed. As she was observing everyone in the living room, a man came out and embraced her and told her how beautiful she was. She could not motion her lips fast enough to say thank you before a woman by the name of Trina blurted out, "She's alright, your acting like you have never seen a beautiful child before."

Cat put her head down. She was used to people telling her she was beautiful all the time. She had never heard anyone tell her anything different. For the first time Cat felt unworthy. Her sister Sabrina, who was one year younger than her, smirked when the women insulted Cat under their breaths.

She turned to Cat and said, "Now you know what it feels like."

Cat had no clue what Sabrina was talking about. Cat would have killed anyone who dared even saying anything ill towards one of her younger brothers and sisters, even an adult. She did notice in the past that people would always ask in disbelief if they were really sisters, but Cat did not think anything of it. All of her siblings ranged in different hair texture, skin color, eye color, and features due to all having different fathers; so Cat thought it was normal that they did not look like one another. Sabrina had a dark skin complexion. Her skin was smooth and looked like someone in a commercial advertising a beauty product for nice skin and her hair touched her waist.

She had hazel brown eyes, and a big rump that Cat wanted. Cat thought Sabrina had a body to kill for. Sabrina would become furious when people would tell Cat she was beautiful and then ask, "Is that really your sister?" So needless to say, Sabrina was having an incredible time watching all the insults be thrown at Cat for once.

An hour after all the insults towards Connie and Cat had been spewed by the women of the family, Cat had settled into unfamiliar territory. She had learned real quick who the gossipers were, the lovable ones, and who were their enemies. She sat in silence as she made sure that Connie's kids did not touch anything that they were not supposed to. One of her female cousins, Nancy, who was the same age, walked into the living room and they instantly noticed one another. Nancy came over and sat next to her and started talking and making jokes to try to make what all had happened a distant memory. Cat clicked with her instantly. Before Cat knew it she was upstairs charging her phone and talking about the newest trends with Nancy. Cat still did not know whose house they were in but by the looks of the room they were in, it was for certain that Nancy lived there. The room had black, hot pink, and white zebra print with Nancy's name spelled out in letters over the sliding glass door that led to a terrace. Cat had never seen a room like it before. She was used to bunk beds with nonmatching comforters and posters that she put up on the room walls. Cat had to ask, it was killing her and because she was the kid that knew everything that was going on, she had to ask.

"Who lives here?"

Nancy replied, "Me, grandma Pie, and Uncle Pettie."

Cat had gotten comfortable in Nancy's room. She had a room that girls where Cat was from only dreamed about. Connie came in the room and proceeded to tell her to "Go get the kids because they are running around."

Cat knew that they were not running around, she knew that her mother did not want to take care of the twins so she went downstairs to get her baby sisters. She picked them up and started to change them, when her grandmother looked at Connie and said, "Are these your babies or does Cat have twins that you never told me about?"

Connie put her head down and picked up a twin out of Cat's lap. Cat could not believe it. This was new. Did someone just tell Connie that Cat did not have any kids? Cat was in shock. In all her sixteen years she never saw anyone challenge her mom about her parenting style. Of course people made remarks but never to Connie's face, with the exception of the women that periodically came to their house looking for their husbands or boyfriends. Cat was going to love visiting Grandma Pie.

Cat had a perception of her grandmother that she was evil and wicked for allowing her husband to molest her mother. However, for some reason Cat did not seem to think negatively of her grandmother anymore. Cat saw an old woman that said what she had wanted to say for nine years, but didn't because of the consequence. Grandma Pie had become Cat's hero. Cat turned because she wanted to see the look on Chuck's face. Of course he did not like Grandma Pie telling Connie to be a mother because that prevented him from getting Connie drunk and running out to every club in town all through the night. Cat had to know if that was the house that they would be living in and she could not remain in limbo much longer so she asked her mother. Cat was careful about her question; she wanted to make sure when she asked she did it in a way that seemed helpful and concerned.

"Mom do you want me to start unloading the truck so I can put the kids in the bath?"
Connie looked at Cat in a way that if looks could kill, Cat would be dead.
Her uncle yelled out, "Unload the truck?" You have these two men standing here and Cat is asking if she can unload the truck?"
Her uncle proceeded to unload the truck when Connie told him very politely that they were not staying there. Cat had never seen a man work around the house. The only work she witnessed a male do was her neighbor's sons that were made to help her at times. Cat was getting more comfortable by the minute. She was quite disappointed that they were not staying there. Sabrina, on the other hand, could not wait to leave. Being only one year younger than Cat, she knew if their family recognized that Cat was the maid then they would be questioning why she was not helping. Connie gathered her clan and loaded them back into the truck. Nancy ran out of the house and told Cat to DM her as she yelled out her Instagram name. Cat was still in so much shock and a little disappointed at all that she had just witnessed, that she did not even store Nancy's information in her phone.
By this time it was nightfall and they were headed to Chuck's family's house in Los Angeles. Even though Cat wanted to stay at Grandma Pie's house, she

wanted to see the glamorous movie stars and all the things that she had heard about in Los Angeles. She could not wait. Thirty minutes had passed and the truck came to a complete stop. Cat jumped up in the dark, stumbling around to find her way to the door. As Ray opened the door, Cat hopped out as though she was intending to plant her feet into the ground, took a deep breath of the California air and looked around. She hardly noticed what house they were at because all she noticed was the woman at the bus stop walking back and forth with little to no clothes on, the police patrolling the streets, and how horrible and trashy the city looked. Cat had a different impression of what Los Angeles would look like. In disappointment she hung her head low as she heard a woman, yelling.

"Hey Chuck Chuck!"

Chuck's brother, Bruce, and sister in-law Susan, ran out the house and hugged and kissed Chuck.

Chuck chuckled and said, "I knew you missed me."

His brother looked at him with a bright smile and held up two fingers with an inch in between them and said, "Just a little bit."

Chuck turned towards Connie, "This is my girl and her kids."

Susan cleared her throat, "Do you mean our kids?" Susan was really short and overweight and had a smile that would light up a room. She was very nice and hospitable.

She looked at Connie, "I know you guys are hungry and I have prepared a dinner; come in and let's eat."

As Cat walked in the house she noticed that their house was tiny and all she could think about was how they were all going to fit and where they would sleep.

11

As she analyzed the house, she could not help but smell the catfish, macaroni and cheese, collard greens, chicken, and sweet water cornbread coming from the kitchen. She instantly turned her attention to the counter tops where all the food was nicely laid out for them to eat. Susan had the food along the counters as though it was a buffet. Cat was walking towards the kitchen and attempted to grab five paper plates to make her siblings a plate when she looked at the table and saw that they were already sitting down eating. Susan had made Bruce's plate and then all the kids. This was another thing that Cat had not been accustomed to. Cat usually made their plates and once she was done accommodating them, it was then that she sat down to eat. The California transition that Cat was initially dreading was now being embraced with open arms. Cat sat down and began to eat her nicely sliced catfish but could only think about where they would all sleep in this tiny house.

The adults bonded over dinner. Connie seemed to be really opening up with the idea of being friends with Susan, which was rare. Connie did not have many female friends. Her philosophy was that you could not trust women. Every time Connie made a statement that referred to women being sneaky and snakes, it confused Cat because she thought her mother's issue would be with men, seeing how it was her mother's husband who had molested her. Cat always pondered on the things that Connie said. She was very analytical. She analyzed everything. You could not get anything past Cat because she would break every word down that a person said, piece by piece, to get a better idea of the person and their story.

Cat wrapped up her thoughts and cleaned off the table after everyone had eaten. She then sat in the corner on the floor, waiting for her cue to take a bath and go to bed. She usually did this on her own at home, but because they were in someone else's house she needed to wait to get proper instructions. Even though Connie had her flaws as a mother, she instilled in her children to have respect for others, especially while being a guest in their home. Her siblings were beginning to fall asleep as the adults talked and laughed. Susan peered over when she saw the children falling asleep and she told them to get blankets out of the hall closet and make a pallet on the floor. Despite the routine they were used to, neither Cat nor her siblings asked about taking a bath or shower since Susan did not offer. Connie had taught them that it would be impolite to ask, but they were all extremely tired from the events of the day anyway. They laid down and fell asleep, despite the adults' loud laughing and late night shenanigans. The next morning, Cat woke up to Bruce getting ready for work. Susan was in the kitchen making coffee for Bruce as he paced back and forth getting his shoes and socks, trying to tiptoe around to avoid waking up the kids. Cat stayed motionless as though she was still asleep but observed Susan and Bruce's every move. This was another foreign thing that was new to her. She had never witnessed a man in a household that was actually the provider. She carefully watched their interactions with one another. Cat was used to watching her mom's boyfriend sit and lay around while she and Connie did everything. Before Bruce walked out of the door, he grabbed Susan by the waist, kissed her with passion, and told

13

her that he appreciated her getting up and making his coffee. Cat laid there and thought to herself that she wanted a marriage like Susan and Bruce's. She felt the love in the home even as tiny as it was. There was a sense of family in their home and Cat wanted that. This excited her because she figured that maybe their relationship would rub off on Connie and Chuck. Cat yearned for a father figure. From the time she was old enough to know that she did not have a man in her life to call dad, she asked where he was but never got many answers. This always left her feeling confused, unwanted, and unloved. As the feeling of excitement settled into her little body, the feeling of rejection came and overshadowed the excitement. Then the hurt of not having a father rushed in and overwhelmed Cat to the point that she started crying. She wiped her eyes and tried to cry as silently as she could but the shakes of her body and the shiver of her cry alerted Susan right away.

Susan looked at Cat, "Get up baby; I feel like you need a mommy hug".

Cat did not really understand what she was saying but got up anyway. As she moved to get up she couldn't get her feet in front of her body to balance herself. Susan grabbed her and embraced her. Cat then knew what a mommy hug was and Cat cried in Susan's arms. When Cat let go, she looked up at Susan and saw that she was crying too.

Cat walked away and started waking up her younger sister and brothers. She wanted to avoid the reason behind Susan crying and she did not want Susan to ask why she was crying. Susan knew Cat was trying to avoid the emotional connection that they shared and because she had just met Cat she did not want to make her any more uncomfortable then she already was. Cat reminded Susan of herself. Susan too was the oldest child and carried the burdens of being parentified at such an early age. Susan identified the hurt and abandonment in Cat from the moment she walked through the door. Susan knew all too well the silent cries and wishes of being in a home where she was loved and adored. Susan also was very observant and analytical.

Susan walked to the back of the house after she stated, "Just know whenever you want to talk, I am always here".

Cat did not respond because her mind was preoccupied with Susan's reasoning behind making the statement that she made.

The younger kids got up one by one and Cat folded their blankets and put them neatly back in the closet just like she found them. Cat sat on the sofa waiting for the day's instructions. She knew her mother would be up shortly because another rule Connie lived by was when you were a guest in someone's home you got up when they got up. Connie walked from one of the back rooms and told the kids to get some clothes off the truck and take a bath. Cat did as she was told and once they were all dressed, Connie and Chuck hugged Susan and said goodbye.

Cat mumbled under her breath "Goodbye?"

Connie overheard her and with a stern voice said, "Yes, goodbye!"

Susan walked to Cat and gave her another mommy hug. They said their goodbyes and walked out the house.

Chapter 2

A week had passed since Connie packed her children up and left Susan's tiny cozy home. They were now staying in a Suburban neighborhood near Grandma Pie. Cat had overheard Connie telling Chuck that he needed to keep a low profile because she was renting the house from her mother's friend and he was not on the lease. The house was a two-story with six bedrooms but yet, empty. Connie had to start from scratch due to her leaving all of her furniture in Brooklyn. The house was big enough for Cat to finally have her own space. This was bigger than any house they had lived in before, and Cat was in awe. It took her back to the day when she was sitting in Nancy's room. Her mind raced through pictures of all the décor that she could add to her huge, oversized room. Before she could finish her thought in her dream room, a doorbell interrupted her. Cat went downstairs to get the door and to her surprise, there was a girl named Samantha with strawberry blonde hair, holding a cake with her hands stretched out. Cat thought it was some type of cruel prank. Cat blurted out, "What do you want?"

Samantha stood in silence for a moment with a big vibrant smile on her face.

"My name is Samantha, I saw your family moving in and thought I would bake you guys a cake."

Cat retrieved the cake from Samantha's palm and closed the door in her face. Cat walked out the garage and to the side door and threw the cake in the trash. Cat was irritated that Samantha could even think that she was stupid enough to eat a cake that a neighbor claimed that she baked out of the kindness of her

heart. Connie walked outside behind Cat just in time
to see her throwing the nicely decorated cake away.
"What are you doing and where did that cake come
from?"
With an annoyed tone, Cat said, "This white girl
thinks I am dumb. She baked us a cake, so she says."
Connie laughed, "Yes, she must really think we are
some type of fools."
Cat took a shower, put her clothes on and ran her
fingers through her hair and screamed downstairs to
Sabrina, "I'm ready!"
Cat went running downstairs to stroll the
neighborhood. The two of them did that all the time
when they moved to a new house to become
acclimated with the community. As they walked
several blocks they stumbled onto an outdoor mall
called The Grove. They walked around and window
shopped as boys continuously asked for their phone
number or their Snapchat names. Cat was not really
interested in having a boyfriend. She observed Connie
enough to see that a relationship was not anything
that she was anticipating. If it required many lonely
nights crying and girls constantly wanting to fight
over a guy, Cat wanted no parts of it. Sabrina on the
other hand, had a distorted perception of what a
healthy relationship was based on witnessing Connie's
dysfunctional affairs. Sabrina gave her number and
Snapchat name to every boy that asked. Cat huffed
and puffed with a subtle eye roll every time Sabrina
would stop and oblige their comments. Most of the
time they were approached, the guy would first
address Cat, and would only engage with Sabrina
when they realized Cat was not interested.

As Cat and Sabrina roamed the streets of the Grove, a person gently taped Cat on the shoulder from behind. Just before Cat could turn around to acknowledge the person with two fingers gently pressed against her shoulder, the voice informed her who the stranger was.

With a welcoming voice, and a slight whisper, "How did you like the cake?"

Cat instantly became annoyed. Cat looked over at Sabrina with an overtly annoyed look on her face.

"Is this girl trying me?"

Sabrina was puzzled, not knowing what to say. They had been in their new house only a week so Sabrina had no idea how this stranger could already be annoying her sister. Cat turned around as though she was in combat. Before Cat could perk her lips up to verbally attack, Samantha cut her off.

"I always bake cakes for the new neighbors. Plus it was a way that I could talk to you and your sister since there are not many teenagers that live on our street. If you thought I did something to your cake all you had to do was ask instead of slamming the door in my face. I overheard you telling your mom that I did something horrible to the cake, but obviously you do not know me because that is not my character. Oh, and I am Samantha by the way, since I was rudely interrupted."

Sabrina, with her mouth so wide open a fly could have flown in, looked at Cat in anticipation of what Cat was going to do next. Was this girl calling Cat out on her behavior? Sabrina wondered. That was a definite no. Cat did not respond well to people challenging her decisions, besides, she made decisions for her mother. Who was this new girl informing Cat

18

that she could have asked instead of slamming the door in her face? Samantha's boldness caught Cat by surprise. She did not have a comeback. For the first time Sabrina watched her older sister look like a deer caught in the headlights. She always had a rebuttal, or what they called a "clap back," when someone her age was being feisty with her. Cat took an instant liking to Samantha. She actually liked the fact that she confronted her. Cat was a leader among her peers and because of that, her friends usually followed her and said things to appease her. Cat actually liked people that stood up for what they believed and whose actions reflected their own way of thinking.

Cat looked at Samantha for what seemed like a lifetime. She watched every syllable that fell from her lips. She intently observed her to see if her words were congruent with her body movement. Samantha and Sabrina started to converse about the local teen fun. Sabrina started asking questions once she realized that Cat was not going to say a single word. To avoid Samantha noticing that her sister was lost for words, Sabrina introduced herself and then turned to Cat, "This is my sister, Cat."

Samantha snickered.

"Oh I see, so you don't have your own tongue?" Sabrina could not help but chuckle too. Sabrina looked at Cat, "You have finally met your match."

Cat knew what Sabrina was alluding to but she wasn't going down without a fight. Samantha had on a black leather jacket, dark blue jeans, and a white t-shirt with some black Doc Martin boots. Cat looked Samantha up and down and pointed to her boots and said in a joking manner, "What are those?! And I think Danny from Grease wants his jacket back."

19

The three girls laughed.

"Oh, she speaks! I thought we had a mute on our hands."

Cat and Samantha went back and forth for the duration of the mall trip. They got so caught up in joking around and having fun that they did not realize that it was getting dark and the sun had begun to set. Sabrina looked at Cat, "We have to go home. You know how your mom gets when her molly maid slash nanny is not at home."

Cat and Sabrina both started laughing simultaneously. Samantha looked confused but did not bother to ask what they were laughing about.

"Do you guys want a ride because my mom texted me and said she was on her way to pick me up."

Cat nodded her head in a yes motion.

"Okay, I will text her back and tell her so she won't bring anybody with her. Let's go stand in front of the movie theatre because that is where she usually picks me up."

The trio stood in front of the cinema while chatting and taking selfies. A white Bentley pulled up and Cat's eyes instantly went into a gaze. She could not stop looking at the car.

"Come on, my mom is here,"

Samantha walked off to the car and Cat and Sabrina followed behind her. Cat and Sabrina climbed into the backseat and Samantha jumped into the passenger seat. A million thoughts raced through Cat's mind during the five-minute ride home. Cat could not believe that Samantha's mother owned a Bentley. Cat always envisioned people that had a great deal of money would act snobbish, but Samantha was the exact opposite; very down to earth and easy to talk to.

Cat felt like she had known Samantha for years. She had the characteristics of a cousin. Samantha's mother was speaking to both her and Sabrina but Cat was so in sync with her thoughts that she would catch a few words here and there as Sabrina and Samantha's mother conversed. They finally pulled into Samantha's driveway and Cat sprung the backdoor open and got out as slowly as possible to take a last look at the elaborate car.

Connie was standing by the front door. Cat just knew that Connie was going to lash out verbally with profanity and putdowns. Cat swiftly walked away from Samantha hoping that they would go into their house as quickly as possible. Cat did not want to be embarrassed by Connie's usual shenanigans. To Cat's surprise, Connie did not say one single word, but instead, greeted Samantha and her mother. Sabrina and Cat looked at one another in complete shock. "Is this a new Connie?" Cat thought to herself. The thought could not completely set in her mind before she saw the dried up tears on the side of Connie's cheeks and the disappointment written all over her face. Cat and Sabrina both knew that something had happened. Chuck came storming out of the house. Sabrina looked at Cat and mumbled under her breath, "The embarrassment is about to begin."

Bruce and Susan pulled up and Chuck had all his belongings in tow.

"I'm done Connie!"

Cat looked in her mother's direction waiting for Connie to bust out a window of Bruce's car or something. She knew Connie had to have the last say and Cat waited in silence for her response. By now, Samantha and her mother had gone into the house,

not wanting to pry in Connie's personal family affairs.
That was odd to Cat as well. Most of the time, when
they were back in Brooklyn when people argued
outside everyone came out to watch the action. They
even recorded, hoping that their video would have
enough views to go viral or get on Grind Face TV.
However, Connie did not say one single word. She
turned around and walked into the house. Again,
Sabrina and Cat looked at one another in disbelief.
Cat did something that she would have never done
before; she reached out to her mother, embraced her,
and hugged her tight just like Susan had hugged her
when she was hurt. Cat did not care if Connie
rejected the hug and to her surprise, she didn't.
Sabrina watched in awe and gave a puzzled look. The
day couldn't get any stranger.
As Cat let go she wiped Connie's face.
"It will be okay Mom. We will manage; we always
do."
Connie did not say a word. She just looked at Cat as
though she heard every word and turned away and
walked in the house with Sabrina and Cat following
behind her. Before, Connie would be angry after a
break up; and Cat already knew she had to step up
and become mini mom to her siblings until her mom
snapped out of her depression state or until she found
a new fling. Cat did as she usually did; she picked up
one of the twins and started giving orders when
Connie interrupted her.
"I got it Cat. These are my kids and I've allowed you
to play me for too long; be a kid. I realize I am doing
to you what was done to me. I have become
everything that I did not want to be— my mom."

22

Connie picked up a twin in each arm and broke down crying as she walked to her room and closed the door behind her. Sabrina, at this point was in a daze, not knowing what to say. This was very bizarre behavior for Connie. Connie being a mother and apologizing for her non-parental behavior, "Wow!" were Sabrina's thoughts.

Sabrina could not be still or quiet for any longer, "What just happened?"

Cat turned toward Sabrina in disbelief and shrugged her shoulders. Cat cued all her younger siblings to take baths and got them ready for bed before she went to her room and called it a night.

Cat was awakened the next day by the sun beaming through her bedroom window. Even if she closed her blinds or put a cover over the window to block the sun she wouldn't be able to sleep because of Kendrick Lamar's new album blasting from outside. Cat threw the blankets off of her out of annoyance, to get up and see who was playing that racket. When she peered out the window there was a boy standing outside with a beat pill, standing in Samantha's front lawn talking to her. Both the boy and Samantha looked up at the window when they noticed someone looking down at them. Cat swiftly fell to the floor and hurt her knee to avoid being noticed lurking. Cat went to the bathroom and then went to check on the twins before going downstairs to grab a bowl of cereal. She peeked in her mother's room to prevent waking her up. When she cracked the door open, Connie and the twins were not in the bed. Connie usually slept in while Cat tended to the twins. Cat ran downstairs, relieved that she did not have to play mommy. When she reached the last step she could see Connie in the family room talking to her aunt Sharon, who also moved back to California. Sharon was Connie's go to person. Whenever Connie was going through a tough time she called her sister. Cat did as she always did when they had discussions. She found a comfortable seat away from Connie and Sharon's view to listen in on their conversation. They always exchanged interesting dialogue that Cat was oblivious to regarding their family matters, plus, Cat admired her aunt Sharon.

Cat listened in.

"Chuck finally left huh?"

"Yes he did. But the thing about it, I am not mad this time. I am aware that he used me for a ride to California. I packed my kids up with hopes of starting a new life with a man that I thought loved me. I listened to everything you said when we talked a few days ago. One thing that you said that stood out to me was when you said I am mom. Even though you are my younger sister I feel like our roles are reversed. I should be speaking into you and guiding you but it has always been the opposite,"

Sharon began to justify her position. "B" was all she was able to get out before Connie interrupted her and continued talking.

"I know you always say you do not mean to be like that but I am glad that you are. You said to me the other night that I needed to learn to love me and you are so right. When Chuck said he was leaving, I reflected on everything you said. It is time for me to change for the better for my kids. I just hope that the damage that I created will diminish within them as I show them what a real mother and woman look like. I

24

want to give them something that mom did not give us. She had multiple kids not knowing who our fathers were. Yeah, mom got her life together but, look at me Sharon, I am mom before she showed us something different."

Connie began to cry and continued, "I am dying to tell Cat about her father, but I can't. I could of slapped Trina when she was rude to Cat. Yes, I slept with your husband but do not mistreat my child because of my wrongdoing"

Sharon cut Connie off.

"Connie, you don't think that your cousin, that you were so close with like sisters, is still hurt about you sleeping with her husband?"

"Sharon, I know I shouldn't have done it but if that's what mom showed me… how was I supposed to know? Do you know how many of our family member's husbands I watched mom creep in and out of our house and screw the life out of right before my very own eyes? Not your eyes, but mine! I am not justifying my actions but that's what I knew. As bad as I did not want to be like her, I became her. The saying, 'it is easier said than done,' is very true. This is what she taught her student and I was the student sitting in the front row of the classroom. Now she is so righteous. Like, is she serious?"

Cat could not even stomach to hear the rest. As the tears filled her almond shaped eyes, she turned and headed to her room with anger and with her hands clinched tight; she thought about running up to Connie and punching the daylights out of her. The doorbell rang before Cat could retreat to her room. Connie yelled out, "Cat get the door!" Cat mimicked her in annoyance, 'Cat get the door.'

Cat opened up the door with anger on her face.
Samantha had a smirk on her face and blurted out,
"Did the floor meet your knees?"
Cat stood in silence waiting for Samantha to finish
her sentence.
"In other words, I saw you looking at us earlier in the
window. Why did you duck when we looked at you?"
Cat's demeanor began to change as she thought about
the cute boy standing outside of her window and
wanting to know the details of his relationship with
Samantha. She wondered if he was already taken
because she wanted a shot at dating him.
"Oh, because, well I didn't want you guys to think I
was lurking."
Samantha snickered.
"But you were, and by the way, he likes you so be
dressed in an hour so we can walk over to his house.
And bring Sabrina if she wants to come because I
don't want to be the third wheel."
After Cat nodded her head while blushing, Samantha
turned and walked away. Connie and Sharon's
conversation was like a distant memory to Cat at that
point. She rushed in the family room and asked if she
could leave with the neighbor and Connie said she
could.
Sabrina yelled from the kitchen, "I'm going!"
Sabrina cleaned the kitchen and ran upstairs to get
dressed. Cat made sure she looked real cute. She left
her hair curly, dripping with water and hanging down
her back. She put on a cute form fitting white dress
with some red sandals, a white and gold watch, and
some gold earrings. Cat and Sabrina then walked out
of the door. As they approached Samantha's door,
she was already on her way out.

26

"Hey guys, someone is looking mighty hot today."
Samantha walked up to Cat and put one finger on her
arm and made a sizzling noise, to reference how hot
Cat looked. They all chuckled.
"So where are we going?"
Samantha looked at Cat and giggled.
Sabrina then looked at Cat and Cat shrugged her
shoulders as if she had no clue why Samantha was
looking at her. They continued walking down the
street as if they had known each other for years. They
strolled, laughing and talking and telling jokes to one
another. A few blocks later they stumbled across
Grandma Pie's house. Nancy was standing outside
watering the front lawn when Cat approached her.
"Hey, do you remember me?"
"Of course I do."
 Nancy skipped to Cat and embraced her so tight Cat
could barely breathe. Cat then turned to Samantha
and said, "This is my cousin, Nancy."
Samantha looked at Cat and rolled her eyes as if she
and Nancy had already met. Being that outspoken
person she was, Cat confronted Samantha.
"Do you have a problem with my cousin?"
Samantha was just as outspoken as Cat. Samantha
turned to Nancy and looked her square in the eyes.
"Of course I don't like Nancy," Samantha said with a
smirk on her face. So ask Nancy why I don't like her."
Sabrina stood as far back as possible in disbelief. She
did not know what would happen next; watching
both Samantha and Cat knowing that neither one of
them would back down. Cat was very protective of
her family. Sabrina wanted no parts of it. Cat took
three steps until she was directly in Samantha's face.

"No, I'm asking you, what is your issue with my cousin?"

Samantha inched her face out to be even closer to Cat's face, as if they were going to kiss and yelled out, "Did I stutter? Like I said, ask your cousin!"

At this point Sabrina was wise enough to know exactly where this was headed so she stood in between Samantha and Cat.

Sabrina looked at Nancy and huffed, "What is the issue?"

"I don't have an issue with you Samantha. You have hated me since the fifth grade and I'm still trying to figure out why."

Samantha glared at Nancy and told her, "You know exactly why I don't like you."

Cat interrupted, "This is not going anywhere. Can we just resolve the issue so we all can move forward and continue with what we were doing prior to this?"

Nancy looked at Cat, "I am willing to apologize but the thing is, I don't know what I've done to Samantha to make her feel this way towards me."

Samantha, in a demanding voice stated, "I will accept an apology and then I want you to think about what you did and come back and apologize again."

Cat, with an annoyed look on her face stepped right into Samantha's face, "You're not going to keep bullying my cousin; either you want to resolve the issue or you don't."

Samantha was the master at being petty and bold, but she realized in that moment, that she had finally met her match.

"Okay Cat, because it's you I will overlook it and let it go."

Sabrina and Cat in unison said, "Thank you," with an
irritated look on both of their faces.

One after the other Sabrina and Cat hugged Nancy
and said their goodbyes and were on their way. They
were back on the path to going to Samantha's friends
house.

Cat, in a soft tone mumbled under her breath, "You
never said his name." Sabrina, with a puzzled look on
her face looked at Samantha and said, "whose name?"
Samantha repeated three times, "Bobby, Bobby,
Bobby that is his name" and burst out with laughter.

"Who is Bobby?" Sabrina asked.

"Oh just a boy your sister likes," Samantha then
giggled.

They walked a few more blocks and they had arrived.
Standing before them was a huge house, unlike any
they had ever seen before except in the movies. In the
driveway there was a black Bentley with a man who
was dressed like a driver opening the door for a
beautiful woman. She looked like she was a movie
star starring in a movie. She had on a form fitting
white dress. She had long blonde hair, blue eyes, and
red lipstick. Her shoes were white with spikes on
them and the bottom of the shoes were red. Cat and
Sabrina looked in awe when they noticed Samantha
walking up to the door. Cat's mind was running a mile
a minute. This could not be the home of the boy who
she saw outside of her window earlier that day at
Samantha's house.

Sabrina and Cat stood at the end of the driveway
when they saw a butler open the front door, "Come
in," he said with a deep voice. Samantha looked back
at Sabrina and cat and waved her arm, gesturing for
them to follow. Sabrina and Cat approached and they

all walked in together. Cat and Sabrina stood in the foyer. The butler spoke as if he only spoke on cue, "Follow me."

They all followed behind him. He walked them through the house and it seemed like it took forever. Cat could only wonder how big Bobby's house was. They finally came to what Cat concluded must be the game room, as there was a bowling alley and a pool table all in a big open space. The carpet looked like a Monopoly game board. There was a bar off to the side with three huge TVs— one for each gaming system— with individual reclining chairs. Sabrina's mind was wandering also. She had to ask the question. She looked right at Samantha and said, "Is this Bobby's house?" Samantha could not respond fast enough before Bobby and his best friend, Mark, came strolling in. Cat was taken aback by everything she had seen. She felt uncomfortable because they hadn't even exchanged words before and for the first time, she had nothing to say.

He took one look at Cat and was mesmerized by her beauty. Even as he spoke to the group he couldn't take his eyes off of her. By now everyone had noticed the chemistry between the two. They watched as if they were watching a movie, as both Cat and Bobby could not stop looking at one other. They both didn't know how to engage one another and introduced themselves. Bobby's best friend Mark took the initiative and introduced everyone in the group to both Cat and Sabrina. Bobby jumped right in, not wanting to look like a scary little boy whose best friend had to speak up for him in his own house. He extended his hand out and introduced himself by saying, "My name is Bobby." He shook Sabrina's hand and then went in for a hug with Cat. Cat embraced him back, not wanting to let go. Samantha eased the tension by mumbling, "Awkward," and they all started laughing.

"How about a game of bowling?" said Bobby.

Mark answered before anyone else could knowing that Bobby wanted some alone time with Cat. "Why don't you two go ahead and play and we all will go play pool."

Bobby looked at Mark, thanking him with his eyes because he knew exactly what he was trying to do, as Mark walked off and motioned Samantha and Sabrina to follow behind him.

Bobby took Cat by the hand and escorted her over to bowl. Bobby asked Cat her name as he punched the names on the keypad and got ready to play a round of bowling. Bobby checked Cat out as she walked back-and-forth to bowl. They giggled, looked at each other, and engaged in endless conversation. Before they noticed, time had passed and it was already 6 o'clock. Samantha walked over to Cat and said, "I know you guys are having fun but I have to go home. Do you want to stay or do you guys want to walk back with me?"

Bobby stated, "I will take you guys home."

They all walked towards the front door and as they walked outside, it was chilly and the wind was blowing. Bobby took his jacket off and placed it on Cat's shoulders. Cat put her arms through the jacket and snuggled up tightly. She stood motionless waiting for the driver to come out but instead, Bobby walked to a black Ferrari, walked back to Cat and grabbed her by the hand and motioned her to the front passenger seat. Cat picked up a Fendi handbag in the seat before sitting down and admired it. She analyzed the handbag not realizing that she was staring so long. Bobby got into the driver seat and noticed that she liked his mom's handbag. Once Bobby got into the car she quickly placed it in the back seat. He looked back at Samantha and Sabrina and yelled out, "My driver will take you home!" As he backed out the driveway, Cat looked at Bobby and said, "But I can't leave my sister."

Bobby said, "Don't worry about it," and picked up his phone and called his driver and said, "They need to go home right away."

The driver walked right out and opened the doors for them to get in the Bentley. Bobby let the driver leave first then backed out and followed behind him. On the way to Cat's house Bobby asked Cat what type of guy she liked. Cat knew that he was only asking because he wanted to see if she was interested in him. To Bobby's surprise, Cat looked right at him, put her hand on his hand as he gripped the steering wheel and said, "You."

He was shocked that she was so blunt. Most girls usually played hard to get or acted like they didn't like the guy when in reality, they did. The radio was playing and "Cater 2 U" by Destiny's Child, came on and Bobby and Cat looked at each other as if they were fascinated with one another. Cat loved this song and for the first time she could put a face to the lyrics as she visualized every word.

By this time they were already in front of Cat's house. Sabrina and Samantha had pulled up and were getting out of the car. Bobby parked the car and looked back at her and said, "Good," as he leaned over to kiss her. Cat reciprocated the kiss, not caring if Connie walked

out the house and saw her. Cat thought to herself, besides, the windows are tinted; and after the conversation she heard Connie having earlier, she didn't care if she would be mad if she saw her kissing Bobby. Cat could only think about the countless guys Connie kissed and actually had sex with. Besides, it wasn't like she was going to have sex with him, it was a simple peck. Bobby took Cat's phone out of her hand and stored his number in her phone.
He licked his lips and whispered, "Call me." Cat smiled and got out of the car and closed the door. Bobby got out the car to walk her to the door.
"No," Cat said, "my mom will be pissed if she knows I came home with a boy." Reality set in. Cat knew Connie could not see her kissing Bobby but if she knew Cat was in a car with Bobby there would be hell to pay. Bobby got back in the car and watched Cat until he couldn't see her anymore. Cat was glowing. All she could do was smile. Sabrina looked at her and rolled her eyes.
"Looks like you had a good time," Sabrina said to Cat out of irritation.
"Yeah I did, you didn't?"
"I was bored and ready to go a long time ago." Sabrina snapped back at Cat.
"Well next time stay home. I didn't ask you to come anyway Sabrina," Cat turned away and walked upstairs and closed her door. She sat at the edge of her bed looking at her phone and Bobby's number, thinking about what a great time she had. Cat didn't want to seem clingy so she decided she would call him in the morning.
Cat was woken up by Connie's loud screaming for all the kids to get up, "You guys are starting school

33

today, you're getting out of my house!" Cat was happy. They had settled into the new home and now everything could be like it was back in Brooklyn once she started school. Cat jumped up and took a shower. She got dressed before thinking about getting her younger siblings ready. To Cat's surprise, Connie had already gotten half of them dressed for school. Cat and Sabrina accompanied Connie as she took the younger kids to the local elementary and enrolled them in school. Cat assisted Connie with filling out all the paperwork to get each kid in school. They were there at least two hours before they left to the local high school, which was called Sunset High. The time was much shorter for Connie to enroll Cat and Sabrina. The office assistant escorted them to class. The first class Cat attended was her third period class-Chemistry. Cat walked into the classroom and stood in the doorway waiting for the teacher to motion her to an assigned seat. The teacher looked over the paperwork in her hand that the office assistant had given her. It seemed like a decade as her eyes paced back and forth on the paper. Cat had gotten tired of waiting and walked to an empty seat that was next to a boy by the name of Stephen. His eyes were tight. He had a bowl cut that made him look like the cartoon character, Dora the Explorer. Stephen had on a white button up shirt with a tie. Cat noticed him because he was dressed so much different than the other students. Cat assumed that it was smart to sit next to him because based on his demeanor, and appearance, he seemed to be very serious about Chemistry. Besides, chemistry was not her best subject; she hated math, and science combined with it was like a bad nightmare. So who better to sit next to

than the serious, over achiever? Cat introduced
herself, trying to get in his good graces.

Stephen mumbled under his breath, "Hello," as if he
were really shy.

Cat had walked in just in time to catch the scores on
the chemistry exam. Ms. Bey was passing the test
back and placed it face down when Cat grabbed it
before it could touch the desk and turned it over to
get a glimpse at Stephen's test score. The students
called her Ms. Bey even though her name was Ms.
Harris, because she looked very similar to Beyonce.
"Excuse me," Ms. Bey said as she snatched the sheet
of paper out of Cat's hand and handed it to Stephen.
Cat had the test long enough just to see the big
ninety- eight percent at the top of the paper.

Cat looked over at Stephen and stated, "You must be
really smart," Cat whispered. Stephen put his head
down and said

"Kind of."

"What do you mean kind of? Looks to me like you
got a ninety eight, which is two points away from a
hundred percent."

Stephen took his focus away from his paper and
turned and looked in Cat's direction. "I can say, it's
not hundred. Therefore, like I said, kind of," Stephen
said in a stern voice. Cat peered at Stephen as if he
were crazy. She could not understand what he was
thinking or what was coming out of his mouth. Cat
thought to herself, this boy is delusional. Ms. Bey
rambled on about the chemistry lesson. Cat did not
understand one word Ms. Bey was saying.

Cat blurted out, "What is this lady talking about,
Stephen?"

A few students sitting near Cat looked at her and chuckled. Stephen turned toward Cat with annoyance written all over his face; he gestured for her to be quiet as he placed one finger over his lips. The bell rang and all the kids jumped up out of their seats running toward the door. It was lunchtime but Cat asked Stephen if he could help her with the Chemistry homework before she left class.

Stephen shrugged his shoulders and said, "Sure, I tutor other people. You can meet me after school in the library."

"Sounds like a plan."

Cat walked out toward the center quad area where everyone gathered during lunch. Sabrina was in the class next door to Cat. She followed behind her big sister avoiding walking with her. Cat picked up on the resistance that Sabrina was displaying. Cat knew she was mad from the night prior but didn't understand what was wrong. Cat perked up her lips to interrogate Sabrina about her bizarre behavior but just as the first syllable flung off of her tongue, they bumped into Nancy.

"I did not know you guys go here," as she ran up to Cat and hugged her.

"Yeah, my mom decided to enroll us in school today so we will be attending Sunset high," Cat said as she embraced Nancy.

Cat could not stop looking at the girl next to Nancy. The mysterious girl looked so much like Cat she could not believe it. Not even her own brothers and sisters looked that much like her. The girl's skin tone was like a brown paper bag, just like Cat's complexion. She had cat eyes—they were very tight, almond shaped and the color was a hazel brown mixed with green. Her hair was very wavy and long just like Cat's. Even Sabrina could not stop staring at her. It was like everyone noticed the resemblance but no one wanted to say anything. Sabrina and Cat stood there gazing at one another with an uncomfortable look on their face. The girl looked back at Cat thinking the same exact thing, which was, "Who is this girl that looks like me?"

It was not long before Samantha walked up. Cat was relieved. She knew that Samantha—with her gigantic mouth—would break the ice.

"Wow, you and Cat look just alike, Yesenia!" Samantha said as she laughed. Nancy rolled her eyes and responded, "Well duh, they are related."

Cat had not seen this girl before nor even heard of her. She did not want Samantha to think that their family was full of weirdos, so she held off on asking Nancy how Yessenia was related to her.

Samantha looked back at Nancy as she rolled her eyes before turning to Cat and saying, "If I didn't know any better I would think Yessenia was your sister, Cat."

Sabrina, in an irritated voice replied, "No, I'm her sister."

Cat observed Yessenia in disbelief. Cat still did not understand what had Sabrina so upset.

Bobby appeared out of nowhere with Mark and two other friends. They were all dressed to impress. Cat could tell that they were the boys that all the girls most likely had crushes on. Cat was attracted to Bobby's swag. Bobby grabbed Cat from behind and gave her a hug as if they had known each other for years.

"I didn't get a call or text from you," he whispered in her ear.

Cat tried to come with a swift reply, trying to avoid sounding uninterested. "That's because I knew I would see you today at school."

"No you didn't. You didn't even know I went to this school." Mark and Bobby both started laughing and the other two boys followed suit. More of Bobby's friends walked up and he could not wait to show Cat off. "This is my new girlfriend."

All the boys looked Cat up and down as if she was a display. Sabrina noticed that all of the boys were hypnotized by Cat's beauty. They could not stop staring. One boy watched Cat so long that drool dropped out the side of his mouth and he wiped it off quickly, hoping no one had noticed. Sabrina rolled her eyes and folded her arms across her chest. Cat kept peeking over to see Sabrina's body language and she seemed to be getting more upset by the second. They all stood in a circle as more of their friends came. Everyone wanted to get a glance at the new hot girl that everyone was talking about. Cat's other name, "the new girl," was spreading like wild fire.

Bobby and Samantha introduced Cat and Sabrina to the new group. Cat could not concentrate on the new people because her only concern was Sabrina. Cat analyzed Sabrina, looking for any clue that would tell her what was wrong with her sister. Cat was also distracted by Yesenia and was curious how this girl was related to their family.

Bobby embraced Cat from behind once more and all she could smell was his Gucci cologne that smelled so good. Cat tried to pretend like she was in sync with Bobby but her eyes would not allow her to take them

38

off of both Sabrina and Yesenia. Cat's over analytical brain was running in a never-ending marathon. Cat was trying to piece the puzzles together while trying to stay engaged in the conversation and be in sync with Bobby's constant display of affection. It was just too much. She could not wait for the lunch bell to ring. Plus, she was anticipating the school day to be over so she could talk to Sabrina to help her find resolution to whatever was going on with her. She had never seen her sister act like this before; or maybe she just had never noticed, being so consumed with Connie's kids.

The rest of the day flew by. The bell rung and Cat was ecstatic; school was finally over. She wanted to talk to her little sister. She hated seeing her upset. They met and waited by the tree near the sidewalk as instructed by their mom. Bobby was on the hunt to look for his trophy to ensure that he gave his queen a ride home. He would not have his girlfriend walking when he had a car. Bobby believed a real man catered to his significant other because that is what he was taught. Sabrina and Cat were waiting by the tree when Bobby approached them. He asked if they wanted a ride home. Cat let him know that she had to wait for Connie. Bobby stood directly in front of Cat trying to make her laugh. Cat realized that he was keeping her company until Connie came.

Cat said in a soft voice, "I do not want to sound mean but my mom will go crazy if she sees me with a boy. I do not want her to know that I have a boyfriend yet. I will text you."

"Are you sure? Because you didn't last night." Bobby reached for Cat's phone.

"I promise I will text you," Cat said as she snatched her phone away before he could grip it. Bobby hugged Cat and motioned his face as if he were going to kiss her. She moved back and put her hand over her mouth. She saw Sabrina peering at her like target practice.

"I will see you tomorrow Sunshine," Bobby hugged and kissed Cat on her cheek.

Cat did not understand why he said 'sunshine'; she thought it was some type of California lingo for 'girl.' Bobby walked toward his car in the school parking lot. When Bobby disappeared, Cat asked Sabrina what was wrong.

"I've noticed that since we've been in California you have been upset here and there, and mainly with me. Usually we are both mad at mom but now it seems like your attitude is directed only towards me. Sabrina, you are never like this."

"I am never like this? Maybe you just didn't notice because you are always soaking up the attention."

"What attention? What are you talking about, Sabrina?"

"Oh, the most beautiful one," Sabrina said sarcastically while raising both of her hands as if praising a Queen. Cat began to tear up. Her little sister's feelings really mattered to her and she did not understand what was going on. This was all new to Cat. She had no idea Sabrina had been feeling this way.

Just then, Connie pulled up right on the curb. She instantly asked the girls how their first day went. Cat slumped over in the front seat and rested hear head on the window while Sabrina went on and on about her likes and dislikes about the new school.

40

Meanwhile, Connie noticed that Cat wasn't her usually talkative self. Connie knew something was wrong. She grabbed Cat by her face and pulled her close so she could get a good look at Cat's eyes. Connie could see the dried up tears on her face. "What's wrong baby?"

"Nothing, just a rough day."

Sabrina folded her arms in the backseat, even more annoyed now that Connie was paying more attention to Cat. Connie tried to reassure Cat that things would get better. Cat poked her head slightly out of the window as they drove off. When until they arrived home, they all got out of the car one by one. Connie did not hesitate to say, "Make sure you guys do your homework."

Cat could not believe that she forgot to meet Stephen in the library to get help with the chemistry assignment. Cat shuffled herself to her room with her head hanging low. Cat did not want to text Bobby. The only thing she could think about was what was going on with her little sister. She felt horrible not knowing why she was so bothered. Cat's thoughts raced back and forth between Sabrina and Yessenia. Too afraid to ask Connie about Yessenia, believing that the skeletons of her mom's past would come flying out of the closet, she decided not to mention Yessenia and the undeniable resemblance that she saw at school today. Cat was exhausted; she laid on the bed and took a nap, which was unusual. She usually attended to her younger siblings and made sure their homework assignments were done before she tended to herself.

Cat woke up two hours later to the aroma of smothered chicken, her favorite. Connie used a seasoning called Arturo and Anise. It was the family's favorite seasoning. It gave the food that extra mouth watering flavor. Cat walked downstairs and saw everyone at the table eating. Cat walked over to Sabrina and nudged her on the arm and said, "I like this Connie."

Usually Sabrina would laugh, but not this time; she just stared at Cat in a way that if looks could kill Cat would be dead. Cat left the kitchen and went into the living room. She had lost her appetite. Cat was acting like a parent that was concerned with their child and had no solutions of how to fix the problem. Cat was in the living room when she heard her aunt Sharon's voice. Cat opened the door and went to help Sharon with the groceries she was carrying. Cat looked over her shoulder and saw Mark and Bobby standing in Samantha's driveway. When Bobby noticed Cat, he ran and removed the bags from her hands and took them into the house. Sharon winked her eye at Cat and said, "He's a keeper."

Cat smiled, not wanting to say that he was her boyfriend and that she already knew him. Connie was loose with the guys but did not want Sabrina and Cat to even look in a boy's direction, which was weird to both Cat and Sabrina. Bobby immediately introduced himself once he and Connie locked eyes. Bobby was so nervous that he introduced himself as Cat's boyfriend.

"How old are you Bobby?"

"Sixteen."

Cat walked into the kitchen and all eyes were on her. Sabrina was sitting at the table with a smirk on her face. She could not wait for the moment for Connie to smack the beauty off of her face.

"Well you are sixteen and a junior in high school. I guess it is time I allow you to date," said Connie. Sabrina immediately got up from the table and slammed her dishes in the sink, breaking the glass plate. Everyone turned, now observing Sabrina's every move. No one said anything. Cat looked at Connie wondering what she would do to Sabrina and she did nothing. Sabrina stomped her feet as loud as she could and slammed her bedroom door behind her. The moment the door slammed Connie headed toward the stairs. The look on her face said Sabrina was about to get the beating of her life. Aunt Sharon grabbed Connie by her arm.

"These kids have been through enough. Maybe you should try talking to Sabrina."

"You are right, I have put them through enough and I am working on the new me."

Cat looked at Connie and mumbled under her breath, "The new me, where was the new me in Brooklyn?" Connie went upstairs to talk to Sabrina and closed Sabrina's bedroom door behind her.

Cat walked outside hoping that Bobby would follow behind her. Cat did not want her aunt to start asking a million questions. Mark and Samantha were still standing in the same spot talking. Samantha asked if they wanted to come in her house and they all agreed to go in. Once in Samantha's house Cat could not help but notice that Samantha's mother was intoxicated. Cat had watched Connie and her men come to the house high out of their minds so many times that it was abnormal if they didn't. Samantha was embarrassed and tried to excuse her mother's behavior by telling them that she drinks wine to calm herself and relax after a long day of work. Cat was not buying what Samantha was selling. Cat was no dummy; she knew that Samantha's mom was a drunk. Bobby got a text and Cat calmly looked at his phone but tried hard to play like she was looking at something else. Bobby placed his phone in Cat's face to give her a better look. He knew that Cat was trying to see who was texting his phone. Bright in red font it said 'mom' as the name and within the text thread it said, "Come home." Cat was embarrassed that he caught on to her insecurity. Cat had watched her mom's heartbreaks and how guys played with her like a toy, and she figured that all males where the same; but in the short time she had been in California, she was beginning to see guys in a different way. Bobby told Cat he had to go but was not leaving without getting her number.

"Sunshine, let me see your phone." He reached out his hand to retrieve the phone. Cat handed Bobby her phone thinking he wanted to go through her text messages to see if she was talking to other guys, but instead, he did the opposite. He texted his phone from hers to get her phone number and went on her social media apps to get all her names to add her. Bobby hugged her and this time Cat went in for the kiss. Bobby was surprised that she wanted to kiss. It caught him off guard. Bobby swiftly turned away as Mark began to laugh.

"You weren't expecting that huh, told you," Mark said.

Cat was confused but as she walked toward the door to walk with Bobby outside, she couldn't help but notice the bulge in his pants that was sticking out. Cat knew what that meant and why Mark was laughing.

They all walked outside and Cat could not resist; she had to ask.

"What does Sunshine mean?"

"It is a name that I like calling you. Why? You don't like it?"

"No, it's cool." Cat smiled while blushing. She never had a guy give her a nickname before. Mark and Bobby said there goodbyes and drove off headed home. Samantha's mom opened the door and held her wine glass up motioning Samantha to come drink. "You and your friend want to have some wine to calm your nerves? I know school can be stressful," said her mom with slurred speech.

Samantha invited Cat in to come drink with her mom. Cat declined. She was blown away that Samantha's mom allowed her to drink. Connie would not be thrilled if she knew this tidbit of information. Cat knew that was some information that she had to lock in the vault. Connie wasn't a great mother but one thing she did not tolerate was the kids that she birthed doing adult things like drinking. Cat told Samantha that she would see her at school before she walked into the house.

Connie and Sharon were sitting in the living room but Connie did not mention anything about Sabrina when Cat walked in so Cat could only wonder what happened. Cat went upstairs and took a shower. Sabrina's bedroom door was still closed and Cat wanted to walk in but did not want to be pushy and make matters worse. Cat went into her bedroom and closed the door. She sat at the edge of her bed letting her thoughts take her on a journey. Her thoughts were interrupted by an alert from her phone. It was a text from Bobby that read, "Good night, beautiful."

Valentine's day was two weeks away and if Cat and Bobby's relationship lasted, it would be the first time she would have a Valentine. Cat lit up like the lights on houses during Christmas time. She laid her head on her pillow and went to sleep.

Chapter 3

The sunrise from the east rested on Cat's face. Cat sat straight up in her bed and stretched her arms out and took a big yawn. She rubbed her eyes and drug herself out of bed. She walked into the bathroom and as she passed Sabrina she gently brushed against her to see if the storm had calmed. Sabrina gave no response. Cat slumped her shoulders over, believing that it was a failed attempt, and slowly walked into the bathroom. Cat was on cruise control; the only thing she could think about was her sister and solutions of how she could repair their relationship. They all piled up in the car as Connie dropped them off at school. Cat saw Bobby coming at a distance, assuming that he was picking her up for school. She didn't ask Connie to let her out because she was too concerned about Sabrina.

The school day took forever to end. Cat shuffled to each class with her head in the clouds thinking about Sabrina. Cat was standing with Stephen by the door of her Chemistry class waiting on Ms. Bey to open the door. Stephen was trying to quiz Cat on the test that they were about to take, even though he was annoyed by the fact that she did not show up for her tutoring session with him. Stephen suppressed his feelings and decided not to mention it and help her anyway. Samantha and her friend Brenda came strolling up, almost falling over and bumping into each kid as they came down the hallway.

"What is wrong with you Cat?" Samantha said in a slurred tone.

Stephen got real close to Cat and whispered in her ear, "Eww, this is someone you are acquainted with? Come on Cat, you can do much better. She is the school's lush."

Cat did not respond to either of them; she was too worried about Sabrina to let her thoughts drift anywhere from the concerns of her little sister. Ms. Bey walked up and Samantha took a step back, trying to compose herself, but the liquor got the best of her and knocked her off balance. She fell right onto Ms. Bey. The stack of quiz papers went flying out of Ms. Bey's hand. The aroma of liquor filled the air and Ms. Bey stared Samantha down; she was furious. Ms. Bey was the kind of teacher that was laid back and really cared about the students; she was more like a mother figure to most. Cat looked at Samantha in despair, knowing that Samantha was about to get the discipline of her life. Ms. Bey grabbed Samantha by the arm and walked her into a corner of the classroom. She did not even bother picking up the papers. Most of the kids that were walking in the hallway gathered around to see what was going on, assuming that someone was about to fight due to the number of kids standing around now forming a big crowd. Once they realized no one was fighting, they eventually left and went to class.

Stephen and Cat began to pick up the quiz papers. Ms. Bey looked at Cat and Stephen as she was escorting Samantha out of the class and stated, "I will be back. Place a quiz on every desk face down." Cat and Stephen followed the directions of Ms. Bey and then took their seats.

Bobby came walking in the classroom shortly after the incident. He walked up to Cat and gave her a kiss on the lips. Cat was confused as to why Bobby walked all the way to her classroom and kissed her. It made no sense to her until she saw the look that Bobby gave Stephen. Cat knew a kid in the crowd must have told Bobby that Cat was standing with him, assuming that she and Stephen had some type of secret relationship. Before Bobby could walk away, Cat introduced Bobby to Stephen, wanting him to know the friendship that she and Stephen shared. Cat knew it was best to tell Bobby who Stephen was instead of letting him speculate. Cat had witnessed enough of Connie's soap operas to know that it could go really badly if she was not upfront with Bobby and let him know the dynamics of the relationship now. Bobby said his good byes and left the classroom. Stephen did in fact have a crush on Cat but after that encounter he knew it was best to allow his crush to remain a secret. Ms. Bey returned to the classroom and Cat went back into isolation, letting her thoughts race through her mind, thinking about how she could mend what was broken within her sister.

All their friends noticed that Cat was quiet and distant during lunch. The fact that everyone kept asking Sabrina what was wrong with Cat escalated Sabrina's frustration about Cat always getting the attention. During lunch Cat made it a point to be near Sabrina. Bobby smoothly approached Cat from behind and Cat pushed him away, knowing that it was him. The only thing that was on Cat's mind was her little sister.

One of Bobby's friends walked up to him and said, "This is your girl?" He was giving Bobby one of those guy code looks, insinuating that he had a good-looking girlfriend.

Bobby introduced Sabrina by saying, "Yeah, and this is her sister, Sabrina." The boy had an astonished look on his face.

Sabrina mumbled under her breath, "Here we go." Cat was in sync with Sabrina's every movement and word. She heard what she had said and wanted to know what she was talking about.

The boy proceeded, "You guys are sisters? You don't look anything alike. She looks mixed and she looks like a regular black girl. She has long hair and she has a weave. She has contacts and she has beautiful eyes."

Sabrina started out speaking but could not finish the first syllable before Cat jumped right in. At that moment Cat realized Sabrina's frustration. Sabrina's eyes began to water as if she was going to start crying.

"First of all, what is the definition of a 'regular black girl'?" Cat said, making air quotes with her fingers. "Second, her hair is real, and longer than mine; and her eyes are real too. So do you mean to tell me in 2016 you are still stuck believing that all black girls' hair is short and that they cannot have colored eyes? You sound stupid. My sister has a body that celebrities pay for, street and book smarts that would run circles around you, and she is lit! So boy, have several seats!"

The whole crowd that gathered as Cat was talking burst out laughing and pointing at the boy, pointing at his shoes all saying, "What are those?!." The boy walked away in embarrassment. Cat looked at Sabrina and smiled.

The day was finally over and Cat could not wait to be at the house to have her one on one with Sabrina. Connie pulled up and Cat jumped in the car without saying goodbye to any of her friends. Once

50

home her phone kept alerting her to texts from Bobby; Cat did not open or read any of them. She was focused like tunnel vision about her pep talk with her little sister. Cat grabbed Sabrina by the hand and rushed upstairs into the bathroom and closed the door behind them.

She looked at Sabrina as tears ran down her face and pushed her in front of the mirror as she stood behind her and said, "Look at you." Sabrina put her head down in embarrassment, not wanting to look up at the mirror, as she silently started crying. Cat knew Sabrina was crying because her shoulders were jerking. Cat took her finger and gently put it under Sabrina's chin and lifted her head up; she held it with her hand to keep it in place.

Cat was still crying and told Sabrina, "You are more than enough. God made you exactly how He wanted you to be because you are a gift from God. You have to believe you are beautiful even when no one else thinks you are. Being mixed is a trend that will soon fade as they always do. I believe that I am beautiful but I also believe that I get to stand next to the most beautiful sister that anyone could have. I realized today that you have envied the way people have always made a difference with us because of one simple thing-our complexion-because everything else is the same. Our eyes are the same, our hair is the same, and oh I forgot, you have a killer body that I want."

They both laughed. They turned and stood facing one another, no longer looking at the mirror. "I vow to stand up for you even when you have the courage to stand up for yourself. You are my little sister and I love you. It wasn't that I did not care how you were being treated. I was naïve because of my own hurt and pain that I was experiencing from Connie. I'm sorry Sabrina. I never realized how my compliments were an insult to you."

They both hugged one another so tight they could hardly breathe, and cried in each other's arms. Connie was standing outside the bathroom door wondering what they were talking about. Connie too was crying after overhearing their conversation. She was crying for two things. One, because of Sabrina's pain, and two, because of the pain that she had inflicted on Cat for so many years. Connie knew she needed to sit Cat down and speak with her about her father once and for all; no more hiding the past and avoiding what could no longer be avoided.

Connie yelled to Sabrina to take her younger siblings downstairs and give them some ice cream. Sabrina knew that meant to keep them occupied for whatever it was that Connie wanted to do, but what she didn't understand was why she was giving the task to her and not Cat. It was Cat that was the mini mother. Sabrina did as she was told and rushed her siblings down stairs into the kitchen where she gave them big bowls of ice cream. She knew the more she gave them the longer it would take them to eat before she had to think of something else to keep them interested and not interfering in what Connie had planned.

"Cat!" yelled Connie. Cat proceeded in the direction of Connie's bedroom. Connie was sitting at the edge of her bed upright with a peculiar look on her face -one that Cat had ever seen before. Cat slowly walked, unaware of what would happen next.

"Yes," she answered. Connie looked at her with watery eyes and patted the bed right next to her. Cat knew that meant to come sit down; but what did she want? This was becoming uncomfortable for Cat. Her insides were screaming "Let me out of here!" An intimate conversation was not one she was used to-- especially not with her mother. It was just as uncomfortable as when she had that odd encounter with Susan. Then a light bulb went off in Cat's mind. She wants to talk about sex. "Easy topic," Cat thought, "all I have to say is that I am not sexually active." Cat was anticipating the question as she relaxed.

Connie began speaking, "Baby, I know that even though you have never talked about it much, not having a dad has had to bother you growing up." Cat's stomach felt like she just hit a thousand foot drop on a rollercoaster. She clinched the covers on the opposite side of Connie and held on tight; she knew she was in for a ride. Cat dropped her head in despair.

Connie proceeded, "Do you remember that woman, Trina, that was mean to you that day at Grandma Pie's house?"

Cat answered with annoyance in her voice, "Yes."

"Well her hu –hu- hu," Connie could not gather up the courage to get the words out. Cat noticed that it was hard for Connie to say so she finished the sentence for her.

"Trina's husband is my dad."

Connie broke down crying, " I am so sorry Cat. I was ashamed that my cousin's husband is your father and that your cousins are your sisters and brothers."

That hadn't even crossed Cat's mind until she contemplated on how sick it sounded that her cousins were her sisters and brothers. Cat instantly felt like she was going to vomit. Cat did not say one word but she cursed Connie out one hundred times over and over in her mind. Cat clinched her fist even tighter. Before she knew it, everything went blank-- and before she could stop herself, she hit Connie right in her left eye. Connie paused in shock, and Cat knew she couldn't back down now; she had already taken the first hit and Connie was going to murder her. They started fighting. They made so much noise rolling around the room that Sabrina ran upstairs. Sabrina busted through the door thinking something was wrong, and something was wrong all right. Cat was so mad that she had Connie's box braids in her hand and was giving her blow-by-blow straight to the face.

"Oh my God! Cat what the heck are you doing? Let mom go!" screamed Sabrina. Cat was so enraged that she could not stop if she wanted to. Sabrina looked into Cat's eyes and saw someone that she had never seen before.

Sabrina could not get Cat to stop and then Cat caught eye contact with Sabrina and gazed into her eyes; she saw so many emotions that it scared Cat. It was in that moment that Cat realized she had just came out of a trance. Cat could see the fear in Sabrina's eyes. Cat immediately jumped off of Connie and ran to her room. She locked the door and smothered her face into her pillow and cried profusely. Cat had lost control for the first time ever in her life. She was now afraid of what Connie might do. She cowered in a corner of her room, anticipating that Connie would bust through the door with some type of object to hit her with. Cat could do nothing but cry and think about how severely she was about to be beaten for what she thought was worse than murder—being-disrespectful in any form toward her mother.

There was a thump at the door and Cat clinched her pillow, waiting for the slap to the face or the kick to the leg or the blow to the head. Cat did not know how it would play out but she knew it would be bad. There were a few more thumps and it had happened, someone came rushing in. Too scared to put her head up and look, Cat held tight to the pillow and smashed her face into it. Cat pushed her head so far into the pillow that she couldn't breathe. She thought death would be much easier to do than to reap the repercussions of Connie's wrath. Cat started seeing stars, then darkness. Cat passed out; she wasn't breathing.

Sabrina stood over Cat in disbelief. Sabrina could not move; her brain was saying, "Yell for help! Call the paramedics!" But all she could do was stand there and look at her sister's motionless body. She was in shock. Connie had called Sharon while she barricaded herself in her room in disbelief of what had all taken place. Sharon had rushed over to the house and ran up the stairs to get to Connie, but noticed Sabrina standing over someone. Sharon could only see a person's legs because the side of the bed was covering the upper body. Sharon instantly knew something was wrong. The only thing that went through her mind was that her sister was about to go to jail for murdering her niece and she would have to be her defense attorney. Sharon covered her mouth and tears started to rush in like a flood busting through a wall. Her tears looked like hurricane Katrina when the levees broke.

Sharon could not contain it as she walked slowly to the body and screamed, "Oh my God! Please don't let her be dead."

Connie overheard Sharon. Connie came running out of her room thinking Cat had committed suicide. The feeling of guilt came over Connie and she ran to Cat's room screaming, "Lord, please don't take my baby! Please, I'm sorry! I will serve you whole heartedly, please bring her back!" Connie ran to Cat like she was a linebacker moving everything in her path to get to her baby. Once there, Connie began CPR.

"Call the paramedics, stop just standing there!" Sabrina could not move. It was as if her feet were stuck in a big pile of cement. She wanted to run and call the paramedics but her body would not allow her to move. Everything was moving in slow motion and all she could do was stare at her sister in deep thought.

Connie pressed down on Cat's chest, "Get up baby, get up," Connie said over and over.

"You're not doing it right!" Sharon, blurted out.

Connie jumped out of the way so Sharon could bring her baby back to life. Sharon got down on her knees and put one of her hands over the other and started pumping Cat's chest and then breathing in her mouth. After the third time, Cat gasped for air and started crying. All three of them grabbed Cat as if she was a mangled doll. Connie kissed her head, Sabrina hugged her legs, and Sharon grabbed her hands and started praying. This went on for over five minutes. They all cried and Connie told Cat and Sabrina that she loved them over and over. This was the most affection that either of them had seen from Connie in this context.

They all eventually left Cat's room and retreated to their space in the house. Cat gathered her thoughts and laid in her bed after lying on the floor for over an hour thinking about how she almost died. The only thing that bothered her about the incident was that she hit and fought her mom. She played the scenario over and over in her head, wishing she could turn back time and verbally express her feelings without allowing her emotions to take over.

Valentine's day was the next day but Cat couldn't care less. She had so many thoughts bombarding her that she stayed up for hours picking through each detail. Would she ever meet her dad? Would Connie ever forgive her? What would her relationship be like with her mom moving forward? Would her dad acknowledge her? Cat eventually rolled over and fell asleep--by this time it was 4 a.m.

Sabrina peeked in Cat's room around 7 a.m. to see if she was almost ready to leave. To Sabrina's surprise, Cat was knocked out sleep. She was usually the first one dressed and getting everyone else together. Connie peeked in over Sabrina's shoulder and whispered, "Let her rest, she has had a long night." Sabrina smiled, she knew Cat had a life changing experiencing yesterday and wanted her sister to be okay. Connie gathered all the kids and put them in the car, and off they went to do the morning drop offs to school.

Cat woke up at noon and jumped up to get ready when she realized it was the afternoon. She went to her mother's room to apologize but Connie was not in there. Cat walked to the top of the staircase and could hear Connie and her aunt Sharon laughing and reminiscing. That was Cat's cue that the storm had cleared and she could go downstairs. Cat entered the family room and hugged Connie as tears rushed down her cheeks.

She couldn't form her words in time before Connie said, "Baby, it is okay. I understand your frustration and even though I did not approve of you hitting me because that is never acceptable in any circumstance, I understand." Cat continued hugging her mom, relieved that Connie was finally starting to act like a mother and understand that Cat needed love and attention and to just be a kid with solid guidance and reassurance. Cat grabbed something to eat and went and sat at the top of the stairs because she knew that her mom and aunt would have a conversation once she exited, and she wanted to hear what they had to say.

Sharon gently put her hand over Connie's hand, leaned in and said, "At some point you have to talk to Reggie and let him know about Cat."

"Well that's why I told her. He actually came to me a week ago and wanted me to tell her before he did. I wanted to be the first to tell her you know. I did not want anyone telling my baby who her father was."

Cat started to see the transformation of Connie. Connie kept referring to Cat as her baby, which was another new thing to add to the list. When

Connie said 'baby,' it was like a term of endearment that flowed preciously off of Connie's lips, as if Cat was fragile and she was shielding a little baby from harm.

"Well when is he coming to see her, or are you taking Cat to see him? How is all this going to work?" Sharon said in an overwhelmed tone.

"I called him crying and told him what happened last night. Of course Trina was upset that I called him crying, thinking I wanted sympathy, but my only concern was our daughter in that moment."

"So is she mad or naw?" Sharon and Connie both laughed. "No, but seriously, is she going to be accepting of Cat or is this going to be a problem in their marriage?"

"Sharon, Reggie has known for years that Cat was his daughter. I never lied about who her father was,"

Sharon gave Connie a stare as if she was saying, "Are you serious?"

"Okay, I lied for years out of embarrassment but once we got here in California, I told him everything. I am in no form trying to interfere in his marriage with Trina even though I think she thinks that."

"Well you have to be real with yourself. I mean, you guys were really close, and for you to sleep with her boyfriend at the time, I mean, come on. Now she shouldn't have stayed with him but who am I to put my two cents in," Sharon said as she giggled.

"My sister, and that is why I love you; because you give me the truth even when I do not want to hear it," Connie replied as she giggled as well.

"Does she know Yesenia is her sister, Connie?"

Cat could not take any more surprises; she went in her room and closed the door behind her. She had one more thing to add to the thought list before turning on her music and putting her earphones in, did Yessenia already know?

Sabrina ran up the stairs and peeked in Cat's door with a big smile on her face, "You have a visitor."

Cat, reading her lips, took her headphones off and got up slowly, while wondering what would happen next. Cat sluggishly walked downstairs. When she reached the door, standing there was Bobby with a hand full of balloons wrapped around his wrist, flowers and candy in one hand, and a huge bear in the other. Cat wanted to smile but her eyes swiftly looked behind Bobby at a Hispanic male. Not knowing who he was or why he was approaching her front door with flowers and red and white balloons, Cat thought to herself, "Here we go again. Connie has a new boyfriend." Bobby noticed that Cat's eyes were not focused on him but behind him. He turned around to see what his girlfriend was so focused on. Cat realized at that point that she was gawking at the dude so she tried to pretend as if she was looking at something else and slowly turned her attention back on Bobby.

"Can I come in or do I just stand here while you keep staring at the old man behind me?" snickered Bobby. Cat moved out of the way to let Bobby in and just as she moved back, the Hispanic man was standing right before her at the front door.

"Is Cat here?" the man said. Cat nodded her head up and down not knowing what he wanted.

Bobby saw Cat's posture and knew she was uncomfortable and came rushing in to protect his girlfriend.

"May I help you?" he said.

"Yes, I am looking for Cat, my daughter,"

Bobby turned and looked at Cat. Cat started to tear up and tried her hardest to fight back the tears but it was not working. She started crying. Bobby and the man both went in to console her. Bobby would not back down. Besides, he could tell by her posture that she did not know this guy. The man stopped in mid hug because he noticed that Bobby was trying to protect her. Bobby embraced Cat and everything in his hands fell to the ground. The balloons went up to the ceiling. Cat buried her head in Bobby's chest.

Meanwhile, Sabrina had informed Connie of what was taking place. Connie patted Bobby on the back giving him a cue to let go. Bobby took Cat by the hand and sat her on the sofa then sat beside her. The man sat next to Cat on the other side and introduced himself, "Cat, I am your dad, Reggie. I'm sorry that I didn't recognize you. The last time I laid eyes on you, you were five years old, and that was on a picture at your Grandma Pie's house." Cat listened in silence not knowing what to say. "I just want to get to know you so that I we can have a relationship with you, if you are willing," said Reggie.

Cat lifted her head, but she could not speak. Her head and face were filled with so many different emotions. She wanted to cry and smile at the same time but then felt anger because no one had ever told her about Reggie. Cat put her face in the palm of her hands and began to cry uncontrollably. Reggie and Connie both looked at one another not knowing what to do. They knew the news would be both hard to deliver and to receive. Knowing that Cat had been through enough within the last twenty-four hours, both Reggie and Connie decided to retreat to the family room, leaving her alone with Bobby. Bobby hugged Cat tight and would not let go. She was overwhelmed by the support of Bobby-- never having experienced anything like it before.

Bobby hugged her without saying a word. He did not know what to do but be there for her. He could only think about his own relationship with his father as he sat and held Cat. Bobby's father was a wealthy man and was successful in his field. He was a banker, the type that worked long days and long nights. Bobby's father thought that he could compensate his love with material possessions. Bobby was happy for Cat that she had a father that took the time out to try to mend what seemed like it couldn't be fixed. On the other hand, he was jealous. Bobby craved a relationship with his father. Bobby's dad was a provider and gave his family the best, but when it came to affection and quality time with his wife and kid, well that was a different story. Bobby was raised by his nanny Grace and did not really have a connection with his mother. At one point Bobby started calling his nanny Mom, being confused with who was who. Grace was his mother in his eyes even though he could tell that his mother despised it. Bobby's family was wealthy and successful from the outside looking in, but from the inside looking out, they were a family that had no connection-- living in a house as strangers-- not knowing anything about one another other than their name. Bobby got lost in thought before Cat looked up at him and noticed that something was bothering him.

"What's wrong?"

"Nothing," mumbled Bobby.

Cat knew by the look on his face that he was troubled but decided to let it go.

"I know that we've only been together for a short time, but I will never be my father and I will always cherish and love you. No matter how much I want to pursue my career, I will want my family even more."

Cat turned toward Bobby with a confused look. "Where did that come from?" she mumbled, hoping that Bobby could not hear her, and he didn't.

The day was almost over and had been a long day. Bobby was disappointed that things hadn't gone as he planned, but he was happy that Cat had met her father and now would have a chance at the type of relationship he longed for with his parents. Bobby kissed Cat on the forehead and said his goodbyes. Cat walked to the doorway and watched Bobby drive away until she could no longer see his luxury car. Cat went upstairs, took a shower, and went to bed. She was so overwhelmed by what had all taken place that day that she told herself she did not want to give it another thought or tear. Cat tossed and turned in her bed until she was comfortable and fell asleep.

Chapter 4

It was a Saturday morning and a month had passed since that long, terrible Valentine's day and Cat had distanced herself from it and left it right there in the past. March was finally here and it was Cat's birthday month. Cat made it a point to let everyone know that she would be celebrating her birthday the entire month. Usually birthdays were not a big deal in their home, but Cat wanted to be celebrated since she had never been in the past.

Bobby figured it was his chance to make up for her emotional Valentine's Day. He wanted to go all out for her and make her birthday special. Bobby knocked at the door. Cat opened the door and Bobby pulled out a little box from behind his back. Cat retrieved the box and opened it up. It was a beautiful shiny diamond ring.

"Is he asking to marry me?" she thought, "We are too young to get married." Bobby could see the confusion written all over her face and preceded to tell her it was a promise ring. Cat blushed. She was falling in love with Bobby day by day. He was like a boyfriend out of an 80's movie, which Cat loved. Cat and Bobby walked outside to have some privacy. They stood on the porch discussing their future. Cat was excited about being a senior the following school year and anticipated applying to different colleges. One of their promises to one another was that they would attend the same college. They had gotten lost in the idea of the college life and how they assumed it would be. They discussed joining a fraternity and sorority. They laughed and envisioned the future together.

Bobby said, "Then after college we will have kids, I cannot wait." The conversation had taken a turn for the worse; in that moment it became very real to Cat.

"Kids!" Cat exclaimed.

"Yeah, kids. What, you don't want to have kids?" Bobby said, as if his feelings were hurt.

"No, I mean, yes, but shouldn't marriage come before having kids? I want it to be done right. I do not want to be like my mom."

"Of course, Sunshine. We will get married and have kids after. I vow to stay faithful to you and to always put you first. You already know I don't want to be like my parents. I love you Cat. I mean, you are more to me than just sex, that's why I haven't even bothered asking you about it. Of course I want you to be my wife." Bobby said in a soft tone as if every syllable was important.

"Why do you keep calling me Sunshine?"

"Because you are my sunshine, you bring the light into my life,"

Cat started laughing, "Really Bobby, you're trying to gas me up and I am not a car."

Samantha came running outside of her house motioning for Cat and Bobby to follow behind her. They walked in the house and observed Samantha's mother sitting at the dinner table, hunched over and slurring her words. Cat and Bobby looked at one another already knowing that Samantha's mother was as drunk as a skunk. Cat had seen Connie in this condition enough times to know. Samantha sat at the table with her mother and motioned Cat and Bobby to come and sit at the table. Samantha picked up the bottle of wine, poured herself some in a glass, and started to drink it until the wine glass was empty.

Samantha said, "Come on guys, take the edge off."

"Everybody needs to wind down and relax after a long day of work," said Samantha's mom.

Cat's mouth dropped and was wide open. Bobby went to pour himself a glass and Cat grabbed his arm and gave him a mother look as though she was threatening Bobby with her eyes. Bobby knew what it meant and placed the glass back on the table. Where most kids would have found Samantha's mom to be considered cool, Cat was actually disgusted. She felt as though Samantha's mother was a bad influence and a poor example of a mother. Cat thought about the day when Samantha came to school drunk and bumped into Ms. Bey, making her drop all of the quiz papers. Cat got up and walked toward the door and Bobby followed close behind her.

"Okay, Ms. Perfect, you act like you have never drunk before. This is normal where we come from. Tell her Bobby."

Cat rolled her eyes and walked out of the front door. Cat was irate and turned around before Bobby could get completely out the door and stated, "Is this what type of stuff you guys do Bobby, get tipsy with your parents?"

"Yeah, I mean no. I mean, I am not allowed to drink with my parents but I have friends that do. I mean, when we have parties most parents provide the alcohol, its normal Cat,"

"Normal? I guess this is a white people thing!" Cat shouted.

Bobby was so hurt. Did Cat just point out their differences of race? That was one thing that Bobby was dreading being honest about—their opposite color of skin. His parents would not care at all but his extended family would. Bobby gave Cat a kiss on the forehead as he always did and got in his car and drove off. Cat went into her house and closed the door behind her.

Later that night Bobby called Cat and asked if she and Sabrina wanted to go to Mark's party. "Will there be alcohol there?"

"Of Course, you know how us White people do it." Cat knew that she had hurt Bobby's feelings earlier that day by the way he responded to her. Cat tried to apologize when Bobby abruptly cut her off and told her that they had forty-five minutes to get dressed and that he would be on his way.

"Sabrina, do you want to go to a party?" Cat asked.

"Not really, but if you want to go then I will go with you."

Cat knew her only obstacle was getting Connie to agree to let them go. Cat peered into Connie's room. She thought if she could see what kind of mood Connie was in, she would be able to determine whether or not it was a good idea to ask if she could go to the party. Before Cat could even ask, Connie saw Cat peeking around her door.

"Little girl, what do you want? I see you peeking in my room," Connie said calmly.

"Uh, can I go to a party with a few friends?"

"Who are these few friends? I need names."

"Bobby, Sabrina, and Samantha." Cat knew she had to say Sabrina and Samantha because she did not want her mom to think that she was trying to sneak off with Bobby.

"Where is this party and what time is it over?"

"I think it is over at 1," Cat mumbled, hoping that Connie would allow her to be out that late.

"The only thing that's open at 1 in the morning is legs. You need to be walking through my door at 12."

"Okay," Cat said as she was walking away from the door. She was so excited and shocked that she had even agreed to let her go.

It was already 7 o'clock and both Cat and Sabrina were fully dressed. Cat and Sabrina stood outside waiting on Bobby as Cat texted him and told him that she was ready. Connie looked out the living room window and did not see Samantha.

She opened the front door and said, "Where is Samantha?"

"Her mom wouldn't let her go," Cat said in a way that Sabrina instantly caught on that Cat was lying. Connie closed the door and went back inside.

"That lie was so unnecessary," Sabrina said under her breath.

"You already know she would've said no if I didn't mention at least two girls that was going with me and Bobby."

Sabrina chuckled, "True."

Bobby pulled up and Cat waited for him to get out the car and open the door like he usually did, but he did not budge. Sabrina noticed the disconnection between Cat and Bobby but she did not say a single word. She opened the back passenger door and got in. Bobby's windows were tinted so you could not see inside the car. When Sabrina got in she saw Mark sitting in the front passenger seat and he was not making motions to get out and let Cat in. Cat went to the front door and pulled on the handle and Mark opened it from the inside. Cat stood there waiting for Mark to get out. It appeared as if they were both standing their ground to ride shotgun.

Bobby looked over at Mark and stated "Dude, what are you doing? Let my girl in the car."

Mark looked back at Bobby and said, "Oh, my bad, I thought Black people rode in the back"

Cat was furious. At that point she knew what the whole fuss was over. Bobby was upset and told Mark what she said.

"Man, get out and get in the back."

Mark got out and got in the backseat. Bobby was nervous about Cat's reaction. He did not expect for his best friend to spill the beans and let it be known what he said when he was venting. The whole fifteen-minute ride to the party was awkward. Bobby played Kendrick to ease the tension in the car but no one made a peep. Bobby tried placing his hand on Cat's leg as a reassurance that he was no longer mad but Cat moved his hand and placed it on his own leg. Bobby knew he had messed up and wanted to fix it but did not want to have the talk in front of Sabrina and Mark.

They had arrived. Bobby parked and jumped out, hurrying to Cat's door to open it before she could open the door on her own. It was his way of showing her he messed up and that he was sorry for not opening her door the first time. Cat was obliged but did not want him to know. He reached to hold her hand and then placed his hand into his pocket really fast, trying to play it off as if that was what he was doing all along. Bobby did not want to be embarrassed if Cat rejected his hand.

Once in the party, Cat walked right in and started dancing. This was her first time at a house party. All the talk about the parents providing alcohol was out the window—all she heard was the music and she couldn't help but to move in sync with the sound. A dark skinned African-American male with a bright, white smile came right behind Cat and started grooving. Cat was so caught up in the music that she didn't even bother to look to see who was behind her; all she knew was that whoever it was, was a really good dancer. Bobby had been so busy greeting his friends that he never saw Cat dancing. He thought that she was behind him. A few of Bobby's friend's from school noticed Cat dancing and looked at Bobby, giving him an eye gesture signaling him to look back at Cat and the guy dancing. Bobby turned around to see what they were cuing him to look at and saw Cat on the dance floor.

Bobby really didn't have much rhythm and he never danced at parties but he felt disrespected by both the guy and Cat. Besides, his reputation was at stake, he had to do something. He walked up to the guy as nervous as he was, and moved him out of the way with his body and attempted to dance with Cat. The guy was not having Bobby moving him out of the way as if he were disrespecting him. Not knowing that Bobby and Cat were a couple, the guy punched Bobby in the face and they started fighting. Bobby's friends came to help and the guy's friends came and it was an all out brawl. Cat got punched in the face by accident. Sabrina grabbed Cat out of the way. Cat was holding her eye trying to figure out what had happened. She couldn't see out of one eye. She felt her eye growing by the second in the palm of her hand. Finally, some parents came in and broke up the fight. They put the guy and his friends out of the party, but he did not leave before approaching Cat and telling her his Snapchat name.

"Aye hit me up on Snapchat—Baby Boy double 07." Cat heard him but wasn't really listening; she could only think of how bad her eye looked.

Mark was furious. He reflected back on what Cat had said to Bobby regarding the White people comment and walked up to Cat and said, "Yeah, this is how us White people party, so we sent your little coon of a boy home."

Bobby's cousins chimed in saying, "Why didn't you guys kick those Black hoes out with their boyfriends?"

Cat had no idea that was Bobby's cousin and Bobby's cousin Michael had no idea Cat was Bobby's girlfriend. Bobby was pissed at Mark and was reconsidering their friendship. He hugged Cat and grabbed Sabrina by the hand and walked them outside of the party. Michael looked at Bobby in shock, finally realizing that Cat was Bobby's girlfriend that he had been bragging about. They all were standing outside by the car.

"What happened? All I know is I was dancing with you and you started fighting," Cat said, seeking understanding. After Cat questioning what had happened, Bobby then knew that Cat had no clue of what happened.

Sabrina chimed in, "You started dancing and this fine, I mean fine, *chocolate* dude came behind you and started grooving; and then Bobby moved him out the way to dance with you and then they started fighting." Sabrina did think the other guy was attractive but she only put emphasis on the word chocolate because she felt slighted about how Mark and their friends were treating them and saying racial slurs pertaining to her and Cat.

Bobby opened the door for both Cat and Sabrina and said, "I will be right back." Bobby went back into the party and confronted Mark. Michael apologized to Bobby, not allowing him to say anything,

"Bro, my bad. I didn't know that was your girl. She is fine. I would never disrespect your girl like that. I just wish you would've given me a heads up about the details of her race."

"Why, why does that even matter? I told you she was dope and beautiful. What else was there to add to the story?"

"Bro, you right. Everyone is just anticipating meeting this girl you have been talking about and I mean, you know how the family is."

"Screw the family!" Bobby said. Then he pointed his finger at Mark and said, "And screw you too!" Bobby stormed out of the party. He walked back to the car, got in, and peeled off, leaving black tire marks on the ground. Cat had never seen Bobby this mad before. She knew the white comment had him pissed but not to this extent. Bobby pulled up in front of Cat's house and Cat leaned over to kiss him goodbye but he turned his head. Cat noticed his eyes were watery, which indicated that he had been crying during the drive over to her house. Sabrina got out of the car and unlocked the door with her key.

Connie looked at her phone and it was only 9. "That party was over quick. What, the police shut it down? Where is Cat," Connie asked.

"No, we were just ready to go; Cat is outside in the car talking," Sabrina answered. Connie peeked out the blinds and saw the car parked out front on the curb. Both Connie and Sabrina went upstairs to turn down for the night.

Cat placed her hand on Bobby's eyes and wiped away the tears that started to flow from his eyes. She did not know why he was crying, but after listening to Sabrina's account of what happened, she knew she was part to blame.

"Bobby, talk to me. What's wrong?" Cat pleaded.

"Man, I am just sick of it all," Bobby said as he was fighting back his tears.

"All of what?"

"When I first met you Cat, all I saw was your beauty and how dope of a person you were. I didn't care about your race. I wanted you because of the person you are. Then the other day when you said this is a 'White people thing,' it made me think about how my family feels about Black people. You are just like them Cat. When I refused to open your door earlier today it was because I was still pissed about your comment; and I know I was wrong for telling Mark but of course he felt some type of way because he is White too. You cannot say things like that and think it is okay. I have to deal with racist comments with my family, I don't want to deal with that with my girl."

"I'm sorry, I didn't know. I said that because you and Samantha were acting as if I was weird because that wasn't my normal."

"Look, all I know is I don't want to be mad at you like that ever again, and you bet' not be dancing with no dude like that ever again. I don't care what race they are, purple, pink, blue or green." Bobby said as he started to laugh. Cat began to laugh as well.

"Never again babe, I promise," Cat said as she kissed Bobby on the cheek. They gave one another a long hug and Cat got out of the car and waved goodbye.

Chapter 5

It was finally Monday and Cat's eye was back to normal. It wasn't as bad as she thought but Cat made sure that she covered her eye with her hair because Connie would notice any slight change and Cat was not taking any chances. Connie dropped Cat and Sabrina off at school after their morning routine. Cat saw Yessenia walking toward them. Yessenia spoke to them and joked about the party on Saturday night and acted like she usually did. Cat wondered if she knew. Cat could only conclude two things; either she didn't know about Cat being her sister, or she was playing it off really well. Cat was not going to mention it if Yessenia didn't. Cat played along. She didn't want anyone else to know what was going on or to notice her thoughts regarding Yessenia. She tried hard to mask her feelings because Cat wore her thoughts and emotions on her sleeve; she did not have a poker face.

The bell rang and Cat went to class. Stephen was sitting slumped over in his chair and seemed sad. Cat tapped him on the shoulder, but Stephen too was wearing a mask and did not want anyone to know what was going on. He sat straight up at attention and said, "Hey Cat, I was studying for the exam that we have today."

Cat knew he wasn't being completely honest but she let it go. Stephen reached for his pen and there were red marks across his arms and wrist. Cat grabbed Stephen's hand and raised his shirt.

"OMG," whispered Cat.

"Please don't tell anyone, please don't Cat," Stephen begged.

"You have to talk to someone about this Stephen. I am your friend and I'm concerned. Clearly there is something going on that has you harming yourself. You have to talk to someone, please talk to someone."

Stephen put his head down and responded, "I know. I'm stressed out. My dad was not even a senior when he knew what college he wanted to attend. My parents are very successful. My sister is a lawyer and my older brother attends Harvard. My family tells me it is okay, that I can pursue whatever path I want, but they have set the bar extremely high. I can't compete with my sister or brother."

"Stephen, follow your dreams. I'm pretty sure your parents will be happy with whatever you decide to do and I know you will be successful. I can see you now coming to our twentieth high school reunion and you being the next Bill Gates or Steve Jobs."

"Cat, you live in a fantasy world. I wish I were half as smart as Bill Gates and Steve Jobs. It's easier said than done. I'm in band, which is all day, and I'm in all advanced placement classes except for Chemistry. I have a rigorous class load, Cat."

"Well maybe you need to quit band."

"See, you just don't get it. Band is my outlet; plus, I want to write music one day. Thanks for being concerned, but there is no way out."

"You're being a bit over dramatic. I'm here for you no matter what," Cat said as she smiled and patted Stephen on the shoulder.

Stephen sighed as if he was hopeless. Cat turned her undivided attention to Ms. Bey. Ms. Bey gave instruction for the day's assignment. Cat and Stephen went right to work. The bell rung and Cat hugged Stephen and said, "Everything will be alright, just wait and see."

The day was half way over and lunch had just begun. Cat found her group of friends that she usually hung out with at lunch. She approached the center quad and there they were, some standing around a table, some sitting and eating, and others laughing and joking around. Cat sat down at the table and Bobby brought her some food as he always did. Cat never had money to purchase lunch but it didn't matter if she did or didn't; Bobby always made sure that he bought lunch for both Cat and Sabrina. Sabrina told Cat about a boy she had a crush on and Bobby sat and ate his lunch trying not to listen in on their conversation. Bobby felt as though Cat's personal life regarding girl talk was not his position to chime in or be nosey when she was having conversations with other females.

Stephen approached Cat's group of friends and stood in front of Cat on the other side. Cat motioned to Stephen to sit down and join them because he was just standing there not saying anything.

Then he began to speak, "Cat, I have always had a crush on you." Everyone was tuned into what he was saying. They started saying things like, "Aw." Bobby didn't find it amusing, he wanted to know where this confession of love was going. Cat did not know what to say, she was surprised that Stephen even felt that way about her. He never displayed any type of affection or gave any indication that he liked her in any way.

Stephen continued talking, "I just wanted to say goodbye." As he said 'goodbye,' he placed one knee on the table and leaned over and kissed Cat right on the lips. Cat sat there in shock, not knowing what to do. Stephen turned and walked away swiftly before anyone could gather his or her thoughts to respond to what had just taken place.

Bobby was upset; for the second time a male had openly hit on his girlfriend in his face, and to make matters worse, this time it was a geek. Bobby felt disrespected by both Stephen and Cat. The last time Cat was actually in the dark and did not know what was going on, but this time, Cat did not confront Stephen about kissing her and that's the part that made Bobby mad. Cat rubbed Bobby's leg trying to calm him down, knowing that he would be upset about Stephen kissing her. Mark, standing across the center quad gave Bobby a smirk, as if he was saying, "That's what you get." Bobby had not talked to Mark since the night of the party despite Mark texting Bobby and apologizing. Bobby got up from the table and walked away.

Cat caught up to follow him and pulled the back of his shirt and said, "Hold on Bobby, let me explain." Bobby stopped and turned around. "Today in class Stephen had cuts on his arm and when I asked about it he said that he was stressed out. I didn't know it was that serious. I brushed him off and tried to tell him to focus on the positive, but I guess it was much more serious than I thought," explained Cat. "Should we let the campus security know that he may harm himself?"

Bobby turned around and said, "I don't care what you do."

Cat knew that Bobby was upset with her. She was conflicted because if she went and notified the campus security Bobby would be mad and think that she cared more about Stephen than their relationship. If she stayed and tried to smooth things over with Bobby then Stephen may possibly be attempting suicide. Cat chose her relationship over her friend and decided to stay with Bobby, even though the two were not talking and just stood around to pass time until the bell rung. She knew in her heart that even though Bobby was still upset he would feel as though her loyalty lay with him. The bell finally rung and Cat kissed Bobby. Bobby did not engage in the kiss but he didn't reject it either. Cat turned in the direction toward her classroom and walked away.

Days had passed and Cat did not see Stephen at school. Feeling guilty that she did not notify the campus security that day, she could only expect the worst.

Friday during Chemistry class, Ms. Bey walked up to Cat and ʲsaid, "Stephen's parents requested that we notify his friends of the date and time of his funeral. Unfortunately, after speaking with all of his teachers, you were the only one that seemed to have had a relationship with him."

Cat could not believe what she had just heard. Did Ms. Bey just say he had no friends? And did she just say the date and time of his *funeral*? Cat snatched the paper out of Ms. Bey's hand and ran out of the classroom. She could not stop crying. She ran into the girls' bathroom, went into one of the stalls, and cried until she could not cry anymore. She slid down the wall of the stall and sat with her head in between her knees and rocked back and forth. This was the first time that Cat had experienced death and she did not know how to deal with it. She blamed herself and began to hit the stall wall over and over. Sabrina walked into the bathroom looking for Cat. Ms. Bey had contacted the front office and had them find Sabrina to go and sit with her sister. Sabrina could hear the sniffles from outside of the bathroom stall. Sabrina stood outside of the stall and waited for Cat to come out. After an hour, Cat came out and hugged Sabrina. It was like time stopped and all she felt was her sister's warm embrace.

"I called mom and she said to wait in the office until she is able to come pick us up," Sabrina whispered. They walked to the office and sat and waited. Connie took forever to pick them up.

School was over and Cat and Sabrina stood in the same spot that they always did. Bobby, Nancy, and Yessenia all gathered and waited with both Sabrina and Cat. By now the news had spread and Bobby and the others had gotten word about Stephen. Cat saw Reggie at a distance and figured that he was there for Yessenia. Cat turned her back to Yessenia, hoping that he would just get her and leave.

Yessenia walked toward Reggie and said, "Dad, what are you doing here? I was going to walk home with my friends like I always do."

"You can still walk home with your friends. You don't have to ride home with me if you don't want to." Yessenia started laughing, thinking it was a joke

"Then what did you come up here for, to talk to my teacher?"

Reggie smiled and turned Cat around by her shoulder and said, "I'm here for your sister."

Connie had called Reggie and asked if he could pick Cat up from school and talk to her. Connie

80

did not want to see Cat like that and wanted to share the responsibility of being a parent instead of always being the only parent there to pick up the pieces when things fell apart within her children's lives.

Everyone standing around looked shocked. Bobby looked at Sabrina to see if it was true and Sabrina looked back at Bobby and shrugged her shoulders. Cat hadn't seen Reggie since their first meeting on Valentines' Day. Yessenia looked embarrassed and walked away, furious. Reggie walked off with Cat and did not see that Yessenia was upset. Reggie assumed that Yessenia already knew because he had spoken to his wife, Trina, and they agreed that she would tell the girls and he would tell their sons.

"I know the last time we talked was on Valentine's Day and I thought I would wait and give you time to speak with me when you were ready. Your mom called me and I left work to be here because I know you are hurting over the death of your friend." Reggie went on and on. Cat wanted to be in the moment with her dad that she longed for but could not concentrate on anything he said because she was thinking about Stephen. Reggie talked for a whole hour and Cat felt like she was watching an old episode of *Charlie Brown*. All she heard was, "whomp whomp, whomp." Reggie and Cat went back to where only Bobby and Sabrina were now standing and walked to Reggie's car.

Cat and Sabrina were getting into Reggie's car when Bobby hugged Cat and said, "I'll be over in a bit; I just have to go to my dad's office and I will be right there."

"Don't bother." Cat was mad at everybody. She was displacing her anger on everyone that she encountered at that point.

Bobby put his head down and said, "Well if you need me, I'm here."

Reggie drove them home. Reggie walked Cat into the house and gave her a long heartfelt hug before Cat headed upstairs and closed her door. Cat sat in the middle of her floor for a while, staring at her carpet. She then got into her bed and lay there until she fell asleep.

Cat stayed in her room for a week, ignoring texts and phone calls and only coming out of her room to go to the bathroom. By this time Cat looked and smelled horrible. She was depressed. Connie had contacted the school and informed her teachers that she would be out until further notice and to excuse her absences. Bobby called and texted non-stop even though she would not reply or answer his calls. Cat wanted to get back into the groove of things but just could not help wanting to sleep. The thought of food made her nauseous.

Connie walked into Cat's room and said, "Baby, today is Stephen's funeral. Are you going?"

Cat sat up in her bed and answered, "Yes, I am going." '

"Well Bobby is downstairs waiting on you. You need to take a shower. Do you need me to help you?"

"No, I'm good."

Cat got up and took a shower. She got dressed and was ready to go. She walked down the staircase and saw Bobby waiting in the living room. Cat had not talked to Bobby so it was a bit awkward.

Bobby, not wanting to upset Cat, said nothing, and just opened the front door and then the car door and they drove off to the funeral. Bobby understood that she was mourning and felt guilty that he acted the way he did instead of letting Cat go and notify the campus security. As in the past when they wanted to let the other one know they were there no matter what, Bobby placed his hand on Cat's leg, and she left it there. This let Bobby know that the coast was clear and he was out of the doghouse. It was the subtle and simple things like that, that allowed them to know where they were in their relationship.

They had arrived and both Cat and Bobby were surprised that the navigation took them to the house. They both observed the scenery and saw all the cars and people entering into the home, which let them know that they were not lost. Bobby opened Cat's door and they walked into the house. There in the family room was the casket. Cat did not want to approach the casket. From where she was standing she didn't know if the casket was opened or closed, and she didn't want to find out. At that point, Cat wanted to only stay long enough to pay her respects. The funeral was nothing like she had experienced before.

An older woman that resembled Stephen walked up to Cat and Bobby and said, "You must be Cat. Stephen talked about you a lot. Thank you for befriending him. He had a hard time establishing relationships with his peers."

Cat just smiled as a tear fell from her eye. The older lady wiped a tear with her fingertip. People were in another room speaking and the older lady swiftly turned around and walked toward the chatter. Cat, feeling uncomfortable and guilty, walked out of the house and told Bobby that she was ready to go.

Bobby opened Cat's door and drove her back to the house without saying a word. "I don't want to go home, drive anywhere but here," Cat said.

Bobby drove her up the coast to the beach. He parked the car and went into one of the shops along the beach and purchased a blanket and something to eat. He went back to the car and got Cat and they walked along the beach until they found a place to sit and laid down a blanket. Cat sat and watched the ocean. Bobby sat with Cat in between his legs and wrapped his arms around her.

"I'm sorry, Sunshine, for not listening to you. I let my ego get in the way when I should have trusted you and listened. I'm sorry." Cat was no longer upset with Bobby. In fact, his persistence of calls and texts and even taking her to the funeral made her realize how much he really cared about her. They sat and watched the ocean for hours without saying anything. Even in complete silence they shared a bond that could not be broken and both felt each other's presence and love. After the sun went down, Bobby told Cat that he needed to get her back home before Connie was upset. Cat agreed and they left the beach that day with a newfound perspective of their relationship and each other.

Chapter 6

It was a week before Cat's birthday and she did not have any plans. Both Connie and Reggie agreed that Cat had been through enough over the last month and wanted to make her birthday as special as possible. They had been planning a surprise party and were talking on the phone often. Trina must have gotten upset over the constant phone calls and text messages and called Connie.

Connie's phone rang and it was Reggie's number. Connie answered in a gentle voice, "Hello."

A woman on the other end said, "What's going on with you and Reggie?"

Connie instantly recognized the voice and responded with, "Trina, I know I hurt you in the past and for that I am sorry. I cannot change the past. All I can do is move forward and pray that at some point our relationship is mended. The phone calls are not about you, nor me; they're about Cat. I kept Reggie out of Cat's life for sixteen years due to shame, embarrassment, guilt, and to keep the peace with you. I can no longer let my own issues, or yours, keep Cat away from her father. It's not fair to her or Reggie. You chose to forgive Reggie and move on with your marriage. You were mad at me for many years and you still are to this day. I did not lay down and have a baby by myself. I'm not saying to leave your husband but I am asking for you to let Cat have a relationship with her father in peace."

Connie paused, waiting for Trina to reply. Connie heard a few sniffles and then the phone hung up.

The day had come, Cat's birthday. When she woke up there were balloons all over her room and she could hear people downstairs. Cat got up and got dressed before she made her grand entrance because she did not know what to expect. She walked downstairs and there everyone was waiting on her. Yessenia was sitting on the sofa with her arms crossed and an obvious attitude. Right next to her was Reggie, another girl, and two little boys. Reggie introduced them as Cat's little brothers and little sister. Of course he did not introduce Yessenia because they already knew each other; and from the looks of it, Yessenia had a problem with Cat being Reggie's daughter. Cat did not let that get her down. She figured that was Yessenia's problem, not hers.

Cat walked up to Reggie and gave him a hug and said, "Thank you for coming dad, it means a lot to me." Reggie smiled and kissed her on the forehead. Cat felt uncomfortable because that was what Bobby usually did. Of course Bobby was sitting in the living room with multiple bags and wrapped gifts. Bobby did not know how to do simple things for Cat. It always had to be extravagant. By now Cat was used to the expensive gifts. Grandma Pie was in the kitchen cooking with Connie and the house was filled with the aroma of Arturo and Anise seasoning, Cat's favorite. Cat could tell that it would be a good day.

Samantha walked in the front door after knocking twice. She had a wrapped gift and a card in her hand. Cat hadn't spoken to Samantha since the day at her house when her mother was drunk. Cat embraced Samantha.

Samantha whispered in Cat's ear, "You know I was holding a grudge with you, right?"

86

Cat laughed and said, "Yes, I know you were mad about me saying, 'I guess this is a White people's thing.' Can we move on now?" They both started laughing.

Reggie asked Cat to introduce Samantha to everyone by saying, "Are you going to introduce your friend?"

"Yes, this is my best friend Samantha."

Samantha smiled and said, "Oh, your best friend, I like how that sounds." They both started laughing again.

Yessenia rolled her eyes and both Cat and Samantha noticed it. "What's wrong with her?" Samantha leaned over and whispered in Cat's ear.

"Girl, I have so much tea to spill, we will talk later," Cat mumbled.

People came in the door in groups. There were so many people Cat felt like a stranger at her own birthday party. There were both African-American and Hispanic people that filled the entire house. Even the garage and backyard were packed with people. Some people hugged Cat and introduced themselves but even though some didn't, it was obvious what person belonged to either her mom's or dad's side of the family. Cat was enjoying the family bonding and all her family. When Nancy and Aunt Sharon finally walked through the door, the party was complete. All the people that meant something to Cat were all under one roof. After hours of laughing and eating, Bobby wanted Cat all to himself. There were so many people in the house that they did not even think before walking upstairs into her bedroom. Cat knew this was unacceptable on all levels. Connie allowed boys to come in the house but never upstairs or in an isolated area. They had to be in a part of the house where anyone could see them at all times. Cat was caught up in the moment and did not really think anything of it. Cat closed the bedroom door behind them and Bobby was shocked because he also knew that he was not supposed to be in her room—especially not with the door closed.

"Sunshine, open your gifts," Bobby sad in a soft voice.

"That is too many gifts to bring upstairs."

"No, just get mine. I want you to open them."

Cat went downstairs to a decorated table were all the gifts were. She grabbed the ones from Bobby and ran back upstairs. She opened each present. Most of the gifts were clothes, shoes, and accessories. Bobby set a gift to the side and gave it to her last. Cat opened the gift and it was a Fendi handbag. Cat was shocked. She loved how Bobby was so attentive to detail. The first day Cat met Bobby she was admiring his mom's Fendi handbag when she got into the car. Bobby never mentioned anything about the purse so Cat did not know that he knew she liked the handbag. Bobby smiled when he saw her reactions and said, "Yes Sunshine, I remembered." It wasn't the gift that Cat was excited about. It was the fact that he paid that much attention to her to know things about her that she didn't speak about.

Cat's happy impulses made her jump up and start kissing Bobby. Bobby started to kiss her back. Bobby became aroused and Cat felt something poking her. She was seventeen and no fool. She knew exactly what that meant. Cat backed up out of embarrassment and apologized. She was not trying to get him excited on that level. Bobby could see the embarrassment in her eyes and sat down on the bed away from her. Bobby did not want to ever pressure Cat into doing something that she did not want to do, but on the other hand, he did want to have sex with his girlfriend. Bobby and Cat had been together for a couple of months by this time and his teenage urges had started to kick in. He sat on the bed thinking that he would not pursue her but if she initiated it he would not stop her. Cat knew that Bobby wanted to have sex but was trying to avoid putting Cat in an awkward position. Cat did not know the first thing about sex; she was still a virgin.

Cat looked out her bedroom door to see if anyone was near her door and no one was standing outside. Cat then locked her door and turned on some soft music. Bobby knew exactly what that meant. He became more excited. That was his cue to take the lead. He got up and started kissing Cat, took her shirt off over her head, and laid her on the bed. Cat was scared but figured she couldn't stop at that point. He unbuckled Cat's jeans and took them off. He got undressed and put the covers on top of them.

He could see the nervousness in Cat's eyes and said, "I will be gentle." Bobby parted Cat's legs and got between them as he kissed on her thighs and breasts. Cat was aroused and anticipated the penetration. Bobby stuck his penis into Cat's vagina. Cat heard that it would hurt but she didn't think it would hurt that bad. Cat fought back her tears. She didn't want to seem like she was still a little girl, even though on the inside, that's exactly what she was. For the first time in their relationship, Bobby was not being attentive to Cat, but rather, focused on his own needs. Cat was so focused on the pain and her efforts to be discreet about how uncomfortable she was, that she didn't even notice.

Three minutes into it, there was a knock at the door and they both jumped up and put their clothes on. Trying to get dressed in a hurry, Cat put her shirt on inside out. Cat sat up in the bed using her covers as pillows behind her because she didn't have time to make up the bed. Bobby unlocked the door and stood on the side so when the door opened he was behind it; he hoped the person would just look in and leave. Sabrina, Nancy, and Samantha walked in. Samantha had a huge smile on her face, already knowing by Cat's body language and her shirt being inside out, that something had just gone down. Samantha closed the door behind her and gave Bobby a smirk. Nancy and Sabrina--oblivious to what was going on--had not even noticed Bobby standing behind the door because they were facing Cat.

"Why are you upstairs in your room by yourself listening to music when it's your birthday?" Sabrina said.

"I was just chilling, you know, opening up some gifts that Bobby got me."

"Well are you coming down?" asked, Sabrina. "Mom wanted me to come get you; they are about to sing happy birthday in the kitchen."

"Yeah, here I come."

Cat got up from the bed and just before Nancy and Sabrina could turn around, Samantha opened the door and shoved Bobby behind it so they wouldn't see him as they were leaving. Once Nancy and Sabrina were out the door, Samantha stepped in front of the door--blocking Cat from leaving--and closed and locked the door. Sabrina saw Samantha closing the door and figured that she wanted to tell Cat something that she did not want them to hear, which was accurate. Samantha pulled at Cat's shirt, hinting for her to look down at it.

"Shoot" Cat mumbled. Cat turned her shirt so that it would be on right. Samantha started laughing. Bobby stood there waiting for Cat's cue of what to do. He was nervous about walking downstairs and everyone noticing that they were missing and were together.

"Is everyone in the living room"? I don't want them to see Bobby and I coming downstairs together," said Cat.

"Look, let's go down first. Wait three minutes and then you come down Bobby," Samantha said.

Cat and Samantha went downstairs into the kitchen and everyone was gathered around waiting on her so that they could sing "Happy Birthday". No one noticed that Bobby snuck in three minutes later. Cat had a huge cake in front of her; it was pink and black with zebra stripes. Bobby muscled his way through the crowd to be next to Cat. Sabrina, Samantha, and Nancy all gathered around her as they began to sing the Stevie Wonder version of 'Happy Birthday.'

"Happy birthday to ya, happy birthday to ya, happy birthday."

They were dancing and singing. It caught Samantha and Bobby off guard; they had not heard that version of "Happy Birthday" before. Cat smiled and then blew out her candles. Connie cut everyone a piece of cake. The cake was delicious. Cat opened her gifts and smiled. She hugged and thanked everyone that brought her a gift. Cat was so excited; this was a birthday that she would never forget.

After the gift opening it was nighttime. Some family members left and some stayed. It turned into family game night. The adults were at the table playing a card game of spades, some of the men were in the garage playing dominoes, and the kids were playing Dance Central on the X Box. Cat was a good dancer and she won every battle against her cousins when playing. After a few rounds of beating everyone, she decided to sit down and let other people play. Cat sat down next to Bobby and they laughed and joked around as they watched her family members play. Reggie approached Cat and gave her a big hug and a kiss on the forehead again and said his goodbyes. Her sister and brothers all said 'bye' and gave her a hug-- all except for Yessenia. Cat walked them to the door and then waved bye and closed and locked the door after they went out.

Samantha came and set next to Cat and said, "Okay, what's the tea." Cat knew exactly what she was talking about; by then everyone had noticed the way Yessenia was acting at the party.

"That is my sister. The guy that hugged and kissed me, that's my dad--and her dad too. I guess she found out when he came to pick me up from school one day; so apparently she has a problem with it I guess."

"Well when did you find out?"

"I actually overheard my mom and aunt talking about it a while back. So I've known for a while."

"Okay, let me get this straight, so when you first met her at school you already knew?"

"No, I found out after that and I didn't want to say anything; it was a touchy conversation."

"Well what is her issue with you?"

"Okay, 21 questions," Cat said and started laughing.

"Well, I need to know!"

"Yeah, I know you do. My mom and her mom are first cousins. Apparently they were really close when they were younger and my mom slept with her boyfriend, or husband, or whatever he was to her at the time."

"Wow, and you had something to say about me drinking with my mom; well I guess *that* is a Black thing," Samantha said sarcastically.

"Let's not go there. This happens in all races; this is a universal human thing," Cat snapped back. They both laughed in agreement.

"Okay, well what happened in the room though?"

Cat became paranoid, thinking someone might be listening. "Shhh, be quiet, that's a conversation for later." Samantha smiled and then looked at Bobby.

Everyone had finally left and Samantha and Bobby were the only two still there. They were now in the family room watching *The Get Down* on Netflix. Bobby was trying to linger around to be the last one to leave, hoping they could sneak off and continue what they started. Connie and the kids were all upstairs asleep, except for Sabrina. Samantha received a text and then stated, "I am spending the night; my mom said it's cool." Cat didn't know Samantha had asked her mother if she could spend the night, but she didn't want Connie to be upset for not asking her so she went upstairs and woke her mom up and asked.

Cat came back downstairs and said, "My mom said that's fine." Bobby was irritated; he was waiting for Samantha to go home and Sabrina to go to sleep so he could have sex with Cat. Bobby wasn't going to give up so easily; he waited around and watched two more episodes of *The Get Down*, and finally after two hours both Sabrina and Samantha were knocked out on the sofa.

Bobby looked at Cat and said, "Can we finish please?"

Cat felt pressured and didn't want to say no. She didn't really want to do it but she didn't want him to know that she didn't. Cat did not have to say she didn't want to have sex, Bobby could tell based on her body language. Bobby was not going to bring up that he noticed that she didn't want to have sex because he didn't want her to say no. He ignored all the signs and waited for her response.

"Okay, but where?" she asked. Bobby got up and grabbed her hand and pulled her into the downstairs bathroom. He locked the door and left the lights off. He picked Cat up and placed her on the counter and then proceeded. This time, even though it hurt, Cat somewhat enjoyed it because he kissed on her while his body thrust toward her body. He was in tune with Cat this time. He kissed on her lips then on her shoulders and neck non-stop.

After seven minutes, he was done. His body stopped moving back and forth and he pulled up his pants and kissed Cat on the lips. Cat pulled up her pants but felt something seeping out. She turned the light on and placed her finger on her leg and looked at it. She looked disgusted. Bobby could tell Cat was really a virgin in all areas. She didn't even know what semen looked like. Bobby took his undershirt off and put soap and water on it and wiped her legs. Cat still felt it seeping on her legs and reached for a towel and began wiping in between her legs and vagina. Cat then pulled up her pants and they walked out of the bathroom.

Bobby was headed to the front door to leave and Cat gave him the most evil look. In that moment, Bobby realized he was doing what he usually did after having sex with a girl; he would just leave. But this was different; it was his girlfriend, someone he actually cared about. Bobby immediately turned around and apologized.

"I am sorry Sunshine. I thought you would shower and then go to bed; we can watch some more episodes of *The Get Down*."

They walked back to the family room and started watching more Netflix. After the first episode Bobby didn't want to just leave so he was nervous on when to say 'bye' and how long he was expected to stay after having sex. He watched episode after episode waiting for Cat to dismiss him but she never did. After the third episode, three hours later, they were both asleep on the couch--Cat wrapped in Bobby's arms.

The next morning Bobby, Cat, Sabrina, and Samantha woke up to Connie going on a rampage.

"You have lost your mind! Since when is it okay for a boy to spend a night in my house?"

Cat jumped up scared. She had fallen asleep and lost track of time. Connie grabbed the first thing she could reach—a broom—and started hitting Cat with it all over her body. She grabbed her eye and started screaming. Connie had hit her in the eye with the broom. Cat tried to run but Connie would not let up. Cat dropped to the floor and curled into the fetal position and covered her face, taking on each blow. Cat whimpered and cried as Bobby just watched helplessly as tears ran down his face. Samantha watched in shock, never having seen anything like it. Sabrina started cleaning up the house trying to avoid Connie's rage.

Connie started coming toward Sabrina saying, "And you, why didn't you tell me her fast tail had a boy in the house?"

Before Sabrina could answer, Cat responded, "She was asleep; we all fell asleep watching Netflix. Sabrina didn't know."

"Well now you know. Don't let it happen again. Now clean up my house!"

Cat could not bear the thought of Sabrina being beaten for something she did. Cat was also relieved that Connie didn't know she had sex because the beating would have been far worse. Cat was bruised and battered but got up and helped Sabrina clean up. Bobby felt bad for Cat and helped her clean every inch of the house. Samantha also helped clean up. No one said anything; they just cleaned until everything from the garage, backyard, and entire house was clean.

Once they were done cleaning, Bobby didn't know what to do. He was conflicted. He didn't want to abandon her but he didn't want her to get in trouble again. So this time he just asked.

"Sunshine, what do you want me to do now? The house is clean. Do you need me to do anything else?"

Cat shook her head no, but that still wasn't telling Bobby anything. He was expecting her to say he could leave now. He followed his own judgment and waited until no one was watching and kissed Cat on the forehead and told her goodbye. Cat went up to her room and went back to sleep. She wasn't tired but she wanted to stay out of Connie's way until the storm was clear. Sabrina, feeling sorry for Cat, went into her room and laid in the bed beside her.

Connie must have called Reggie about Cat having a boy spend the night because within thirty minutes after she went to her room, he was in their living room talking to Connie. Cat woke up to them talking and Connie being dramatic about the situation. Sabrina woke up too.

"Dang! Is she going to call him for everything? I'm starting to think she just wants to talk to that man. Everything that happens over here does not warrant a phone call," Sabrina said.

Cat rolled her eyes and said, "Really." Reggie came into Cat's room and instantly got upset when he saw that she had a black eye and bruises all on her arms. He couldn't see the bruises on her legs because she was under the covers. Connie was expecting for Reggie to back her up so she wouldn't be the bad guy. She wanted him to justify Cat's beating.

"What did you do to my daughter Connie?!" Reggie screamed.

Connie, not expecting Reggie to respond the way he did, responded with, "I –I— I— ..."

Reggie cut her off. "I don't want to hear it! Cat, get your stuff; you're coming home to live with me." Cat got up and started getting her clothes out of her closet. Cat actually wanted to leave.

Connie was livid. She grabbed Cat by the arm and pushed her to the floor, preventing her from getting her clothes, "She is not going anywhere."

Reggie stood in front of Connie, shielding Cat from her and said, "Cat, get your stuff. Connie, if you touch my daughter one more time or try to stop her from leaving, I am going to call the police. When they come and see her they are not just going to take Cat, they are going to take all your kids. So do yourself a favor and let me take my daughter."

Connie backed up. She knew Reggie was serious. In the past when neighbors and family members called Child Protective Services she always got out of it some way, but there was never one of the kids' fathers fighting for them. Connie knew that this was a battle that she would lose so it was better that she retreated--and she did. Cat got all of her clothes and put them in plastic trash bags and left with Reggie.

Cat was met at Reggie's house, which was fifteen minutes away, with eye rolling from Trina and Yessenia. This let Cat know she wasn't welcomed. Trina stormed off into her bedroom and Yessenia went the other way into another bedroom. They lived in a very small, one-story apartment. You could see the entire house by just standing in the living room. Cat stood by the front door with two trash bags in her hand, waiting for instructions.

Reggie walked Cat into the room where Yessenia was and said, "You can share a bed with Beep." Beep was five years old and her real name was Betty. Reggie walked out of the room to go and talk to Trina. You could hear Trina from the other room screaming that she didn't want Cat in her house.

Reggie was going back and forth defending Cat, saying that his home is his daughter's home.

Beep walked in the room where Cat was and hugged her and whispered, "I want you here, Cat." A tear fell from Cat's eyes. In all her years being on earth she had never felt more rejected than in that moment. She laid down on the bed after placing her bags behind the room door. Cat didn't even bother trying to talk to Yessenia; she already knew from her birthday party that Yessenia was not sold on the idea of them being sisters.

Cat stayed in the room until it was dark outside. By this time the arguing had subsided and she was in the room by herself. Reggie walked into the room and brought a plate of food to Cat. He handed it to her and left the room and closed the door behind him. He felt bad that she overheard Trina and that she had been beaten. He was saddened by the thought that the two women who could have pivotal roles in Cat's life were failing her. Cat ate her food; her body was sore and she could barely move. When her siblings were in the room, she made it a point to not act injured. She didn't want to be a victim.

Bobby texted her, "Missing you." She replied with a heart.

Yessenia entered the room and said, "You finally are getting what you want—a daddy." Cat usually was one to have a quick come back but she was so exhausted she thought, why even bother. Plus, she could already tell that she was not going to like living with Reggie. Cat rolled over and went to sleep.

Chapter 7

Cat woke up to a text from Bobby that said, "Let me know when you get your period."

"OMG!" is all she could think. He did not use a condom. "Bobby, you did not use a condom?" Cat replied.

"No, I didn't have one on me."

Cat wanted to talk to Bobby in person so she just ended the text with, "ttyl," meaning talk to you later.

Bobby responded with, "I love you."

Bobby didn't know how to read the text. He didn't know if Cat was mad or just saying she didn't want to talk or couldn't talk at the moment. Bobby called Cat because he didn't want to go back and forth on text and he needed to find out what that text meant. She sent the call to voicemail and sent an automated response saying she couldn't talk right now. Bobby still didn't know how to read her response but he figured he would just leave it alone. She had been through enough and he didn't want to add to her stress.

Reggie and Connie both agreed to keep Cat home from school for a week to avoid Child Protective Services being called on Connie for Cat's bruises. Reggie was not trying to hide what Connie had done. He knew Connie meant well, but her form of discipline was too extreme. Connie was disciplining her kids the way her mother disciplined her, so she did not know any better. The days that Reggie was at work, Trina treated Cat horribly. She would cook and make just enough food so there wouldn't be any left for Cat. Most of the time Cat stayed in the bedroom

100

to stay out of the way. Yessenia ignored her and acted as if she wasn't there. Cat yearned for Sabrina and the connection she shared with her sister.

Trina walked into the room two hours before Reggie had gotten home from work and told Cat to sit in the living room because Yessenia needed to clean the room.

Cat responded, "I can help her."

"No, come sit in the living room."

Cat went and sat in the living room where Trina was seated with her mother and sisters. Yessenia was in the room for two minutes and then joined the family on the sofa on the opposite side of the room as Cat. Yessenia had a devious look on her face, as if she already knew what was about to take place. It became clear why Trina ensured that Cat was in the living room. Trina, her mother, and sisters went on and on about how Connie was promiscuous and slept with most of their cousins' husbands and boyfriends. Their conversation was very calculated. Yessenia laughed every time they said something horrible about Connie, wanting to rub it deeper in Cat's face. Trina wanted Cat to hear all the horrible things about Connie. Cat laughed to herself. She had overheard enough conversations between her mom and Aunt Sharon to know all of what they were saying. The news that they were desperately sharing was not news to Cat.

Grandma Pie walked through the door and the conversation ended instantly. Cat didn't know if they shut up because she was Connie's mother or because she would let them have it. Cat wanted to go back in the room; she had had enough of two hours of gossiping. She got up and headed to the room, but after hearing the first part of Grandma Pie's sentence, she decided she wanted to sit in on the conversation.

"How dare you talk down on my daughter when the DNA test proved that Beep is not even Reggie's daughter!"

"Cat and Yessenia, you can go back into the room," Trina said in a cowardly voice.

Yessenia got up and went in the room. Cat crossed her arms and looked at Trina as if she would kill her and said, "No, I'd rather stay right here."

Cat was tired of all the antics. When she first got there she was allowing a lot to go on, but not today. She had had enough and Trina was about to meet the real Cat. Trina's face turned stone cold when she caught on to what Cat was doing. Trina was angry.

However, Grandma Pie did not stop there, she went on, "You and Connie were real close. See Connie told me about the men you both slept with because I beat it out of her, and if those vagina walls of yours could talk, I don't think you would be sitting high and looking low."

Reggie had walked in the door, and he was not happy about what he was hearing. He knew Trina well enough to know that Grandma Pie was only defending Connie because of something Trina had said. Reggie looked upset.

He looked at Trina and said, "I need to talk to you."

Trina's bold persona had diminished. Trina had guilt, embarrassment, and fear written all over her face. Trina followed Reggie into the room and closed the door behind them. Cat couldn't hear Trina but she heard Reggie all right. He was laying into Trina.

Reggie was going off and telling Trina how dare she disrespect his daughter's mother in front of her. Cat felt loved. She loved how her dad fought for her. Cat had heard enough of their argument. She felt at that point that continuing to listen was just being vindictive. Cat went back in the room. She texted Bobby. It was time that they finished the conversation that Bobby so badly wanted to have.

Cat called Bobby. He waited for Cat to speak so he could feel her vibe out.

"Hey, can you come over? We need to talk."

"Yes, text me your dad's address. Sabrina told me you were not at school because you were with your dad."

Cat gave him the address and walked outside to the pool area and waited for Bobby. Yessenia watched from her window trying to see what Cat was doing. As soon as she saw Bobby pull up, Yessenia went right into the living room to tell Trina. She wanted Cat to get in trouble.

"Cat is outside at the pool with her boyfriend mom!" Yessenia shouted.

Reggie looked at Trina and said, "You have my daughters against each other because of the things you keep saying in front of the kids. Yessenia has been acting funny with Cat since she got here, or better yet, since she found out she was my daughter. This was a conversation that I let you have with her because you asked me to let you tell her; and come to find out, you never even told her. This should have been dealt with a long time ago."

Reggie sounding hurt and upset at the same time. Trina just put her head down and Grandma Pie shook her head in disgust. Reggie went and looked out the window to see what Cat was doing. Cat was sitting with her feet in the pool and Bobby was beside her. He walked away from the window and went into the bathroom to take a shower. Yessenia was disappointed that Cat didn't get in trouble.

"How are you? I was worried about you and when you didn't call me back, I didn't know what to think," said Bobby.

"I hate it here, but I don't want to talk about that right now. Why didn't you use a condom, Bobby?"

Bobby shrugged his shoulders with his hands out in front of him, "I didn't have one. It wasn't intentional. When you started kissing me in the room I just couldn't help myself; and the second time, I mean, I couldn't resist."

"When you gave me your shirt to wash up it was like you did this before."

Bobby became silent. He knew they had never discussed the specifics of sex but he didn't know that Cat thought he was a virgin. He didn't know how to respond. He was scared of what her response would be regardless of whether he told the truth or lied. Cat waited for him to respond; she was not giving him an out by talking and leading the conversation.

Bobby knew Cat wanted an answer and he gave her one, "I watched porn and other movies, that's how I knew what to do."

Satisfied with his response, Cat let it go. Cat did not necessarily believe it but for the first time, she did not want to hear the truth. The lie was easier to deal with and she knew the truth--that she had given her virginity to someone that had possibly been with many other girls--would hurt too badly. Cat and

Bobby talked for two hours before Reggie yelled over the balcony for Cat to come in.

"Well, looks like that's my cue to go in the house." Bobby went in for the kiss and Cat turned her head and gave him her cheek because she knew that Reggie was watching. Bobby knew why Cat turned her head. He gave her a hug, walked her to the door, and then left.

Chapter 8

Cat had been living with Reggie and Trina for a month and she was home sick, but she knew Reggie was not going to let her go back home to Connie's. Trina was a little better. She did not fully embrace Cat, but she wasn't overtly mean and rude either. They had just learned to stay out of each other's way. Reggie's brother often came to the house and stayed over night. Yessenia always seemed uneasy when he came around. Cat was very observant, but because Yessenia still was giving her the cold shoulder, she did not know what to make of it.

Reggie's brother, Cat's uncle Ray, came over one day. All the adults were in the living room playing dominoes and the younger kids were in the living room watching a movie. Beep always slept in the living room when Uncle Ray spent the night. It was getting late and Trina and Reggie retreated to their room. Uncle Ray peeked in and Yessenia clinched her covers with her fist. Cat knew something was wrong, but she couldn't pinpoint it. Cat rolled over toward the wall. Cat felt someone come and lay right next to her so close that they were cuddling. She turned around thinking it was Beep and it was actually Yessenia. Yessenia looked scared but didn't give an explanation as to why she was in Cat and Beep's bed. Cat felt awkward. She didn't know if Yessenia was trying to be mean or was trying to apologize. Cat couldn't figure it out. She knew Yessenia wasn't scared of the dark, because she slept in the bed by herself all the time. Cat got up and got into Yessenia's bed and went to sleep.

106

Cat had been sleep for hours before she felt someone slide in the bed behind her. Thinking it was Yessenia, Cat said, "Yessenia, move; I'm trying to sleep."

Cat felt something poking her in her butt, similar to what she felt when Bobby was aroused, but thicker. Cat turned around to Uncle Ray's eyes. It was pitch dark but there was a beam of light from the blinds that gleamed in, which allowed Cat to see his face. Uncle Ray placed his hand over Cat's mouth, realizing that it was Cat and not Yessenia. He turned her on her back, snatched her pajama pants off with one hand, and got in between her legs and began to rape her.

Cat froze. Tears ran down her cheeks but she could not move or scream. In her head she was screaming and yelling, "Get off of me!"

Cat felt numb. It seemed like time was standing still and all Cat could do was wish that he would be done. After what seemed like forever, he was finally finished.

He kissed her on the forehead and whispered in her ear, "You better not tell or I will kill your mom."

Cat's body started to shiver. She wanted him to hurry up and leave so she could scrub the smell off of her. She laid in the bed motionless until she heard the front door close. Cat scurried out of the bed and ran into the bathroom and got in the shower. She scrubbed herself so hard that her skin started bleeding. Cat slid down the shower glass door and sat there for hours and cried. After a while the water was no longer hot; it had started to run cold.

Cat went to the door but forgot her clothes in the bedroom and there was no towel to dry off with. She peeked her head out of the door to see if she could dash back to the room and grab her clothes, hoping everyone was still asleep. Yessenia was sitting by the door with Cat's clothes in her hand. Cat grabbed the clothes and Yessenia hugged Cat.

"I know exactly how you feel," she said. "Everything that you just did I also did the first time."

They both started crying, standing there while Cat was naked, holding one another. Cat realized all the hurt and resentment that Yessenia was holding was only displaced anger from the hurt that she had endured. Cat put her clothes on once they separated and they went back into the bedroom. Cat turned on the light, not wanting to be in the dark ever again. Cat could not go back to sleep and Yessenia climbed in the bed with Cat--consoling her and empathizing with her.

It was morning and Cat was not going to keep quiet like Yessenia did. She knew that Reggie would believe her. He always defended her. Reggie and Trina were in the living room and Cat knew it because she could smell the bacon and eggs that Trina was making.

Cat walked out into the living room and cried with her voice trembling, "Uncle Ray raped me." Trina dashed into the living room and looked at Reggie in disbelief.

Cat turned and looked at Yessenia and said, "He has been raping her too." Yessenia shook her head in a no motion. Cat was furious, "Tell them Yessenia! Don't let him get away with this," Cat pleaded.

Yessenia yelled out, "She is a liar! Uncle Ray would never do anything like that!"

Reggie and Trina, conflicted about what to believe, took Cat to the hospital for an exam. The doctor examined Cat and concluded that she was not a virgin and that there had been some type of penetration. The doctor asked Cat if she was still in the same clothes that she had on when she was raped.

Cat replied, "No, I took a shower and then changed my clothes."

The doctor told Reggie and Trina that her skin looked like she tried to clean his scent off of her because of the fresh bruises, which is common in many cases. The nurse contacted the police immediately, as well as Child Protective Services. The police went to the house to collect the clothes and Yessenia was acting suspicious to the police. Yessenia gave the police the clothes that Cat had on from the previous day. The female officer noticed that it was daytime attire and not pajamas, as Cat had reported, so she called Reggie and Trina and asked if she could enter into the house. When she went into the kitchen, she saw a pair of pajamas lying in the trashcan in a plastic bag, leading her to believe that that was the actual clothing that Cat had been wearing when the assault had taken place.

Yessenia had lied about the article of clothing that Cat was wearing, which led to the officer taking Yessenia down to the police station for questioning. Child Protective Services came to the house and eventually picked up all the kids and said that they needed to question them regarding the incident.

Cat was still at the hospital. Reggie was upset that he had to contact Connie in the same situation that he had threatened to put her in had she not let him take Cat. Connie came into Cat's hospital room and hugged her. Cat broke down crying. She felt violated on so many levels. Connie was furious.

She told Reggie, "Why would you have Ray around my daughter?! He has been doing this mess for years! Your dad used to molest your sisters when they were kids. You know this is a cultural issue that runs in your family. We talked about this many times when I lived here in California!"

Reggie could not deny it. Within his family it was known for the fathers and uncles to sleep with the daughters, nieces, and some nephews. It was a Hispanic taboo that was not openly discussed. Sometimes the mothers knew and would turn a blind eye, silently promoting their husband's behavior. Cat did not want to hear any more secrets. Everywhere she looked, whether it was her mom or dad's side of the family, it was full of dysfunction.

Cat turned and looked at Connie and said, "Mom, I want to come home." Connie nodded her head in a yes motion and hugged Cat and comforted her by rubbing on her back. The doctor asked Trina to leave out of the room, concluded the exam, and then released Cat from the hospital.

Trina felt bad. Her eyes were watery and even though she never said she was sorry, her actions displayed it. Before departing from the hospital, Trina hugged Cat and then Connie. She patted the top of Cat's head, knowing what she said was true. Cat knew on the surface that Trina felt bad, but Trina's deep rooted hurt stemmed from knowing that what Cat said about Ray molesting Yessenia was also true. Cat could tell that Trina also had reservations about Ray and it was like she was thanking Cat for telling for Yessenia.

Connie drove off and Trina and Reggie got into their car and drove in the opposite direction. Reggie got to the house and packed all of Cat's clothes in a bag, put it in the car, and they made their way to the police station. Once there, the social worker spoke with Trina and Reggie and informed them that Yessenia had been molested by Ray too.

The social worker said, "Yessenia did not want to tell what he did at first, but after the police officer asked her why she tried to hide Cat's clothing to cover up what Ray did to her sister, Yessenia broke down and told it all. It is a bit much and I'd rather that she tell you."

Both Trina and Reggie knew that it had to have been going on for some time for the social worker to suggest that Yessenia tell them what happened on her own. The lead detective came into the room and asked Reggie for all of Ray's personal information. Reggie was very cooperative. He wanted the police to catch Ray because he knew if he caught him, he would kill him. The children were returned to their parents. The family left the police station and headed to Connie's house to deliver Cat's bag of clothes

Once at Connie's house, all the kids went inside while Trina, Connie, and Reggie stayed outside talking. Cat overheard Reggie mention something about counseling. Yessenia sat on the sofa while her younger siblings went to play with Cat's younger siblings. Cat went and sat on the sofa next to Yessenia. Cat was mad at Yessenia at first, but then she realized that she was scared.

Cat hugged Yessenia and said, "Its okay, I'm not mad. I get it."

Yessenia cried uncontrollably. Cat comforted her, no longer seeing her as Yessenia, but as her sister. She was treating her the same as if it were Sabrina. Cat had established a bond with Yessenia that they both thought would never happen.

Reggie and Trina walked into the house and gathered up the kids. Reggie kissed Cat on the forehead and Cat went ballistic. She started screaming and kicking Reggie. Instantly Reggie realized what he had done. Reggie watched Ray kiss most of their nieces and his own daughters on the forehead just as his dad used to do to his sisters.

Reggie pleaded, "I'm sorry baby, I'm sorry."

Cat ran to the kitchen and started cutting herself and saying, "You are just like Ray! You and Bobby. You kiss girls on the forehead to rape them!"

Cat took the knife and slit her wrist. Blood started gushing everywhere. Cat looked as though she was in a trance. Everyone in the house was crying and pleading with Cat to put the knife down, telling her that it would be okay. Cat had snapped; it was just too much too carry. That one kiss on the forehead had triggered Cat's recollection of her awful experience of being raped. Sabrina called 911 because they couldn't get Cat to stop bleeding. They wrapped her wrist with towels but the blood continued to gush out excessively.

The emergency medical technicians arrived and took Cat back to the hospital so she could be examined and stitched up. They then transported her to the local psychiatric hospital and told Reggie and Connie that she would be on a 72-hour hold. The

112

intake therapist informed them that Cat was experiencing post traumatic stress. Cat was placed in a room by herself and given medicine to get her to calm down and sleep.

Cat did not wake up until the next day. The therapist came into her room and spoke with her. She was an African-America woman who was very soft spoken and gentle. She made Cat feel safe. She validated Cat's feelings and continuously told her that it wasn't her fault. Cat opened up to the therapist and before Cat knew it, she was telling her about Stephen committing suicide, the rejection from Trina, having sex with Bobby, and then the rape by her very own uncle. The therapist could not hold back her tears. She felt bad for Cat; she had experienced so much in such a short amount of time. The therapist diagnosed Cat with Major Depressive Disorder and Post Traumatic Stress Disorder.

The therapist left Cat's room and then some staff came in and escorted her to a room with other teens where they were sitting in a circle talking about depression and different things that they were going through. Cat observed each kid and, listened to their stories. She focused in on a white girl with pink hair. Cat was annoyed with her because there was a boy there that tried to commit suicide because he had bad grades. The white girl with pink hair, whom she later learned was Sarah, kept telling him how he was a spoiled rotten brat and how having bad grades is not a reason to commit suicide. Every time Sarah made a smart remark, Cat thought about Stephen and how he tried to tell her that the pressure of getting good grades and making a career choice was too much for him and how it ultimately led to him killing himself. Cat ripped into Sarah. Sarah started crying.

The therapist came into the room and asked Cat to follow her into her office. Cat was viewed as being aggressive in the group therapy session. Cat felt very comfortable with the therapist and she seemed to know how to calm Cat down.

The therapist said, "I am going to teach you some coping skills. You have been through a lot. Therefore, you lash out when memories of hurtful things that have happened to you arise. Instead of lashing out, I need you to take a deep breath and write down all of your thoughts in this journal that I'm giving you. Write down everything that you're feeling, and then when you come and meet me we will discuss the things that you have written down. I want you to come and see me once a week. I have already let your parents know. I'm going to release you in 2 more days and then you can go home with your parents."

Cat was disappointed, "I wont see you anymore?"

"Yes, after you leave here you will see me once a week at my private practice."

Cat was ready to crack open her journal and write. She had a whole lot to say.

After being released from the psychiatric hospital, Cat stayed in her room and isolated herself. Sabrina would come in and lie in the bed next to her and play music on her phone as they laid there in silence. Sabrina understood what Cat had gone through and she wanted to be the sister that Cat had always been to her. Connie completely took Cat out of school and put her on home teach where a teacher came to the house for an hour a day and gave Cat assignments and instruction. Cat would turn her phone off and ignore all her phone calls and text messages from all of her friends, including Bobby. Bobby came over several times and Cat would not leave her room to see him. Connie told Bobby to try again tomorrow. That went on for a week before Cat started replying to text messages. Most of the texts were extending empathy and letting her know that they would be there if she needed to talk. Sabrina told Cat's closest friends what was going on, and that consisted of Nancy, Samantha, and Bobby even though Nancy was her cousin and not her friend, they were really close.

Sabrina planned a movie night for all of them to come over and surprise Cat to spend time with her. Sabrina also extended the invite to Yessenia. Sabrina started to view Yessenia as a sister because she knew Cat did, just by watching their interaction on the sofa before Cat went ballistic and got admitted into the psychiatric hospital. Everyone agreed to come over.

Bobby had been confiding in Mark because he did not have anyone else to talk to. Mark felt bad about Cat and wanted to apologize to her for how he had been treating her. Mark asked Bobby if he could accompany him at the movie night gathering. Bobby agreed to Mark going. Bobby did not know if it was a good idea but he felt like he needed him there for his own moral support. Bobby had been sad over everything that had been going on with Cat. He felt like he wanted to shield her from harm but it was out of his control. Most of his fiends gave him the advice to end the relationship because it came with too much drama. Mark was the only one that continued to tell Bobby to stay by her side. Bobby respected Mark for that because he wanted to be there for Cat. She was the only girl that he had ever been in love with.

The day had arrived and Cat was in her room and Sabrina let them all in and led them into the family room. Sabrina took Bobby to the side and told him whatever he did to not kiss Cat on the forehead. Bobby did not ask any questions, he just did as he was told. He figured it had something to do with what happened when she was raped. He felt conflicted because that was one of the ways that he expressed his love to her. Sabrina went and got Cat from her bedroom. Cat had not showered and Sabrina begged her to take a shower, making her believe that her therapist was coming to the house to see her. Seeing her therapist was the only time she left the house. That seemed to be the only reason that Cat would ever get dressed.

She showered and walked downstairs into the family room. Everyone jumped out and yelled, "Surprise!"

Cat nearly had a heart attack. She jumped back, holding her heart and let out a sigh. She instantly walked up to Yessenia and gave her a hug. Cat knew what Yessenia was also going through and did not want to make it all about her. Bobby and Samantha both looked confused, not understanding the new connection between the two. Sabrina told everyone the details of what happened to Cat but not Yessenia. She felt as though that was Yessenia's choice to disclose what happened to her and she was right. Both Cat and Connie would have been mad at Sabrina for discussing Yessenia's business. Connie was an open book about her own life, but she wouldn't dare discuss someone else's personal business; and Cat was the same exact way.

Cat hugged everyone and then went to Bobby. She hugged him and when he went to kiss her on the lips, she turned her head. She sat down on the recliner—a one-person seat. Cat usually snuggled up with Bobby as they watched movies. Everyone instantly noticed the change in Cat's behavior. Mark patted Bobby on the back, reassuring him that it was okay.

Mark broke the awkward silence and said, "Hey Cat, we all missed you."

Cat looked at him and smiled and said, "I missed you too, Mark."

They started up their favorite series, *The Get Down,* and watched episode after episode. They were binge watching. Sabrina made popcorn and gave everyone a glass of soda. Connie peeked in from time to time to see how things were going. She was happy that Cat was engaging with her friends and not isolating herself in her room. Throughout the episodes, Bobby kept glancing over at Cat to see if she was okay. Bobby felt as if there was a significant change in their relationship, as though he was just another friend instead of her boyfriend.

It was 10 o'clock and Cat was falling asleep in the chair. Mark had to go home and Bobby didn't want to leave without saying goodbye. He went to kiss her on the forehead and remembered what Sabrina had told him. He leaned down and kissed her on her lips. Cat instantly woke up and frantically started swinging.

Bobby grabbed her arms and said, "Its me Sunshine, it's me."

Cat opened and closed her eyes like she was trying to get a better visual and then calmed down. He hugged her and Cat started crying. She was embarrassed. Bobby had scared her when he kissed her. She reflected back to that dark moment in the room with Ray. Cat did not want that to be her response but it had become a natural reflex when anyone got close to her when she was asleep—and sometimes even when she was awake. Bobby wiped her tears with his hands.

He looked at Mark and extended his keys. "Aye bro, you can just drive my car home."

Mark grabbed Bobby's keys and gave Bobby a special handshake and then left. Bobby left the room to find Connie and ask her if he could sit in the recliner with Cat. Bobby did not want another episode of Connie beating Cat. Connie agreed and told him that she thought Cat needed all the comforting she could receive right now. Bobby squeezed into the recliner with Cat. She laid her head on his chest and went back to sleep. Bobby texted his parents and told them that he wouldn't be home until the morning. Bobby had no intentions of leaving Cat alone that night. He planned to fall asleep in the chair with her, hoping that Connie would be okay with it since he had asked her permission to sit with Cat

Cat and Bobby woke up to Connie making breakfast; the aroma was in the air and it made Bobby hungry. This time when they woke up it was quite different. Bobby was at peace when he opened his eyes and saw Connie cooking with a smile on her face. Bobby looked around and saw that Nancy,

Yessenia, and Samantha were still there as well. Everyone was spread out on the floor and sofa of the family room.

Cat lifted her head, wiped the saliva from the side of her face and watched Connie intently. Cat did not want another episode of black eyes and bruises over her body. Connie caught Cat watching her and knew why she was staring and analyzing her every move.

Connie smiled at Cat and said, "Good morning baby."

Cat stretched, barely having room in the chair and said, "Good morning mom."

Sabrina smiled. She was happy that Cat was out of isolation and not freaking out to a simple touch and words. Sabrina was enjoying every moment of it.

Connie fed the younger kids and walked them to the local park a few blocks away. She whispered something to Sabrina before she left. Cat figured she was leaving Sabrina in charge, which was a first. Cat didn't mind; she knew she was in no condition to be taking charge of any situation. Cat figured that her mom told Sabrina to watch her and make sure that everything remained calm at the house. These were the same instructions she gave Cat when she left her with the other kids when she was younger. As Cat got older, she no longer needed instructions on what to do. Connie just left, and Cat knew that meant she was in charge and to maintain order. Sabrina was a newbie in training.

Cat went to the kitchen and made Bobby a plate, wanting them all to know that she had not completely lost her mind. She could tell that everyone was walking on eggshells, monitoring what they said and how they said it. Cat didn't want the people she loved to feel as though they could not relax around her.

Samantha hugged Cat. "I missed you friend."

Cat smiled and said, "How much?" They both started laughing.

That broke the ice. They all grabbed a plate and started grabbing what they wanted.

Nancy ate a piece of bacon and said, Auntie Connie got down on this."

Cat and Sabrina stopped in their tracks and said at the same time, "Aunty Connie?"

Nancy looked at them and said, "Yeah, Aunty Connie. That is respect. How were you raised?"

Cat and Sabrina thought about it and let it go. They figured she was calling her 'Aunty Connie' because she was older, but Cat did wonder how Nancy was related to them, or if she was really Grandma Pie's foster kid.

Cat sat at the table with Bobby, and the others sat on the sofa in the living room, trying to give Bobby and Cat their space. It was obvious that they had missed each other based on their subtle interactions with each other. Bobby would feed Cat with his spoon and they would both smile.

Bobby told Cat about the things that were happening at school and how he wanted to attend UCLA right after high school without taking any time off.

"I want you to come with me Cat. You will have a full ride. My dad already said that he would pay for you. I always wanted us to attend the same college. Remember, that was our dream? I want to major in film and make movies. What do you want to do Cat?"

"I don't know. I like how my therapist interacts with me and if I can help other kids like she is helping me that would be fulfilling. I want to be a therapist."

Bobby went on and on about the type of movies that he wanted to produce. Cat got lost in her own thoughts and could only think about the limitless possibilities of what her life would be like after high school. She loved the fact that Bobby looked out for her and always wanted the best for her. Cat always felt like God sent Bobby to her. She was thankful that Bobby's dad considered paying her college tuition without ever meeting her.

"Bobby, I want to meet your parents. I want to tell your dad thank you."

"I would love that. I always talk to my dad about you. They would love to meet you. I'm about to text him now and see if he could fit us into his schedule."

Bobby starting texting on his phone and a few minutes later he received a text.

"Cat, if you want to meet my dad he will be available tonight. He said he would be home today."

"Today?" Cat said with curiosity.

"My dad is a banker and he is so busy wanting to be successful in his career that he spends most of his time in meetings and on business trips. My dad is a great guy but that is the one thing I hate about him, he never has time for us. My parents only had one child because they knew they did not have the time to raise kids; and that is why my nanny raised me. Well, I take that back. My mom has always been a stay at home mom, so her reasoning for having a nanny raise me really makes no sense at all, but I guess shopping and spas were more important than being present with her child."

"Promise me Bobby, that will never be us. I want to be successful, but never at the expense of time with my family."

"Sunshine, that will never be us."

After eating and an hour of chatting, everyone was leaving to go home except for Yessenia. Cat, Sabrina, and Yessenia spent hours taking selfies and snap chatting. They formed a tight bond. Cat was having so much fun, the thought of being raped was a distant memory. She was living in the moment and experiencing one moment at a time like her therapist encouraged her to do.

Yessenia loved being with Cat and Sabrina and not being at home where her Uncle Ray had raped her on multiple occasions. It was a new scenery and she could spend time with people her age that she could relate to. Plus, she was tired of the constant third degree and answering questions that Trina and Reggie asked over and over. At one point they were asking out of concern and then it turned into asking to know what all he did. Yessenia avoided telling them because she could see that it only made her parents angrier. She understood their anger, but she didn't want her dad to go to jail. So when she was asked a question that she knew would hurt her parents she would either lie or give minimal details.

With Cat and Sabrina there were no questions and that allowed her to feel free. Cat did not ask because she too did not want to keep reliving the rape over and over. Reggie and Trina did not realize that when they bombarded Yessenia with questions, it resurfaced the hurt and the pain of each encounter. Yessenia was tired of hurting over it. She, too, was receiving therapy and felt as though it was beneficial. Cat and Yessenia shared a connection that no one could understand and Yessenia did not feel like she was on the stand when she was with Cat.

Connie had returned from the park with all the kids when the three girls were cleaning the kitchen and putting everything back in its place in the family room.

Cat turned to Connie and asked, "Mom can I go to Bobby's house tonight to meet his parents? Bobby said his dad is going to pay for my college tuition for all four years, and I want to tell him 'thank you'."

Connie was not thrilled about Bobby's father offering to pay for Cat's tuition. She hated feeling like a charity case. She could tell by Bobby's car and the things he purchased for Cat that he came from a wealthy family, and was fearful of his family looking down on Cat upon meeting her. On the other hand, she was happy to see Cat getting out of the house and interacting with people, so she told her she could go.

A few hours later, Cat was getting ready. She made sure she was looking her best. She knew that first impressions were long lasting. Bobby texted Cat and told her he would be there in thirty minutes.

Bobby was excited and could not wait for his family to meet Cat. Bobby pulled up to Cat's house and she was already waiting outside. Bobby got out of the car and opened the door for Cat as usual, before getting back into the driver seat and taking off. Cat was nervous. She had heard a lot about Bobby's parents and had some idea of their personalities but still did not know what to expect.

Bobby opened her door and took her by the hand, and they walked into the house. The whole family was in the dining room around the table eating. Cat assumed that it would be just his mom and dad, and based on Bobby's face, he was thinking the same thing. It was Bobby's aunts, uncles, grandmother, and his cousins. Cat smiled and greeted everyone. She instantly noticed the boy that was with Mark at the party when Bobby got into a fight. Some responded and others just looked at her as if she was invisible and continued with their conversation. Bobby's dad waved for Cat and Bobby to sit between him and Bobby's mom in the two empty chairs. Bobby's dad stood up and embraced Cat with a hug and pulled out her chair. Bobby put his hand on Cat's thigh under the table to put her at ease.

Bobby introduced Cat, and all of a sudden they all spoke as if they did not hear Cat speak the first time. Cat would have assumed that they did not hear her but because of their facial expressions, she knew they were just being rude. There was one elderly woman that did not say a word. In fact, she rolled her eyes, making it obvious that she was not going to speak. The server brought out the food and placed it in the center of the table. The food looked delicious. Cat felt like she was at a fancy restaurant. Bobby's dad blessed the food and they started to eat.

Cat leaned over and whispered to Bobby's dad, "Thank you for offering to pay for my tuition."

Bobby's dad smiled and said, "Anytime kiddo. If you make my son happy, then you are a keeper in my book. Bobby has never mentioned any girl to us, so that speaks volumes."

The elderly woman must have heard what Cat said because she looked at Cat with disgust before she spoke.

"Now we are paying for the trash? We eat with the trash and now we're paying for tuition? What's next, mating with the trash?"

Cat noticed that some of his relatives smirked and outwardly laughed as if they were in agreement with what the elderly lady said. Bobby slammed his hand on the dinning table.

"I am so sick of you making racist comments about anyone different from you! I know times were much different when you were a child but it is a new day, and no one will disrespect my girlfriend—not even you Grandma!" Bobby hollered.

His grandmother looked at him as if she were in shock. You could hear a spoon drop in the room, it was so quiet. Bobby had had enough of his family's racist views towards others and he knew if he did not put a stop to it, other family members would chime in.

Cat felt uncomfortable. She just wanted to meet his family. She was not expecting to be the topic of a racist debacle.

Bobby's dad was embarrassed for Cat and said, "Son, you are absolutely right. This type of thing has gone on for far too long. If you don't respect my guest in my home then you can excuse yourself, regardless of who you are. I will no longer tolerate my friends, colleagues, and my future daughter in-law to be disrespected at my own dinner table."

Cat smiled inwardly. Did he just say daughter in-law? Those were the words that she concentrated on until she thought of how Bobby and his father were standing up for her, making her feel more secure than ever. Cat had lost a sense of feeling safe after being raped by Uncle Ray. She had never told anyone, not even her therapist, that she felt resentment toward Reggie for not protecting her. She knew that he was unaware of what was going on, but she still felt that since she was a girl, it was her father's job to ensure her safety. Being with Bobby and his dad made her feel loved and safe. Bobby and his dad reacted the same way that both of her parents would have. However, after being violated by Ray, she needed reassurance of a man protecting her to feel safe.

Cat was expecting Bobby's grandmother to get up from the table. However, a table of twenty people had only seven people left once everyone excused themselves, and that consisted of Cat, Bobby, Bobby's parents, his cousin Michael, and his parents, which were Bobby's dad's brother and sister in-law. They all apologized continuously to Cat, especially the adults. Cat was comfortable once all his family that brought negative energy was no longer at the house.

They finished dinner and the adults went off to a separate space in the house. The men went into an office and discussed Wall Street and business. The women were in the family room discussing plastic surgery and the latest shoes, which were shoes that Cat had never heard of. Bobby, his cousin, and Cat went into the game room and played arcade games, laughed, and joked around.

It was getting late and Bobby knew that he needed to get Cat home. Bobby asked Cat if she was ready to go and she nodded her head yes. Cat said goodbye to Bobby's cousin and headed toward the garage to get in the car and leave.

While driving, Bobby knew he had to ask Cat about her menstrual cycle and he thought it was the perfect time.

He leaned over and whispered with fear in his voice, "Cat, have you had your period?"

"No," Cat said in a low, disappointed voice.

The one thing she never wanted to be was like her mother. Having children by different men and having kids before being married was not ideal. Cat wanted to marry Bobby and was deeply in love, but she also was very insightful. She knew that they were young and that even though he consistently professed his love, it did not mean that they would be together forever. Cat was a realist, and one thing that she did not do, was lie to herself. A million thoughts were racing through Bobby's mind and he was scared. Financially, he knew that the baby would be taken care of, but he was fearful of being a teenage father.

"Do you think it's late or do you think you're pregnant?" Bobby mumbled in a shaky voice.

"I don't know."

They both waited for the other to speak due to feeling uncomfortable and not knowing what to say. The fear of becoming a parent scared them both. Bobby pulled up to a twenty-four hour Rite Aid. Cat did not question why they were there because she already knew. Bobby parked, and looked at Cat as if he was asking if she was going into the store. She looked away towards the window, which let Bobby know that Cat was not going in.

Bobby went into the store and within five minutes he was already back to the car with a bag in his hand.

He got into the car and looked at Cat and said, "Where do you want to take it?"

Cat did not respond. Even though she knew what he wanted her to do. Bobby pulled off and when he arrived at Cat's house, he opened her car door.

"After you take the test, can you call and tell me the results please?"

Cat nodded her head as she looked at the ground and attempted to walk away, but not before Bobby grabbed her chin and kissed her on the cheek, rather than the forehead, because he didn't want to trigger her. Cat hugged Bobby and tucked the pregnancy test in her pocket. She gave the bag back to Bobby and walked into the house.

Cat went straight into the upstairs bathroom. She took her clothes in with her so if someone was watching, they would just assume that she was taking a shower. She undressed, sat on the toilet, and peed on the stick. Nervous, and not really wanting to know the result, she got into the shower.

Cat had been in the shower for forty-five minutes—trying to avoid looking at the test results, when Connie knocked on the door.

"Cat, get out the shower before you be paying my water bill."

Cat knew that meant to turn the water off immediately and so she did. She got completely dressed and threw the test into the trashcan, avoiding looking at it, and went to lie down in her room. Her phone was sitting on her bed with three missed calls and a text from Bobby that read, "Did you take it?"

Cat sat at the end of her bed. She jumped up, instantly realizing that she had thrown the pregnancy test in the trashcan and someone might find it. She ran into the bathroom and got the pregnancy test out of the trashcan, still refusing to look at it. She tucked the test into her pocket and went downstairs to grab a bag to put it in.

Cat headed to the trash outside, grabbed the test out of her pocket and wrapped it up, making sure that the test was turned over on the side where she couldn't see the results. Her phone rung and it was Bobby. She answered.

"Did you take the test?"

"Yes, but I haven't looked at it. I am scared."

"Call me on face time and let me see if you don't want to know."

Cat agreed and hung up the phone. She called Bobby on face time and turned down her volume so no one would overhear the couple's conversation. She turned the volume low enough that she had to put the phone close to her ear to hear him. She took the pregnancy test out of the bag and turned it where he could see it. Then she wrapped it up and hurriedly threw it into the trash. Bobby was quiet and tried saying good night but Cat could tell in his voice that he was disappointed. He told her the results of the pregnancy test without telling her.

Cat started crying and Bobby tried to console her over the phone.

"I'll help you. I'm not going to leave you, I promise," Bobby exclaimed.

Cat was crying and could not stop. Bobby knew Cat did not want to be pregnant, but he thought she would be afraid or disappointed. He quickly saw that Cat was neither of these. Cat looked angry.

"He will pay. I am making sure, he goes to jail," Cat said over and over.

Bobby realized that Cat didn't know who the father of the baby was. Bobby was so scared of being a father that he didn't even think about Ray possibly being the father too. That had completely slipped his mind. Bobby panicked. He didn't want Cat to start freaking out and be admitted to the psychiatric hospital. He jumped into the car with her on face time the whole time. He was consoling her through his words. His only thought was getting to Cat as fast as he could before she tried to hurt herself. Bobby felt guilty. He had wished that he didn't push her to take the pregnancy test. Bobby was running red lights and driving erratically trying to get to Cat.

Chapter 9

A drunk driver hit the side of Bobby's car. The car hit a tree and spun around in a complete circle, ejecting Bobby from the car. Bobby's phone flew out of his hand. Cat was watching the whole car accident on face time. She started screaming hysterically. Connie came running outside to see what was wrong with Cat.

Cat could not get the words out, "He, he, he, he-."

"Who Cat, who is he?!" Connie screamed.

Cat could not say anything; she was in shock. She froze. Connie took Cat's phone out of her hand and looked at the phone. She saw Bobby's name but could only see the sky, as if the phone was lying on the ground faced in an upward position. She heard sirens in a distance. Connie knew deep down in her heart that Bobby and those sirens were in some way connected. Connie grabbed Cat and rushed to the car and drove to where the sirens were.

Two blocks away, Connie's mouth dropped, and she started sobbing when she saw Bobby's car mangled and wrapped around a tree in a front yard. Connie parked and Cat stayed in the car, fearing the worst. Connie ran up to Bobby's body and saw that he was unresponsive. Medics were trying to do CPR and do everything they could to get a pulse. After five minutes of working on Bobby, they pronounced him dead on the scene of the accident and documented the time of death.

Connie looked back at Cat. Cat's head was slumped over on the window. Connie tried to hold it together but she couldn't. She lost it. The medics had

131

to grab her and calm her down. After five minutes of Connie screaming, she was finally calm and was able to walk to her car. Connie was not ready to deliver the tragic news to Cat. She had already been through so much. Just like with Bobby, Connie did not have to say anything; her screaming outside of the car already alarmed Cat that Bobby was dead.

Cat kept looking up to the ceiling of the car and Connie was worried that she was going to flip out. Cat was actually looking up at the ceiling of the car praying and asking God why she was going through everything that she was going through. Cat could not understand.

Connie pulled up to the house and Cat gathered herself out of the car and went straight into her room and closed her door. Connie walked up behind her and opened her door, thinking that she would commit suicide. Cat fell to her knees and cried out to God. Pleading with him to bring Bobby back. Cat prayed and cried for so long that she fell asleep in the middle of her floor.

Connie never left the bedroom door. She watched Cat hopelessly. She did not know what to say or how to console Cat. In her head, she too was pleading with God and wondering why Cat was experiencing the things that she was facing at such an early age. Cat's siblings passed by the door, trying to get a glimpse in her room to put the pieces of the puzzle together. Connie went and grabbed a blanket off of the bed and snuggled up next to her.

Connie woke up to a pound at her front door at 4 in the morning. Police officers were questioning her of the relationship between Bobby and Cat. They stated that they needed to speak with Cat. One of the officers remembered Cat from when they admitted her into the psychiatric hospital. He knew that Cat was a teenager that had been through enough. The lead officer was requesting to speak to Cat and wanted Connie to wake her up and take her to the police station for questioning.

The officer that had been to the house in the past took the lead officer to the side, after which they both approached Connie and the lead officer said, "Just bring her in the morning. I can imagine that she has been through enough already."
They handed Connie a business card and walked away from her front door. Connie was curious of the conversation Cat and Bobby were having moments before his death. Connie went back to the same spot she was in before the officers came, and fell asleep.

It was morning and Connie was contemplating how to tell Cat that Bobby was dead. She kept looking at Cat. Cat finally opened up her eyes.

Cat looked at Connie as calm as ever and said, "I know, mom."

Cat knew that Connie felt sorry for her and was trying to find the words to tell her and she could not keep watching her mother in despair. Connie looked surprised— not because Cat knew, but because of how calm she was. Connie envisioned Cat flipping out and crying. Connie waited until Cat was completely up before she told her that she had to go down to the police station. Cat got up to go to the bathroom and Connie waited for her to return to her bedroom.

She looked at Cat as she walked in the room and said, "The police want you to go down to the station so they can talk to you."

Cat looked confused. She couldn't imagine what they wanted to speak to her about.

Connie said, "It will be okay baby."

Cat did not even acknowledge what her mom said. She turned toward her closet and proceeded to get dressed.

Connie drove Cat down to the police station. Cat was intimidated. She didn't know if they were blaming her and thinking she killed Bobby. Connie approached the receptionist and then sat down next to Cat.

The receptionist offered Connie and Cat some water and said, "I just sent him a text. He should be arriving shortly."

Cat didn't know who she was referring to but sat there patiently waiting. A man in a gray suit arrived. He was tall and slim and had a beard.

He approached Cat and said, "How are you doing?"

Cat did not respond. She thought it was a rhetorical question. He positioned his hand in a way to tell Cat, "This way." Connie got up out of her seat to go to the interrogation room and the detective informed Connie that she did not need to be in the room.

Connie ignored his statement and said, "Is my daughter under arrest? Because if she's not I want to be in the room. She is a minor and I'm her representative."

The detective did not try to debate with Connie, but instead, he let her join them. The detective asked Cat what she and Bobby were talking about before he died, because according to witnesses, he seemed to be in a rush. Cat's eyes got big, and she knew she would have to tell the detective about her being pregnant; but the worst part was that she had to say it in front of Connie.

Cat could not avoid the question. She thought of a lie that would make sense but then she thought if they subpoena the phone records and listened to the conversation, they would know she lied, and possibly think she killed Bobby. Cat paused for a while, not knowing what to say. She finally answered the detective's question.

"He was rushing to me because we found out that I was pregnant; and I was angry because I didn't know if it was his or my uncle's baby."

Cat put her head down in embarrassment. She felt ashamed to mention that she was pregnant by her uncle. She never considered it being Bobby's baby because she was too focused on being raped by her uncle. The detective looked confused. Connie started crying and tried to turn her head to shield her hurt from Cat but Cat felt her hurt; she did not have to make a sound.

The detective then asked, "What is your uncle's name?"

Connie cut him off; she knew where the questioning was leading.

"We have already pressed charges. He was picked up and incarcerated yesterday."

Cat did not know that Reggie was in jail. The detective's demeanor changed and he became soft and warm.

"Do you two need anything before you leave?"

"No, but thank you," Connie answered.

They walked out of the room and Cat zoomed in on the detective's face as he looked at Cat displaying great empathy. Cat acted as if she did not see his face and then thought about Bobby. She cried after she left the police station.

Chapter 10

It had only been a week that Bobby had passed away, but for Cat, it felt like a lifetime. Cat continuously had nightmares and sometimes woke up screaming in the middle of the night. Things were no longer the same. Everything looked different, smelled different, and felt different. Cat would daydream and reminisce of the good times she shared with Bobby and Stephen. She often isolated herself in the room and cried herself to sleep. Sabrina would check in on her from time to time and did as she did before, just lie in her bed without saying anything. It was the most soothing thing that Sabrina could do even though Cat never verbalized it to her.

Connie informed Cat of the funeral. Cat was reluctant to go. She thought that Bobby's parents blamed her. Cat refused to go and Connie sat at the edge of her bed and talked to her.

"Cat, Bobby was your boyfriend. You have lost two people less than 6 months apart. You need to mourn the death of Bobby; attending his funeral will definitely help. Bobby would love for you to go to his funeral. His parents are expecting you. They have called me everyday checking on you. I think you should go, because if not, you will regret it."

Cat listened to what her mother was saying. Cat had no idea that Bobby's parents were checking on her. She thought that they would be furious with her. Knowing that his parents wanted to see her brought relief. She felt like she owed it to his family to attend his funeral because they were really good to her.

Cat and Connie arrived at the funeral. Cat looked at how packed the funeral was. She didn't know most of the people that were there. She saw a few of his friends from school and right in the front row was Mark, sitting with his parents. Cat swiftly grabbed a seat on the very back row. Someone knelt down and said something in Bobby's dad's ear. He walked to the back, grabbed Cat by the hand, escorted her to the front and sat her right between him and his wife. Cat felt uncomfortable. She cried for herself and Bobby's parents, but smiled because she admired the fact that they understood that she was also hurting. Cat sat there and waited for the service to start.

They played a slide show of Bobby's life. It started with him as a baby and progressed to his latest pictures. As it got towards the end, the slide show included pictures of Bobby and Cat together that his parents must have retrieved from his phone. There was one picture that Bobby took of her and he captioned it "The love of my life." His parents showed the picture and it was captioned "The love of Bobby's life." Cat and Bobby's mom broke down crying once the slide show was over. Cat felt like it was an interpretation of Bobby's life being over. She knew that she would never see her boyfriend again. Unlike Stephen's funeral, Cat wanted to see Bobby in the casket. When the pastor was done speaking, Cat walked up to the casket and stood there, looking at Bobby and caressing his face. His parents came up behind her and held her as she observed her boyfriend for the last time. Bobby's mom put her hand over Cat's stomach and started crying all over again. Cat did not pay attention to his mom. She figured it was her touching her by accident because

138

she was distraught. Cat hugged both of his parents and left to go find Connie.

"I'm ready mom," Cat said as she walked passed Connie toward the door.

Connie followed behind her and they left. Before they were completely out of the building Connie grabbed Cat an obituary.

Cat got to the car and out of nowhere, the elderly lady from Bobby's house walked up behind her and said, "I'm sorry."

Cat turned around to see who it was. Cat embraced her and said, "It's okay."

Cat got in the car and they drove off. Connie did not know what all that was about but she was not going to ask. She did not want to stress Cat out anymore than she already was. Connie put some soothing jazz on as she drove.

The next week Cat went to see her Therapist, Mrs. Mayo. She was the same therapist from the psychiatric hospital. She was very warm, but very direct. She would tell those she worked with the truth, whether they wanted to hear it or not. Cat had never known her name because she never thought to ask, until they started to build a stronger rapport. Cat viewed Mrs. Mayo as not just her therapist, but also her mentor. She gave Cat practical advice that she could apply to everyday, real life situations. Most people that Cat encountered just said things like, 'It will be okay'. Cat thought it probably would be okay but in those moments, it wasn't, and Mrs. Mayo allowed Cat to be in the moment with her emotion. Mrs. Mayo taught Cat the importance of verbalizing her feelings either on paper or by speaking to someone. Cat did both. She talked to Mrs. Mayo during her sessions but she also wrote down her thoughts and feelings in her journal. Cat took in every piece of advice Mrs. Mayo gave her.

Connie was trying to keep Cat from isolating herself by doing family activities together. Mrs. Mayo recommended that Cat not be alone for long periods of time. Connie and all the younger kids were at the dinner table playing Monopoly, while Sabrina and Cat lay across the sofa watching *Bring It*.

There was a knock at the door and Sabrina got up to answer it. It was Bobby's parents. The last time Cat saw them was at the funeral. Connie got up and spoke with them in the living room. Connie summoned Cat and she joined them. Bobby's mom got up from where she was already sitting and sat next to Cat. They asked her how she was feeling and explained that they were checking on her to see how she was doing. Cat felt like they really cared. She was thankful that they still wanted to be connected with her after Bobby's death. Bobby's mom rubbed her stomach and it dawned on her the actual reasoning for their visit. Cat could not figure out how they knew about the baby.

"You know we will always be here for you and the baby," Bobby's dad said.

Cat put her head down and started to cry. She was embarrassed and did not want to disappoint Bobby's parents by telling them that the child she was pregnant with may not be their grandchild.

Connie asked to speak with Bobby's parents in private. They stepped outside and were outside for over thirty minutes. Connie came back in and they followed behind her. It appeared as if both Connie and Bobby's mom had been crying. Cat assumed that Connie told them about Uncle Ray.

Bobby's mom held Cat tight and said, "Whatever you decide to do with the baby we will still be here for you."

Bobby's dad came and sat on the other side of Cat. and looked her in the eyes.

"A man never goes back on his promise, and I am still going to pay for your college tuition. My son bragged about you all the time. As I told you before, you are the first girl that he has ever wanted us to meet. I want you to still come over for dinner and be family Cat, because that is what Bobby would want."

Cat nodded her head as tears ran down her face. Still confused about how they knew she was pregnant, Cat turned her attention to his parents and was feeling and thinking in the moment just like Mrs. Mayo told her to do. Mrs. Mayo had been telling Cat to verbally express herself and to stop thinking about something that she was curious about and just ask.

Cat asked the question, "How did you guys know that I was pregnant?"

"The officer told us that was the reason that Bobby left the house in a hurry, and no, we do not blame you, Cat. Sometimes things happen that only God will understand," replied Bobby's father.

They hugged Cat and said their goodbyes.

Before they were completely out of the door, Bobby's mom turned around and said, "Cat please contact us and let us know what you want to do with the baby before making any final decisions. I want you to know we will be here for you."

Connie closed the door behind them and hugged Cat. It was time for her to discuss the baby and Cat's options. Connie sat on the opposite sofa directly across from Cat so that she could look directly in Cat's eyes and have a serious conversation.

"So I know I haven't mentioned anything about the baby and that's because I wanted to wait until it was time. I want you to know, whatever you decide, I support your decision."

"What do you mean you support my decision? You're saying it as if I had a choice in the matter. I mean, with Bobby it was consensual, but with Ray—because he is not my uncle—I will not even call him Ray. His name is The Molester. The Molester raped me! Everyday I look at my baby it will be a constant reminder that his dad is The Molester," Cat said in a frustrated tone.

It dawned on Connie that Cat thought there was a slim possibility that it was Bobby's baby and she was not thinking clearly about her options. Connie, knowing her daughter, knew that she had not thought about adoption or abortion.

Connie got up from where she was sitting and sat next to Cat, placing Cat's hand in the palm of hers and said, "Cat, you do not have to keep this baby. There is a chance that it is Bobby's baby but there is also a chance that it's Ray's."

Cat cut her off and said, "You mean The Molester."

"Cat, what I'm saying is, you do not have to have this baby."

Cat looked up at her mom with a shocked look, "What?"

"You do not have to have the baby; you can abort it or give it up for adoption. There are options and that's why I said I support your decision."

142

"What if it is Bobby's baby and I abort it?"

"But what if it's not? You have to make the best decision for you Cat, and I will support what ever that decision is."

Cat paused for a few seconds and said, "I do not want to risk my baby being by The Molester and then having to explain who the father is. I do not want my baby going through that mom. I hate what he did to me. I am not having this baby."

"Is that your final decision Cat? Because if it is, we need to schedule you an appointment."

"Yes. I don't want to keep the baby."

It was obvious that Cat was conflicted. Guilt started to set in with Cat. She did not want to kill her baby but she did not want to chance it being Ray's.

"Mom, can you call Bobby's parents and let them know? I don't want them to be upset about my decision."

"They won't Cat and yes, I will call them."

Cat went into her room while Connie made the phone calls. Connie scheduled the abortion for the next day because she did not want Cat to change her mind. Connie did not want Cat to have the baby. Just like Cat, she also thought about the results of the situation if it were Ray's baby.

The next day, Cat was at the clinic sitting in the waiting room filling out paperwork. Cat was hoping that no one saw her there. She did not want people to know that she was pregnant and now having an abortion. She was embarrassed about the whole situation. Connie had to help her fill out the paperwork. She was anxious and didn't know what to expect. They called her back and Cat looked at Connie, but she remained seated.

The staff member said, "Oh, no one can go back there with you Sweetie."

Cat was scared; she did not know what they were going to do. She was escorted to a room where she removed her clothing and changed into a paper hospital gown and some blue paper shoes. She was then escorted to another sitting area. All Cat could think about was Bobby. As she sat in the waiting area she closed her eyes and began to pray. She whispered to make sure that no one could hear her.

"God, I don't understand why I'm going through this. Mrs. Mayo said that I will get through this but I don't see how. Just when my life started getting better it has turned for the worse."

Tears started to roll down her face but she kept praying, "I cannot take one more thing happening, I've had enough. Ever since we moved to California, my life has been going downhill; and every time something good happens it's followed by a tragic event. God, I am begging you to make it stop. I cannot take anymore. My baby, my baby."

Cat started crying. Just as she started crying a staff member had walked in another younger girl. Once the staff member was gone, the teenage girl walked over to Cat and hugged her.

"We will be okay. This too shall pass."

Those simple words were so comforting to Cat that she felt as though God was speaking to her through the girl. As soon as she let Cat go, another staff member walked in and called Cat. Cat got up and followed behind the lady and went into another room. When she reached the third room, she saw beds all laid next to each other—five in total—with lights over each bed like an operating room. She laid down on one of the beds. The nurse found a vein and put an IV in Cat's arm. The nurse asked her name and before she could respond, she was asleep.

Cat woke up later and she felt dizzy and nauseous. She tried to lift her head when she noticed that the teenage girl that was in the room with her was in the bed next to her asleep.

The nurse came and told Cat, "Calm down and lay back. The dizziness will go away in a little bit. Just lay back and relax."

The nurse could tell by Cat's face how she was feeling. The nurse had seen enough people to know what Cat was thinking and feeling. Cat followed the nurse's instructions and relaxed. Just like the nurse said, after awhile, the dizziness and the nausea had subsided. The nurse helped Cat get up and pulled up her paper panties with a pad in it. The nurse escorted Cat back to the room to get dressed and told her to see the receptionist once she was in the main lobby.

Cat got dressed and entered into the lobby. Sitting there was Connie, Reggie, and Bobby's parents. Cat went to the front desk and told the receptionist her name. The receptionist handed Cat some pills and had her sign a paper and told her she was free to leave.

Bobby's parents hugged Cat. Bobby's mom walked outside. Cat followed her with her eyes to see what she was doing. She saw Bobby's mom break down and cry. The last thing Cat wanted to do was disappoint Bobby's parents. Bobby's dad observed Cat looking at his wife and turned her head by her chin toward the opposite direction.

"It's okay," he said, "she will be okay."

They all walked out to the parking lot. Reggie got into his car and Bobby's dad took out a big box of some of Bobby's things that he thought Cat would want to have. It was filled with pictures of the two of them, among many other things. He placed the box in the trunk of Connie's car. He hugged Cat again and looked at his wife.

"Come on Cupcake; come give Cat a hug. She thinks you are disappointed because she had the abortion."

"Oh, no Cat, I'm just still mourning Bobby's death, that's all."

Cat could tell even though she was saying that, it was not true. She could see it in her eyes. Cat thought that Bobby's mom was hoping that Cat had the baby so there could be something left behind that she could remember Bobby by. Cat got into the car and they drove away.

Cat arrived to her counseling session that Connie had scheduled. Cat could not wait to see Mrs. Mayo because she had so much that she wanted to talk to her about. Cat walked into her office and sat down in the chair. Mrs. Mayo could instantly tell that there was something wrong with Cat so she asked what was wrong.

Cat answered, "I had an abortion yesterday and Bobby's mom was mad that I did not keep the baby. I mean, she didn't say that, but I could tell."

Mrs. Mayo gave Cat some advice, "Cat, in this life people will not always agree with your decisions, however, they are not decisions that others have to live with. Bobby's mom was not going to raise that baby, you were. So it really doesn't matter how she

146

feels. The only thing that matters is how you feel about not keeping your baby. So now I ask the question, how do you feel?"

"I wanted my baby, but could not live happily if it turned out that it wasn't Bobby's. To me, that would be reliving what *he* did to me every day and I did not want to do that. It wasn't just about me, but my baby also because eventually, I would have to explain who the dad was. It was just a messed up situation. Trust me, if I could have kept my baby, I would have—especially since Bobby died," Cat said as she cried.

Mrs. Mayo handed her some tissue and explained to Cat that she had to be comfortable with her decisions regardless of other's views. Mrs. Mayo displayed empathy but she did not allow Cat to have the mindset of a victim.

"Okay, you believe that Bobby's mom did not like that you aborted the baby. However, never mind her; what have you been doing for yourself to move forward?"

"I take it day by day and focus on the positive instead of always thinking about the negative—replacing the negative thoughts with positive ones."

Mrs. Mayo was always about the solution. She did allow Cat to express her issues but she would redirect her, not allowing her to ruminate on the problem, and that was what Cat loved about her. Others treated Cat as if she was fragile, and empathized, but Cat knew that she needed someone that would tell her the truth even when she didn't like it. Mrs. Mayo often ruffled Cat's feathers by saying things that Cat didn't like, but Cat never had a rebuttal because she knew what she was saying was true. It was rare that people challenged Cat, but Mrs. Mayo did not hold back. Mrs. Mayo left Cat with a sentence to think about.

"Cat, in life we have the choice to be the victim or the conqueror. Twenty years from now you do not want to be a grown woman, but yet, still a broken little girl."

Cat didn't know what she meant but it sounded good.

Chapter 11

It was already May 19th, the last day of school. Cat had not been to school but decided that she wanted to attend on the last day. Cat got dolled up. The last time she saw everyone was when she was last at school right before her birthday in March. Cat walked through the hallways. One part of her wanted to be back at school, but the other part was her wanting to conquer her fears of being in a place where Bobby and Stephen were no longer there. She knew in order to be healed she had to do things that would make her uncomfortable like Mrs. Mayo had told her once before.

She had finally gotten to third period. She looked at Stephen's seat. Everyone watched her in amazement to anticipate what she would do. The kids at school knew that she was Bobby's girlfriend and that he had passed away. Cat acted as she did in the past. She spoke to her peers and joked and laughed.

The bell rang. She had conquered the hurt of Stephen, but now she faced the biggest challenge of all, lunch. Cat was used to Bobby buying her meal and spending time with him. Most of the time that Cat spent with Bobby was during lunch at school. She walked out to the center quad where all her friends were. They were all gathered there laughing and making jokes. Even Mark was hanging out with Cat's friends, which was unusual because he only hung out with them because of Bobby.

Mark walked up to Cat and hugged her for a very long time.

"I heard you were here today and I was waiting for you to come so that I could just see you.

You know Bobby loved you, right? I haven't seen you in so long and seeing you reminds me of Bobby. You two were inseparable. I'm not going to lie, at first I was a tad bit jealous, like you were taking all my boy's attention."

He held up his fingers an inch apart as he said, "A tad bit," and laughed. "But I have love for you Cat. You are the only girl that made Bobby light up like he did. I mean, bro, you made him stop talking to me because he felt I disrespected you, and we've been friends since elementary. I know I'm babbling, but I just missed you and Bobby, that's all."

Cat smiled and held up her fingers an inch apart and said, "I missed you too; just a tad bit."

They both laughed and Mark hugged Cat and walked away. Mark approaching Cat and saying what he said really made Cat feel warm inside. She loved how even in Bobby's death, the love between the two of them was just as radiant as before he passed away. No one could deny their bond. Cat had gotten through the school day, and when the last bell rung, she was ready to say goodbye to school and get to summer.

Before, she often thought about how summer would be, but she followed Mrs. Mayo's advice. Cat knew that it would be challenging without Bobby. Mrs. Mayo taught Cat that challenges were a time of growth, to become a better person, and Cat believed it. She could see the benefits just in the short time of seeing Mrs. Mayo. Cat's mindset was beginning to change.

Cat waited out in the front of the school with Sabrina as she always did. Nancy and Yessenia joined them. Yessenia informed Cat and Sabrina that she would be going home with them and spending the weekend. Cat and Sabrina did not mind; they loved having her around. Besides, she was Cat's sister and Sabrina felt like she was her sister too. Cat could tell that Nancy felt left out.

"Ask Grandma Pie if you can come too Nancy,"

"Okay." Nancy got on her phone and texted Grandma Pie, "She said yes."

Cat and Sabrina were excited that they were going to have a girls weekend. Sabrina was especially happy because she cherished the moments when Cat was really happy. Sabrina took them as they came and enjoyed every moment of them. There were days when Cat was happy, and others when she was sad. Sabrina knew that she had to cherish each moment since she didn't know what Cat's mood would be an hour later, because anything could trigger her, whether it was a song, a smell, or something someone did or said; it could change in a moment's notice.

Connie had picked the girls up. She was happy to see Nancy and Yessenia coming over because she too cherished the moments when Cat was having a good day. Connie figured that things must have gone well at school. Connie was nervous about allowing Cat to go to school with Bobby not being there.

Later that night the girls did what they always did when Connie retreated to her quarters of the house and the younger kids were in bed. They binged watched *The Get Down*. Connie had ordered some pizza and Cat went to the door to talk to the delivery guy while Sabrina dashed upstairs to get the money for the pizza. Cat left the delivery guy at the door once Sabrina was on her way downstairs.

She walked back into the family room and overheard Yessenia telling Nancy, "Tell Cat, I think she deserves to know."

"I need to know what?"

Cat was irritated because she was thinking, "What now?" She did not want to hear anymore bad news. The irritation in Cat's voice put Nancy on edge and she didn't want Cat to think they were gossiping about her so she told Cat what they were talking about.

"Cat, I should have told you this before, but I didn't think that you were going to ever meet Ray."

Sabrina walked in on Nancy talking and knew it was going to get real in a few seconds. Cat intently listened as both she and Sabrina grabbed a seat, almost in unison.

Nancy continued, "There has been a long dysfunctional history in our family. I never told you why I lived with Grandma Pie."

"Because I never asked," Cat said in an agitated tone.

Cat was getting annoyed with the prolonged speech. She wanted Nancy to spit out what she wanted to say, without hesitation.

Nancy proceeded, "Cat, Ray is my dad."

Cat and Sabrina's mouths were wide open. Neither of them were expecting that.

"Well then how are you related to us? Well, I get how you are related to my sisters but why are you living with our grandmother?" Sabrina asked.

By this time, Nancy was annoyed because of the constant interruptions.

"Well if you would let me finish, I would get to that."

Sabrina gave her a very crazy look. Cat patted Sabrina on the chest as if she were telling her to calm down.

"Let her finish Sabrina," Cat said.

"Well I live with Grandma Pie because that is my grandma. Your mom's sister, the one that they never talk about is my mother; she died when I was three. Grandma Pie fought for me in court after Ray raped me. On our dad's side, that's what they do. When I was younger, I was around them because I lived with Ray. Uncle Reggie doesn't deal with them anymore, but I don't think he ever knew about Ray. He just knew about our Uncle Pedro, who molested me too.

That's when Child Protective Services first came out and they found out that Uncle Pedro was molesting his own daughters. The women in the family knew what was going on. They acted like they didn't know. I remember when Pedro's daughter, Alicia, told her mom that he was molesting her and her mom told her she was a liar, and continued the relationship. Ray was mad when I told him about Pedro and he pressed charges, but a few years later he started doing the same thing to me, so I didn't understand his logic.

One day I was at your dad's house and I got caught having sex with three boys in the laundry room. Uncle Reggie whooped me and I called Grandma Pie before he could call Ray. I told her everything, and that's when she fought for me in court."

A million thoughts were going through Cat's mind. She did not believe that her dad didn't know about Ray, and now, she was just as disgusted with Reggie as she was Ray. All she could think about was that when she saw him she would have a whole lot to say to him.

"Wow, so you guys' family are sick in a major way," Sabrina said in disbelief.

"I guess it is something that just runs in their family," Nancy replied.

Cat had drifted out of the conversation; all she could think about was how she was going to tell Reggie how she felt about this whole situation. Cat went from feeling great, to being so furious she could not hold it in. She went upstairs to grab her phone. Sabrina was still questioning Nancy about the details of their family history. Cat called Reggie.

The phone rang three times before he answered.

"Hi baby."

"Don't 'hi baby' me. You let The Molester around me and my siblings and you knew what he did to Nancy?! How can you call yourself a father?!"

Connie overheard Cat from her room and got up to see what was going on. The younger kids started crying, thinking that Cat was going to try to hurt her self again. The screams and cries from her younger sisters and brothers made her calm down because she realized that she was controlling the thermostat of the house through her behaviors, which was another thing that Mrs. Mayo talked to her about.

"Calm down, Cat. What is going on?" Connie asked in a calm voice as she was putting her robe on over her panties and bra.

"He knew that The Molester raped Nancy and yet he had him around us!"

Connie did not have to ask what Cat was talking about because she already knew. For many years the whole family made Nancy out to be a liar. They said she made it up because when they questioned Pedro's kids and other family members, they all denied it. It left Nancy out in the cold and isolated from her Hispanic family. Grandma Pie never doubted what she was saying because she knew the signs of a child being molested. Grandma Pie recognized the signs when her husband molested Connie. So when Nancy came to her, she knew it was the truth.

Connie grabbed the phone and told Reggie, "You need to come over and have a conversation with your daughter. This is something you need to speak with her about in person."

Connie had been gone for many years; all the old stuff that she ran from was resurfacing. Connie suppressed a lot of memories to numb the pain of her own hurt with her family. When Reggie picked up Cat from her house after the beating, it never dawned on her about the story of Nancy. But once Cat said it, all the hurt and family secrets came rushing into her memory like a flood.

Reggie did not hesitate, "I'm on my way, Connie."

Connie could feel her emotions rising. She was trying to control it but it was too late. She then called Grandma Pie and screamed and cried and asked why she saved Nancy but turned a blind eye when it was her. Cat looked at her mom and saw that broken little girl that Mrs. Mayo had talked about in therapy. All these years had gone by but Connie was that same little girl from when she was raped twenty years ago. She left California running from her problems, but she never addressed her hurt and fears. Even though she was free to go as she pleased, she was not free mentally and emotionally. Connie had been carrying the baggage from her childhood for many years. Cat realized that people could be adults but emotionally and mentally still be little girls. Cat saw her mother from a different vantage point. Realizing that Nancy was promiscuous after she was molested, explained why Connie went from man to man. Connie was craving a man's genuine love. Cat did not want to become Connie but she already was Connie.

Connie cried and said, "Thank you, mom. Do you know how long I waited for that apology?"

Cat walked out of her room and closed the door fearing overhearing another family skeleton. Cat's days of wanting to hear the family gossip were long behind her; she couldn't take another scandal. Cat determined in that moment that she was not going to wait for Ray to apologize for her to be set free. She was going to set herself free by forgiving him and moving on with her life. Cat could not fathom the thought of being as old as Connie and still hurting and begging for apologies and acceptance. That was the day that Cat snapped back and decided that she would be free of it all.

The doorbell rang. It was Reggie. Sabrina answered the door and Yessenia looked confused as to why her dad was there. Cat came down to face the person she was angry with. She was no longer going to act out with tantrums, but be assertive and direct, just like Mrs. Mayo.

"So answer the question," Cat looked at her dad and bluntly said.

Sabrina, Nancy, and Yessenia knew where this was headed. Nancy instantly left and retreated to the family room, being afraid that everything would be blamed on her. Nancy saw that Cat meant business and she did not want to receive the backlash of it all.

Reggie looked fragile, he did not want to disappoint his daughters more than he already had.

"I'm sorry you guys," he looked toward Nancy's direction and continued, "It was never proven what Nancy-," he abruptly stopped and rephrased his sentence. "I'm sorry. I know now that Ray raped Nancy. I wanted to believe my brother and I overlooked the facts that were right in my face, and for that, I was wrong. You and Sabrina are really close, and if someone said she did something that you couldn't imagine her doing, you would believe your sister."

Cat thought about it and she had to be fair, because her dad was right. If someone told her Sabrina were a child molester, they would have to have video footage to convince Cat it was true. Even then, she might argue that the video had been tampered with. Cat had to be honest with herself. She knew that her dad was being a good brother--just like she would be a good sister to Sabrina. She could no longer fault him for believing his brother; as mad as she wanted to be at her dad, she couldn't.

Cat hugged her dad and said, "I apologize; and you are right, but the only thing I ask is for you to apologize to Nancy."

Reggie looked at Cat, then turned and went to talk to Nancy. Even though no one had mentioned Nancy being a liar in years, Cat felt that Reggie needed to apologize and make it right. Cat believed that the reason Yessenia lied for so many years was because she saw how they treated Nancy when she told. Mrs. Mayo constantly said things happened for a reason and that was one of the things she said that often made Cat mad, but Cat now understood what she was saying. Had Cat not gotten raped, Ray would have continued to hurt other children, and most importantly, her sister. It took Cat to stand up and confront the unspoken truth that had been occurring in their family for many years. She redeemed Nancy of being a liar, and Yessenia from the constant guilt, shame, and hurt.

Cat mumbled to herself, "This is what Mrs. Mayo meant when she said, 'you will either be a victim or a conqueror'."

Cat was using what happened to her to help Nancy. She could have stayed focused on her issue with Reggie but instead, she wanted him to acknowledge his wrong doing with her cousin and how he handled the situation. Cat felt relieved. At first, she thought she started a hurricane; but it seemed as though both Nancy and her mom found relief in the storm. Now she had to figure out what Yessenia's relief was. Yessenia did not verbally express how she felt about being raped. In fact, she avoided the conversation all together.

Cat walked into the family room to Reggie and Nancy hugging, and Nancy crying. Cat looked back at Yessenia and realized that Reggie needed to apologize to Yessenia too. Yessenia had become the shadow to Cat the moment she stepped on the scene, and everyone knew it. Cat never looked at it from Yessenia's perspective. The focus was on Cat-- especially since the rape. Everyone had been concerned about her because she was the most vocal, but Yessenia was the one that needed the most attention. She kept everything locked inside.

Cat walked up to Yessenia, embraced her very tightly, looked her in the eyes, and said, "I'm sorry. I walked into your world taking your father and then hogging his attention. It was never intentional, but I know that you are hurting too; and because you don't say much, people see you as the strong one, but it's actually the opposite. You are the weaker one; internalizing everything and bound to break at any given moment."

Yessenia started to cry. Cat looked at Reggie as he wrapped up his conversation with Nancy and said, "You owe Yessenia, your *first* daughter, an apology too."

Reggie looked at Yessenia crying and knew that he had focused more on Cat. He was trying to overcompensate for not being present in Cat's life. Reggie did not realize that he was actually minimizing Yessenia's experiences with the rape and finding out that Cat was her sister. Reggie started walking toward Yessenia and Cat went to go apologize to her younger siblings.

It was like a domino effect. Once Cat figured out her wrongs, she wanted to make each one right. She went into the room where all her younger siblings were and hugged them. She was like a second mom to them and since she had been with Bobby, she did not spend as much time with them as she used to. She was glad that Connie had stepped up, but she had removed herself from her siblings altogether. Cat was usually locked in her room enjoying her privacy. She forgot to be their sister once the mother role was taken from her. She kissed on them and really looked at them for the first time in months.

Sabrina walked in the room behind her and said, "Cat, I want to apologize for not being there and focusing on my own hurts in the past."

Cat looked at Sabrina and said, "You have been in my corner even when you didn't realize it. Being my sister was enough for me. Now I want to know how I can help you. Growing up, you always resented me and I never knew why until a while ago when we had the conversation in the bathroom. But tell me about you. Make me understand you because I can only assume," Cat begged.

"It has been hard growing up standing next to a beautiful, brown skinned sister that everyone admired. I always felt like I was not good enough because of my skin color. I was always the after thought. Boys always chose you because you were lighter. Cat, it's like going through life being the leftovers. They only want you after all the good food has been chosen and there is nothing else left to eat.

"I was jealous of you-- not that it was your fault- but I didn't understand that you were also a victim. So I was angry. I wanted to feel beautiful. I wanted people to walk up to me and compliment me like they did you. I hated that they never thought we were sisters or how they would ask what kind of hair I had. I'm always viewed as having fake hair and fake eyes, and why? Because I am dark skinned. Cat, being dark skinned is a stigma that I don't think you will understand until you've lived it. I even hate when black guys say they don't like dark girls or black girls. I can't explain it. It's just one of those things that you have to experience to fully grasp how it makes me feel," Sabrina replied.

Cat could not follow up with a long speech because she felt like it would make Sabrina feel like she was minimizing what she was saying. Cat didn't know how she would let Sabrina know she understood, but when the opportunity presented itself, she would. Cat apologized and embraced her sister.

They walked back downstairs. Connie was sitting on the sofa with Reggie, who was apologizing to her.

Reggie looked at Cat and said, "We have our own Iyanla. She has fixed the family's life."

They all started laughing. Reggie walked to Yessenia and hugged her.

"Come on baby, we need to have some father-daughter time."

Yessenia smiled and went to gather her things and they left. Cat could tell that that really made Yessenia's day. Once Reggie and Yessenia were gone, the rest of the family pulled out the Monopoly game and stayed up until 6 am playing.

Chapter 12

It was now time for Cat to take her senior pictures--a week before school was starting. Connie took Cat to the local shop and got her hair, nails, and make-up done. While Cat was getting her hair done, she could not avoid the gossiping that was taking place in the shop. The hair stylists talked about their relationships, other co-workers, and client's hair, among many other things. Cat was in disbelief and annoyed at the same time. She kept thinking about what they would say about her after she left since they had something to say about everyone else.

Cat dismissed most of their conversations, but one in particular caught her attention. She listened to women discuss how they remember when they were in high school and how they wished they could go back to those days. They discussed only being a kid once. Cat held on to those few words. She knew after high school, there was adult life, and there was no going back. She wanted to cherish each moment of her childhood that she had left.

Cat's hair was flawless and it was time to get out of the stylist's chair. Cat left with the decision of never returning. If she had to get her hair done, she would not go to a hair salon after observing how much they gossiped.

Cat left from the hair salon and went straight to the photo studio to take her senior pictures. She loved them. They were absolutely amazing. The photographer let her see the final results right after shooting so she and Connie could decide which ones they wanted to purchase. Neither Cat nor Connie could make a conscious decision of which ones they wanted to trash and keep, so Connie purchased all of them, which was a pretty penny. Afterwards, Connie dragged all the kids from store to store doing her last minute school shopping.

It was the first day of school and Cat was ready to turn over a new leaf. It was a challenge going to school and not seeing Bobby and Stephen. Cat figured she would get through it like she did on the last day of school. Cat was looking forward to joining clubs and meeting new people. Mrs. Mayo had taught her that when your mindset changes, so should your actions and people around you. Cat knew she needed to connect with new people to help her grow and to be exposed to new things--not just the people that she was comfortable with. Cat made it a point to talk to someone that she had never spoken to each period. It wasn't going to always lead to a new friendship, but she wanted to expose herself to the possible opportunities that were out there. In order to grow, she had to challenge herself. She was eager to become the conqueror and not remain a victim; she knew it was imperative that she followed Mrs. Mayo's advice as if it were prescribed.

It was the end of the day and Cat had connected with some amazing people, but the most important thing she did was join Black Student Union. She was happy to be a part of something while causing change, instead of attending school and allowing time to pass her by. She made a conscious decision to live in the moment and enjoy her last year of being a kid.

Cat was nominated as the President of the Black Student Union club. During the second meeting, one of the boys by the name of Rakheem, stated that he did not like black girls because they were all 'ghetto and demanding.' Sabrina later reminded Cat that he was the boy from the party that was dancing behind her last school year. Cat did not address his opinion; she let it go. Then she thought about what Sabrina said about being dark skinned and Cat immediately thought of a plan she could put in motion.

Cat made fliers to bring awareness to the Black Student Union club. Cat did not just want to focus on African Americans, she wanted to incorporate all races, but not too many other races wanted to join. Week after week Rakheem worked Cat's last nerve with his stereotypes of black females. Cat knew she had to address it. After months of meetings, she thought of how she could cause change by provoking thought. Cat was on a quest to provoke thought by changing lives and she would not detour from it. Cat knew the perfect person that she needed to talk to.

The following week during Cat's counseling session, she told Mrs. Mayo her thoughts about Rakheem talking bad about his own race. Mrs. Mayo gave a brief history lesson of slavery and how self-hatred started from slaves when they were made to feel like they were not good enough. It was based on the color of their skin and it bred a generation of hating self within the Black community. Mrs. Mayo was the type of therapist that did not let her clients focus on others; she always redirected it back to the client. Mrs. Mayo always said that focusing on other people did not help Cat. She asked Cat how it made her feel when others hated their own race of people.

Cat said, "My sister told me about it before, but there's this boy named Rakheem; he always downs black girls and it annoys me."

"Why does it annoy you?"

"Because who does he think he is to say that I am not good enough?!" Cat said in frustration.

"You cannot control how he feels. His view is based on his own experiences and vantage point. The only thing that you can do is provoke thought. Provide a different experience by allowing him to see that every Black girl does not fit into the mold of his preconceived stereotype."

Cat thought about what she said and was going to think of an activity that she could do in the BSU meeting to provoke thought. Cat left her therapy session that day feeling optimistic.

After hours of sitting in her room thinking, she had the perfect plan. Cat was so caught up with the idea of provoking thought and being the best BSU leader possible, that her mind had shifted from the victim and her problems to being a problem solver, and it felt good. At the next BSU meeting, Cat told her peers to get in a group based on gender, then skin complexion. Rakheem was in the dark skinned male group.

Cat asked the question, "Who is comfortable with being the race that they are?" Everyone raised his or her hand. Cat then asked, "How do you feel about being the complexion that you are?"

The answers ranged from okay, to not liking it. Some light skinned students complained of being looked down on because of others thinking that they acted superior to their darker skinned counterparts. A dark skinned student said that they are treated poorly based on being darker. Cat noticed a common theme, a stigma within the African American culture. The darker skinned people felt like they were mistreated because they were not light enough, but then the light skinned people felt mistreated because they were not dark enough. Cat shared her story of Cat and Sabrina's experience and informed the groups that they were all victims, and it was not their fault. Cat informed them that they had to decide if they were going to remain victims or be conquerors. They were intrigued by what Cat was saying.

The next week the students all joined for the BSU meeting, and this time Cat noticed new faces. There had been talk around school regarding their last meeting, and new students came to see the show. This time Cat told the students to break off in groups based on dating preference. She did two separate groups, Black and others. She gave a five-minute speech on how it is perfectly okay to be attracted to other races, because in reality, there is only one race, and that is the human race. She then asked why they preferred the race they had chosen. Their answers varied, and some were legitimate. One girl said she likes to date Asians because she's attracted to their eyes. However, Rakheem went on a tangent, spewing hate and saying how he dated White girls because Black girls were controlling and ghetto.

Samantha was in attendance and did not like what Rakheem had to say, so she challenged him.

"I'm offended; you're saying you only date White girls because, according to you, we would be more submissive, which ultimately translates into you controlling us. Only someone that's weak is unable to walk side-by-side with a strong person. Only weak

166

minded individuals want to be among weaker people because it feeds their insecure ego."

Samantha had all the kids chattering after that speech. She was right. Rakheem was insecure, and since the Black girls that he dated did not allow him to walk all over them, he twisted the reality instead of addressing his own insecurities. For the first time, Rakheem was quiet. Both Samantha and Cat had a way of making complete fools out of people. However, Cat knew if she was the one that challenged Rakheem, he would twist reality and turn it on her. Cat was relieved that it was coming from Samantha and not her because it was coming from the perspective of a White female.

Another male student also challenged Rakheem and said, "Well what does that say about your mother? Most importantly, what will you tell your daughter? You can have children by a White woman and they can come out looking just like you. So what do you tell your daughter if she looks just like you?"

Again, Rakheem did not say anything. For the first time it appeared as though he was being challenged to think about his perspectives and because it was by his peers, it seemed to have resonated with him. Cat closed the meeting with a speech on loving yourself from where you are and embracing your strengths as well as your imperfections. The students clapped when Cat was finished and then left out of the meeting room.

Rakheem stayed behind and waited until it was just he and Cat in the room. He approached Cat and said, "Did you have your friend say that, because it sounded more like something you would say?"

"No, she said that on her own; and to be honest, she is my best friend and our personalities are quite similar."

They talked for thirty minutes and were so engaged in the conversation that they did not hear the bell ring.

"Everything my mom said is what you have been talking about. I'm convinced that you two had a previous conversation." Rakheem laughed and then went on, "I want to apologize for my arrogance. The truth is, a girl that I dated two years ago went around and said my penis was small after we had sex, so in return, I went around and said that she was ghetto. Was it childish? Yes, but it felt good at the moment. Plus, I needed to redeem myself. I had sex with White girls that never publicly discussed our sex life so when she did this, I was pissed off. The girl still goes here and that was my way of belittling her like she did me. The worst thing you can do to a man is compare him to somebody else and step all over his manhood and ego. You are a dope person, but to be honest, when I saw you dating that White boy, I felt a little shunned. Here I am dancing with one of the cutest girls in the entire party and I get pressed by a White boy. So Black girls do the same thing in a different way."

"Bobby was the first White boy that I ever dated; and besides, I did not date him because he was White. I dated him because he was a cool individual and I liked him. That is totally different from downing Black boys that look like my little brothers."

They both felt like they got to see past the surface and learned a significant detail about one another that day. From then on they were as close as ever.

Chapter 13

Cat was having a great year. The day she fell to her knees and prayed it was like life turned for the better. She was no longer in pain. She was living in the moment and her family did not feel like they had to walk on eggshells when they were around her anymore. Cat was back to her normal self.

The school year was flying by and it was Christmas break. Reggie asked Cat if she wanted to spend the Christmas Break over his house. Cat had not been over at Reggie's since the incident with Ray. Cat arrived at Reggie's house and went straight into the room where she was raped. Cat did not want to avoid her fear. Mrs. Mayo had been using exposure therapy as a tool to help Cat get over the things she had gone through that had traumatized her. Both Reggie and Trina noticed that Cat walked straight into the room. Yessenia knew what she was doing but did not bother to address it.

Yessenia waited and stopped her younger siblings from entering into the room to greet Cat so she could have the time that she needed to deal with her rape experience. Yessenia understood what Cat was doing because for many years she hated that room. It was where she was raped, so she knew exactly how Cat was feeling and what she was thinking. The only thing was that Yessenia did not have a choice but to see that room everyday. Yessenia resented Trina and Reggie for a long time for never moving. However, after talking to her own therapist and watching Cat, she realized they were doing the best that they could and they could not afford to move. Trina and Reggie were not aware that Yessenia felt that way. Watching Cat immediately go into the room upon arrival and Yessenia guarding the door alarmed them both of what was going on.

Cat finally came out of the room when Reggie told the kids that they were going to share Christmas Day at his mother's house. Cat was uneasy, and it was written all over her face. She did not want to meet his family based on the different stories Nancy had told her. She felt like her dad's family was dysfunctional and she had no desire to meet them.

Reggie noticed the look on Cat's face and asked, "You don't want to go, Cat?"

"Not really."

"Ray will not be there and we won't stay long."

It was Christmas Day and they drove over an hour to Pomona, California. The houses looked old and dilapidated and put Cat in an unhappy mood. She already did not want to go. They walked into their grandmother's house and it wasn't anything like Grandma Pie's. It was very small. It smelled really bad. The carpet was filthy and there were people all over the place.

They had food on the counters and stove and it looked disgusting to Cat. Cat could tell that Trina also felt uncomfortable. Reggie got a bowl of posole and laughed with his brothers and sisters. They spoke mostly in Spanish and no one understood what they were saying, except for Reggie. Cat convinced herself that they were speaking in Spanish on purpose because all of her cousins were speaking in English. Reggie's mom approached Cat and hugged her. She said something in Spanish, but Cat did not understand a single word of what she said.

Cat watched how all the women catered to the men of the family, almost as if the women were slaves. One of Cat's teenage boy cousins did not like the food. He dropped the plate on the floor and told his younger sister to get it up. She rushed over to clean up the mess as if she was an employee at Molly Maids. Part of Cat knew that was how things worked within their family, but another part of her knew that her male cousin was showing off because guests were over. However, Cat, Trina, and Yessenia were not impressed. They were actually infuriated by his actions. In fact, Cat was turned off by the way the men were treating the women. Reggie was the opposite. He catered to his kids and his wife. They were there only an hour and Trina was ready to go. She leaned over and told her husband that she wanted to leave. Cat was happy because she was counting down the seconds to leave. Reggie spoke in Spanish and said his goodbyes.

Once in the car, Cat could not hold her thoughts in. She remembered that Mrs. Mayo told her to verbally express her feelings instead of internalizing.

"Why do the men treat the women like that in your family, Dad?"

"It's the culture. The males are the dominant figures in the family and many men feel like the woman is supposed to obey."

"So why are you not like that then?"

"Because I chose not to be like that. Just because it's a tradition doesn't mean they have to act like that, they choose to. You guys bet' not ever let a guy treat you like that."

Cat was quiet for a moment and then said, "It makes sense. That's why the men in the family were able to molest girls and nothing was done about it; because they are to be obeyed. It's almost as if they feel as though the females in the family are their property."

Reggie didn't say anything, as if he was analyzing what Cat said and picking it apart to grasp what she had said. Reggie acted as though he never gave thought to that analogy before.

"Exactly," Trina added her two cents and did not say another word.

Once back at Reggie's house, Cat opened her gifts. She didn't really care what she got. Bobby had bought her so much stuff before he died that she had a closet full of stuff. She opened her gift. It was an iphone 6. She thanked both Trina and Reggie. They watched "A Christmas Story," Cat and Sabrina's favorite holiday movie of all time. They loved the part when they said, 'Ralphie shot his eye out!'

Cat wanted to go home but she did not want to look ungrateful. Cat texted Sabrina and told her to tell Connie that she wanted to spend Christmas with Cat so she could come pick her up. A few minutes later, Reggie's phone rang and Connie was on her way to pick her up. Cat gathered her things and was ready. Then Connie texted, telling her to come outside. Cat went outside to go home.

Chapter 14

Christmas break was over and it was time to go back to school. Her guidance counselor, Mr. Hoffman, called Cat out of class the first day back at school. He told Cat about taking the SAT and the ACT's. He told her about the different scholarships that were available. Cat told him what she wanted to do and how she wanted to become a therapist. He told Cat to research the different schools that had that major. Cat told him that she already had and she was looking into going to Cal State San Bernardino. Mr. Hoffman informed Cat that he had a friend that worked there and asked if she wanted him to schedule a meeting so she could visit the campus. Cat told him that she did, and the date was scheduled.

Cat knew that she and Bobby had made plans to attend a specific college, but she realized that she had to let go of the past to move forward. She had to rewrite the script in her movie called life. Holding on to the past meant that she could not walk into her future. Cat also did not want to take Bobby's parents' money for college. She asked Mr. Hoffman about every scholarship possible. He gave her a list of scholarships that she could apply for. Before Cat left, Mr. Hoffman told her to have her mother help her do a free application for federal student aid.

Cat spoke to Connie about the application for financial aid when she arrived home. Connie pulled out her laptop and helped Cat fill out the forms online. They had to wait to see how much Cat qualified for. Cat lived with Connie, therefore she only had to use Connie's income to see if she qualified and Connie did not make that much. Connie worked as a caregiver for family members and their friends while they were at work. Connie got paid under the table, due to not having a daycare license. Because she had so many kids, they fell within the low-income range on the application, which meant that Cat would most likely qualify for the maximum amount. Cat was not going to put all her hopes in the financial aid. She was going to find other resources just in case she was not eligible. Cat wanted to make sure she had all her bases covered.

The next week, Connie took Cat to her scheduled appointment at Cal State San Bernardino. She met with the director over the psychology department and some students walked her around campus and let her see the college atmosphere. Cat was impressed with what the school had to offer. She loved the fact that it wasn't too far from home, but not too close either. Connie wanted to ride around the city to see how it looked. Over the past year San Bernardino had been on the news for one of the worst cities to reside in in California. They got into the car and drove around; Connie was impressed. They drove down past some railroad tracks and Connie's idea of the city swiftly diminished. The only nice part of the city was by the university. The rest of the city was very raggedy and looked run down. The city was bankrupted, and it looked like it. Connie was apprehensive in regards to sending her daughter to school where the crime was high. She did not want Cat to not attend the school of her choice, but she was concerned for her safety. Cat did not like how the city looked either, but she really wanted to attend the university.

"I don't know about you living on campus out here, Cat."

"Mom, I really want to go here."

Connie wanted to say no, but she knew Cat would soon be eighteen, old enough to make her own decisions. She didn't want Cat to feel as if she was holding her back from her dreams. Cat had made so much progress and she did not want to hinder her in any way.

"What if I stay at home and not live in the dorms?

"Deal."

Connie had to compromise somewhere, and the fact that Cat was agreeing to live at home and only come on the days she had classes was a win -win situation for Connie.

Cat had put all her energy into applying for scholarships. Most were based on essays on a specific topic. She knocked them out one by one and waited for the responses. Cat was notified that she was granted the full amount of financial aid, which meant her tuition would be paid for. She wanted to follow in her aunt Sharon's footsteps and become something and change lives. Connie was happy that Cat was taking the initiative to get funds to attend college, rather than depending on Bobby's parents. Connie thought the gesture of them paying was nice, but it made Connie feel like a charity case, and she did not want anyone to do things for her and her family out of pity. That was just one of Connie's own insecurities. Cat was not worried about being perceived as a charity case because she knew when Bobby's parents said they would pay for her tuition it was coming from a good place.

Cat wanted to figure things out on her own instead of her first option being to rely on someone else to solve the problem. When Cat presented Mrs. Mayo with a problem she was facing, Mrs. Mayo provided her with options to solve the problem, but never gave her the answer. It taught Cat that she was very capable of solving her own issues when given resources to solve them. Cat had found a resource in Mr. Hoffman when she asked about the different scholarships, which helped her figure out how she would apply for college. Like Cat anticipated, she was provided with four different scholarships totaling in the amount of ten thousand dollars, which, combined with her financial aid, was more than enough to cover her tuition.

It was the month of March and Cat's birthday was approaching. Cat did not want to celebrate her birthday. She wasn't in the mood. She requested that if Connie wanted to do something, she would just have their household attend with some cake, ice cream, and pizza. Connie was disappointed. She wanted to go all out for Cat's eighteenth birthday. It was the last year that her baby would be a minor under her roof without a choice. Connie felt that Cat deserved a big birthday bash but she also wanted to respect Cat's wishes. Connie knew her daughter well enough to know that if she said she did not want a birthday party then she meant just that. Sabrina was the total opposite. When she said that she did not want something, it was her passive way of saying what she actually wanted.

The day had come, and when the kids came home from school, they entered into the house with a living room full of balloons, cake and ice cream, and pizza; just like cat requested. They played Phase Ten and watched movies the remainder of the day. Before Cat went to bed that night she walked over to Connie and whispered in her ear.

"This, by far, was the best birthday ever. Thanks Mom."

Connie accidently kissed Cat on the forehead because Cat turned her face before Connie could allow her lips to connect with Cat's cheek. Connie was immediately aware of what she had done. She knew that a kiss on the forehead was something that triggered horrible memories for Cat. She tried to apologize but Cat cut her off and told her that it was okay.

A month had passed and it was time to get ready for the prom. The girls at school obsessed with what they were wearing, who they wanted to go with, and how they wanted to be asked. Cat couldn't care less. She didn't care about having a date. It really didn't matter to her if she went or not.

After a BSU meeting Rakheem asked Cat, "Who are you going with to the prom?"

"Nobody. Who are you going with?"

"Nobody. Who is Sabrina going with?"

"Sabrina? She's a junior. What, you have your eyes on my sister?"

"Yep, I do. Do you think she will say yes?" Rakheem said in an insecure voice.

"I don't know, ask her." Cat smiled from ear to ear. She was so happy that Rakheem was going to ask her sister and could not wait to see the expression on Sabrina's face when he asked.

Samantha overheard the conversation and told Cat that she was going alone as well. They agreed to be each other's date. Cat was over the whole dating thing after Bobby. That was one last fear that she hadn't conquered. She was content with going with Samantha and just enjoying the night. Cat and Samantha agreed to go looking for dresses after school.

While Cat and Samantha were at the mall, they ran into Samantha's friend, Kyla. She accompanied them while looking for dresses. Cat would usually be picky, but because she was not really feeling going to the prom, she tried on a few dresses and picked the one that she liked best out of the three she had picked up. It was a cute dress, but not a gorgeous dress. Cat sent Connie a picture of the dress she was planning to purchase. Connie told her that she was on her way to the mall to help her pick out another dress because the dress she had picked was too plain for the prom.

Connie knew by the dress Cat picked that she was not really in the mood for the prom. Cat put all the dresses back and roamed the aisles looking at different dresses while she waited for Connie to get to the mall. Cat ran into a few girls that she knew from school who were also looking at dresses. She watched them and quickly realized that they were interested in the same styles that she had been interested in. Cat decided if she was going to put her all into getting a dress then she most certainly did not want to look like everyone else. Cat told Samantha and Kyla that she was going to the store at the other end of the mall to look at dresses. She texted Connie to give her the new location.

Connie walked in the store and saw Cat roaming up and down the aisles looking at dresses. Connie picked out six dresses that were to Cat's liking; and they were much different than the styles the other girls were looking at. Connie had great taste and was really into fashion. Cat loved all the dresses that her mom had picked but she could only choose one.

The dress that Cat chose was a soft pink and white, with gold trim. It was absolutely beautiful. Cat looked flawless in the dress. She knew that most of the girls at school would never consider putting those colors together. Cat wanted to stand apart from all the other girls. She made the prom about her outfit and put her energy into her dress and her look for the prom. Once Cat had purchased her dress, Connie left Cat to hang out with her friends.

Cat texted Samantha and met up with her and Kyla. They were done shopping and were ready to leave the mall. They had had enough of shopping for the day. Kyla asked Samantha if she could join them and Samantha told her she could.

Cat went to Samantha's house before going home–which she rarely did. Samantha's mom was a drunken mess as usual, and Cat knew she was not going to stay over much longer. Kyla and Samantha joined Samantha's mom with drinking. Cat left, not wanting to be a part of what they were doing.

Kyla asked Samantha, "Why did she leave?"

"She is a prude. She's too good to drink. She thinks it's a 'White people thing' for kids to drink with their parents. I should have told her it must be a Black people thing when her mom beat her with a broom and gave her a black eye," Samantha said sarcastically.

Cat heard Samantha before leaving completely out of the door but she was not upset, because she started the whole race fiasco with her 'white' remark. She knew Samantha was putting her down to justify drinking with her mother.

Cat showed Sabrina her dress and tried it on for her. While Cat was walking back and forth as if she was in a fashion show on a runway, Sabrina said, "Guess what?"

"What?" Cat answered.

"Rakheem asked me to the prom!" Sabrina screamed as she was smiling from ear to ear.

Cat smiled in silence.

"OMG you knew, he told you?!"

"Yeah, he did."

Suddenly, Cat and Sabrina heard sirens outside and looked out the window. The paramedics were headed to Samantha's house. Cat and Sabrina raced down the stairs and out the front door. Kyla was on a gurney and Samantha's mom was in handcuffs.

"What happened, are you okay?" asked Cat.

"I don't know what happened; we were drinking and she just passed out. Samantha said while crying. "She said she had drunk before. I told her to slow down, but she said she drinks like that all the time. So I figured she knew what she was doing, Cat. I thought she could handle her liquor."

"What happened to her? Why is she leaving in the ambulance; and why is your mom in the back of the police car?"

"She passed out and we couldn't wake her up. My mom is going to jail for providing alcohol to a minor. I tried telling them that my mom didn't offer it to her, I did. She drank it on her own. My mom did not force her to drink the alcohol—God's honest truth."

Cat shook her head in disbelief. She knew that Samantha was in shock and that she knew that it was illegal for her mother to provide alcohol to minors. Cat knew it was not the right time to bring that point up to Samantha, so she let it go.

A social worker tapped Samantha on the shoulder and told her to that she was going with her until everything got sorted out.

Samantha held on to Cat cried and said, "I can stay over my best friend's house. Cat, tell her that I can stay with you until my mom gets out of jail."

Cat tried to convince the social worker that it was okay for Samantha to stay over, but the social worker informed Cat that because she was not biologically related to Samantha, she could not stay with her. Cat felt bad. She had told Samantha many times before that it was not right for her mother to be drinking with Samantha and her friends. All the inappropriate parenting and poor decisions had finally caught up to Samantha's mom. Cat hugged Samantha and after she drove off, Cat and Sabrina went into their house and told Connie what happened.

Days had passed and Cat had not heard from Samantha, and her mother was not back at the house. Cat knocked on the door everyday to see if she had returned, but no one was home. There were rumors around school that Kyla was still in the hospital in a coma. Someone had given Kyla's mom Cat's name and told her where she lived, and Kyla's mom stopped by to question Cat about the behaviors of Samantha and her mother. Cat would not give her any information. Even though Samantha's mom was negligent in her decisions, Cat did not want to be the one to tell on her best friend's mother. Cat could not find it in her to turn on Samantha. Cat simply redirected the questions back to Kyla.

"Why don't you ask your daughter?"

"I would but she is in a coma and cannot talk," Kyla's mom said sarcastically before she turned around and walked away.

Cat felt horrible. The rumor had been confirmed. Cat was conflicted; she wanted to do the right thing and tell Kyla's mom, but she did not want to disappoint Samantha. Cat made a pact with herself that if Kyla did not pull through, she would go ahead and tell on Samantha and her mother; but, if Kyla woke up, she would leave it to Kyla to tell her mother the details of what type of people they were. Cat made her decision how she would handle that situation, and then let it go.

Cat arrived to school the following day to more rumors. They were centered on Samantha and her mom being charged with attempted murder, and if Kyla died, murder. Cat had been texting Samantha but was not getting a response. The rumor about Kyla being in a coma ended up being true so Cat didn't know what to believe. During lunch Kyla's friend Brenda and a few others approached Cat.

"Your best friend's mom is scum. She *should* be locked up in jail for what she did to Kyla."

Cat was taken aback because Brenda, who seemed to have the most to say, was often at

Samantha's house, and Cat could only assume that they were drinking. When Samantha had friends over, they played drinking games. That was the reason why Cat did not like going over there. Besides, every time Samantha was drunk around school, she was with Brenda. Cat was irate and had to defend Samantha.

"Her mother is scum? Well, it takes one to know one. Last I checked, you all would often be over drinking with her scum of a mother, right?!"

They didn't make a peep. Cat went on and on calling them hypocrites. Spectators observed with their mouths wide open.

The girls had been bashing Samantha and Samantha's mom all around school and omitting the part they played. Cat was not going to let them off the hook—especially since they approached her with a crowd of people, trying to play the hero that was standing up for Kyla. Well Cat was not having it. She exposed them for the individuals they really were. They were only complaining now because their friend was in the hospital.

It was sixth period, the last period of the day. The Assistant Principle of Discipline, Ms. Maggie, called Cat into the office. She questioned Cat about the incident that happened with Brenda. Cat did not understand why she was asking her questions about responding to someone that approached her.

"Do you know about Samantha's mom providing alcohol to Samantha and her friends before arriving to school?" Ms. Maggie asked.

Cat did not understand why she was asking her about Samantha's mom when the incident with Kyla did not happen at school.

Cat just kept answering, "I don't know."

Cat was overwhelmed. She had not talked to Samantha since she had been taken by the social worker and she did not understand why the principle was now involved. Cat went into defense mode. She was going to protect her friend by any means necessary.

Cat inquired, "Why are you asking me all these questions about Samantha's mom when she is not a student?"

Mrs. Maggie dismissed Cat from her office, never answering her question.

Cat tried texting Samantha again but she never replied. Cat tried speaking to Samantha's other friends and questioned them about her whereabouts but they all appeared to be acting strange. Cat saw Mark in a group talking and laughing.

"Mark, what is going on with Samantha? Have you heard anything?"

"You haven't heard? Since Kyla has been in a coma, her mom has been rallying all her friends to come forward and inform the police if Samantha's mom had ever offered them alcohol at her house. You know, a lot of times kids come to school drunk and high, but now kids are coming out of nowhere making up stories. Some stories are true but others just want attention. I can't believe her own friends are turning on her. I don't know if it's because they're scared and don't want to get in trouble, or they feel bad because Kyla is in a coma. Rumor has it that Kyla's mom is putting pressure on the school because Brenda has been telling people that Samantha's mom got her drunk before school."

"Well we all know that's a lie. Samantha's mom does let them drink alcohol in her house but

Brenda and Samantha always got drunk at school. Why are they lying like this?"

"I don't know. You know when there is a big story kids always want to involve themselves to be a part of the story."

Mark reached out and hugged Cat because he could see the frustration on her face. Cat reciprocated his hug and then walked away.

After school, Sabrina ran up to Cat out of breath, "Cat, they are trying to implicate you in drinking with Samantha because you guys are best friends. I had to press a girl in class because she was lying, saying you were there when it happened and that you tried to cover it up."

"I am getting so sick of them lying! The next person that lies on my friend and I hear it, is getting socked in the mouth. Period." Cat was becoming frustrated.

Connie pulled up and caught the end of their conversation. "Whose mouth are you going to sock?"

Cat started to explain and Sabrina jumped in and told all of the accounts of the rumors and everything that was going on at school.

"Well Samantha's mom is home but the media is all out in front of the house trying to get a story, so just walk in the house and do not bother speaking to them," Connie instructed.

They pulled up to the house and every major news channel was there. Someone must have told them who Cat was, because a few members of the news crew were pointing at Cat and when she got out of the car, they walked right up to her.

"Is your name Cat?" One of the news crew staff asked.

Cat did not respond.

"Did your best friend Samantha's mom provide you and your friends with drugs and alcohol?" the news crew staff asked.

Cat was furious. The story went from alcohol to now drugs. Cat could not believe how the story kept changing.

"No, she never gave kids drugs and every kid that went to Samantha's house and drunk was because they wanted to, not because they were forced to!" Cat said angrily.

"So you are admitting that you all have drunk alcohol at Samantha's house in the presence of her mother?"

Cat could not believe how he was trying to twist her words. "I have never drunk alcohol at Samantha's house," Cat explained.

Connie snatched Cat by the arm before she could dig herself further in a whole. The reporters chased behind Cat trying to get more information. They were like leeches, trying to suck everything up that they could.

It was obvious that Connie was irritated, but Cat didn't know if it was because she failed to follow her instructions about not talking to the media, or because of her answer. Cat tested the waters and tried speaking to her mom to see if she was upset with her, but based on her response, she was upset about something else. Connie had a way about her when she was mad. Cat knew if it was her Connie was upset with, Connie would have no problem making it clear to her, and since she hadn't, Cat knew her mother's anger had nothing to do with her.

Relieved that Connie was not mad at her, Cat went into her backyard, jumped over the fence into Samantha's backyard, and knocked on the backdoor. Samantha's mom answered the door and let Cat in.

"What is going on and where is Samantha? The prom is in two days and we are supposed to go as a couple."

"I am being charged with attempted murder, Cat. Do you really think I care about the prom?" Samantha's mom asked in a frustrated voice.

Cat realized the way she worded her question made it appear that she was being shallow and only concerned about the prom, when in reality, Cat was concerned about Samantha's well being.

"I'm so sorry. People just keep asking me questions and I haven't talked to Samantha. I just want to know if she is okay."

"They are trying to take her away from me, saying that I'm an unfit mother."

Cat stood there in silence with an awkward posture, not knowing what to say, and because she did not have a poker face, her true thoughts were written all over it.

"Do you think I'm an unfit mom, Cat? I noticed how you are her only friend that never comes over and you live next door. Samantha always makes excuses for why you don't want to come over, but I know my daughter well enough to know when she is covering for somebody."

"I mean..."

Cat paused. Mrs. Mayo had been talking to Cat about being honest with people. Being honest could potentially allow them to look in the mirror and recognize their flaws and when they are lied to, it only enables their behavior. Cat thought she was a terrible mother.

"I mean, I just have to be honest. From what I've observed, you are an unfit mother."

Cat could not just stop there; she took a deep breath and explained her reasoning. Cat thought that answering the question without providing the reason was not allowing her to see her faults.

"You allow Samantha and her friends to drink, which is against the law. Most of the time I came over you were drunk. Even though you would say you were 'calming your nerves after a long day,' the reality is, you are an alcoholic."

Samantha's mom did not say one word, and Cat could tell that the truth hurt. Hearing that she was unfit from a kid was more hurtful than any other time she had heard it. Adults told her that all the time, but the fact that a kid noticed it was not only embarrassing to Samantha's mom, but the dagger dug deep.

"Wow Cat, you really know how to kick someone when they're down."

Samantha's mom then closed the door in Cat's face. Cat stood there for a moment and pondered over everything she had said. Cat could not find anything wrong with what she said. Samantha's mom asked a question but did not really want to hear the truth. Mrs. Mayo had also taught Cat that when telling the truth, people would not always be willing to hear and be receptive to it. Cat knew that she did the right thing by telling the truth.

Chapter 15

Cat was scheduled for her weekly counseling session and she did not want to miss it. She had so much she wanted to tell Mrs. Mayo. Mrs. Mayo always knew when something was bothering Cat. Cat didn't even have to mention it because Mrs. Mayo would bring it up before Cat could. Sometimes she didn't want to mention it but Mrs. Mayo knew how to get Cat to open up even when She didn't want to.

"You seem like you're slipping back into depression. The last time I saw you looking disheveled with your hair not combed and wearing sweats and a t-shirt, you were depressed. What's going on?"

"I am sad all the time. I cry in the shower so no one knows that I cry and I don't know why."

"Well we think of losing people when they die and that's when we mourn them. A break up or someone being absent from your life can sometimes feel just like them actually dying. You are mourning the loss of your best friend, which is normal. You miss her. However, I want you to use your coping skills, which consist of journaling and verbally expressing your feelings. I don't want you to slip back into a deep depression. Your prom is tomorrow, and even though Samantha will not be there, I want you to live in that moment. This is your last year of high school and the only prom that you have ever attended. Be present and have fun.

"Many times we miss the opportunity of taking in the moment. What you are experiencing is very hurtful and I don't want to minimize it in any way, but you also have to realize that being a victim and walking around looking homeless is not going to bring Samantha back. So what can you do to put your mind at ease and enjoy your prom?"

She always had a way of giving Cat a lecture but making her think as well, challenging her to provide a solution to the problem. Cat felt good talking to Mrs. Mayo.

"I'm going to live in the moment and have fun, so when I see Samantha, I can tell her about the prom."

Cat left the counseling office that day feeling optimistic about the prom and couldn't wait to be free and live in the moment.

It was the day of the prom and Cat figured she would just go by herself. Connie ensured that Cat was all dolled up. Cat kept thinking about Samantha and how she was doing. Cat didn't even care that Samantha wasn't going to the prom. She just wanted to make sure that her friend was okay.

Sabrina and Cat both looked like a million bucks. Cat walked into the prom. It was an Indian theme. They had chocolate fountains with strawberries. The students really put thought into the prom. Cat reflected on what Mrs. Mayo had said in the previous session and wanted to be present in the moment. Cat walked around and gathered with her friends. She did not have a care in the world. She relaxed her mind and was having fun. Someone tapped her on the shoulder and then smacked her butt. Cat turned around immediately and was about to give them the scolding of their life. Half way around, she noticed Samantha's hand. Cat was hesitant for a moment. She did not know if she was really seeing Samantha or was just thinking about Samantha. She then turned fully around and saw her best friend dressed like Cinderella with a big smile on her face, with her arms wide open, anticipating a big hug.

Cat jumped into Samantha's arms. They laughed and joked. Cat wanted to know all the details of what happened but she knew that they would spend hours talking about everything like they always did. Cat did not want to ruin the moment of being at the prom, so she pushed those thoughts aside and let Samantha know that she missed her. Cat loved the music so she stayed on the dance floor the entire night. Cat and Samantha literally danced the night away.

It was time to leave and everyone was gathering on the party bus to be dropped off in front of the school. Samantha said goodbye and told Cat she would call her. Cat didn't bother to ask her why she hadn't returned her texts; she was too tired. Cat got on the bus and instantly realized that she did not see Sabrina. Cat walked off of the bus and repeatedly asked people had they seen her. Cat saw Sabrina coming from a distance. Sabrina was fixing her hair and kept tugging at her dress, pulling it down. As Cat got closer she saw that her lipstick was across her face and on Rakheem's as well. Cat instantly knew that they had had sex.

She grabbed Sabrina by her arm and walked her over to the side like a mother getting ready to reprimand her child.

"Do not tell me that you had sex with him and he is not even your boyfriend."

"Yeah, I did. I am not a little girl Cat, and furthermore, I am not your child. The last time I checked, you are only one year older than me, and I am pretty sure you had sex with Bobby so, poof, be gone!"

"Is that alcohol I smell on your breath? So a guy asks you to the prom and you drop your panties? Yes, I did have sex with Bobby but he was my boyfriend and it was not a week after I started talking to him. Wait a minute, you're not even talking, he just asked you to the prom. So what, you're mini Connie now; dropping your panties for any guy that smiles in your direction? I mean, have some type of standards!"

Sabrina started crying. Sabrina knew that every word Cat said was true. She had only slept with Rakheem because he told her what she wanted to hear and she felt pretty in that moment. Sabrina knew that she was acting like her mother. Sabrina and Cat sat separately on the bus and when they got home, they went their separate ways.

The next day Cat received a call from Samantha.

"I had so much fun last night!"

"Yeah, I did too. Where are you?"

"I'm in a group home. You have to get on a certain level by earning points in order to have your phone, and because I was new, I had to work up to level four to get my phone. Everything is all bad. Can you believe Brenda and her little imps gave statements to the lead detective that my mom got us sloppy drunk before going to school? I will admit that my mom does allow me and my friends to drink, but she has never sent us to school drunk. I think it's pretty crappy of Brenda, being my so called friend, to outright lie like that."

"Wow Samantha, I don't know what to say. I just want you to come back home."

192

"I can already tell you that I'm not going home. They made it clear that they're not giving me back to my mom. I will be eighteen in a week so I can leave and be on my own. The social worker said she will assist me with getting my own place as long as I stay in school. My dad lives in Manhattan and I am not leaving my senior year to go to Manhattan."

"I would rather you be in Manhattan than to not be around some type of family, Samantha."

"I *am* around family—you. After I turn eighteen I will have my own place, and to be honest, my dad or mom will pay for my apartment. So realistically, I don't need the social worker to help me financially. After we graduate my dad has already said he would pay for my tuition to attend Yale or Harvard. I wanted to stay here and go to school with you but my dad said he's only paying for my tuition if I go to an Ivy League school. Hey, but what's up with Sabrina letting Rakheem and his boys get down with her?"

"What?!"

"Yeah. She didn't tell you? How didn't you know and I'm in another city and I know?"

"OMG, are you serious? I knew she had sex with Rakheem, but I didn't know that she had sex with his friends too. Let me call you back. I need to talk to her," Cat said with an irritated tone.

Cat marched into Sabrina's room. Sabrina was lying on her bed, and from the looks of how she was talking, she was talking to a guy.

"Who are you talking to?"

"Rakheem."

Cat snatched the phone and Sabrina snatched it back, hanging up the phone by accident. Connie walked into the room during the tug of war match and told Cat to go to her room. Cat badly wanted to say what was going on but she did not want to out Sabrina. Even though she disagreed with what she did she still had an allegiance to her sister to hold her secrets just as Sabrina had always done for her.

Cat went to her room and texted everyone in her contacts asking for Rakheem's phone number so she could tell him off, but no one knew his number. Cat tried to find Rakheem on social media but he was not under his real name. Kids made profiles with nicknames instead of their government names, which made it hard to find them. Cat told herself she would leave it alone for now.

The following week the rumor was all over school about Sabrina and Rakheem, and his friends. Cat confronted Rakheem as soon as he entered into the BSU meeting.

"Why would you—"

Rakheem cut Cat off and said, "Cat, I know what you are about to say, but I had no idea Sabrina had sex with my bros until yesterday. Your sister and I got into a big argument over it. It was not something that I planned. Yes, I wanted to have sex, but I was really feeling your sister until I found out she messed with my bros. Your sister is a thot, straight up. I was literally pressing people behind the rumor until I talked to my bros and they confirmed that it was true. They had sex with her after I did. After the prom I thought she went home, but apparently they hit her up on Snapchat and met her at your house. I didn't know until after the fact. I'm cool on your sister in a real way. She's a hoe."

Rakheem walked away toward the back of the room just as Sabrina walked in and walked out, as if she was embarrassed. All the boys she slept with were in BSU. Cat could not wrap her brain around why Sabrina would do something so stupid. Cat let the group know that the meeting was cancelled until the following week.

Cat waited until she was home to speak to Sabrina about what happened. When Connie was preoccupied with the younger kids, Cat knew it was her chance to talk to Sabrina without Connie overhearing. Cat went into Sabrina's room and closed the door behind her. Sabrina was lying down listening to music. Sabrina already knew what Cat was in her room for. Cat started speaking.

"I do not understand why you put yourself in a position to be called the school ho. We promised that we would never become mom. What were you thinking? I was ready to go to war for you and then to find out that you slept with his friends too! I thought it was a lie."

Sabrina swiftly sat straight up in her bed and said, "Do you know how it feels to always be overlooked? No, you don't. So don't tell me about mom. I know it was stupid, but in that moment, for the first time, I felt wanted, desired--something you wouldn't know about because you're Cat. They always chase you. You have a dad that worships the ground you walk on and 'Cat' is all the boys' first pick. When they messaged me, I thought they liked me. Was it dumb? Yes. Do I regret it? Yes, but until you experience what I have, you will never understand how it feels Cat. You are the only person that tells me I'm pretty. I look at your pictures on Instagram and it can be a simple picture and you will get over a thousand likes and I may get twenty. Sometimes, Cat, I just want to feel loved and pretty like you." Sabrina cried in embarrassment.

Cat didn't want to add insult to injury, so she hugged Sabrina and let her cry in her arms. Cat knew giving her a lecture was not what she needed in that moment. Sabrina recognized her faults and this was a situation that Sabrina had to fix on her own. Cat knew she could not fix it for her.

Cat waited until her next counseling session to process her thoughts with Mrs. Mayo. Cat walked in her office, ready to spill the beans. Cat wasn't in her seat before she started talking.

"Sabrina had sex with three guys in one night—two at the same time," Cat spewed out.

"Okay, Cat, slow down; and it would have been nice if you walked in and greeted me before spilling the tea all over the table," Mrs. Mayo said in a joking manner.

"I'm sorry, hi, Mrs. Mayo. I was saying that Sabrina has turned into my mom and I don't understand why."

"You have to understand that many people will do anything, even if it means disrespecting themselves to feel loved or to get a compliment. That's why you see people degrading themselves on social media and posting pictures half clothed for attention. You may not because you know your value. Someone struggling with low self-esteem may compromise who he or she is just to feel loved, even if it is a lie, because it feels good in that moment. How does all of this make you feel?"

Mrs. Mayo always had a way of redirecting Cat to focus on herself and not others.

Cat paused and then responded, "I'm embarrassed, not for me, but for her."

Mrs. Mayo cleared her throat and said, "Are you sure you're only embarrassed for her?"

Cat had a love-hate relationship with Mrs. Mayo. Cat wanted to vent and talk about Sabrina. Cat sometimes hated when Mrs. Mayo challenged her and did not allow her to focus on others during a session. Cat wanted to discuss Sabrina and not herself, besides, it was Sabrina who had had sex with three guys in one night.

Cat thought about what she was going to say and then said, "I mean, well of course it is embarrassing. Who wants a sister that is known as a thot? It was embarrassing enough that we had to deal with that with Connie and now we're in a whole new state and it's no longer Connie, but now Sabrina."

"What does Sabrina and Connie's actions have to do with you? Are they not allowed to experience life through their own lens and make their own mistakes just like you have?"

Now Cat was really annoyed because Sabrina and Connie making mistakes was not the point. She wanted Mrs. Mayo to feel and understand how their behavior was an embarrassment to the family. Cat rolled her eyes and Mrs. Mayo caught it right away.

"So if I don't agree with you and allow you to focus on others versus yourself then you become disrespectful? Now, should I be embarrassed of you based on your presenting behavior?" Cat was even more frustrated.

Cat realized it was a lose-lose situation and Mrs. Mayo was not going to allow her to focus on others.

"Cat, if you came here every week and we fixed everyone else's problems and not yours, how does that benefit you?"

"It doesn't."

"Focusing on others is a way to not focus on self. It's a way that we mask our own hurts, insecurities, and frustration. So what is it that you are trying to mask when you keep focusing on Sabrina?"

Cat had to stop focusing on Sabrina and be honest with herself. The issue was not Sabrina, the issue was that Cat was concerned about how others would view her based on Sabrina's behavior. Cat was too embarrassed to admit it so she didn't respond, and she didn't have to because the alarm went off, signaling that her one-hour session was over. Mrs. Mayo had a smirk on her face, conveying that the bell saved Cat from answering the question.

On the way home, Cat ruminated over the session. She thought about the question that Mrs. Mayo had asked her. She was mad at herself for being a hypocrite. She preached to her siblings and everyone around her about being a leader and not caring how others perceived them. Cat realized why she was avoidant in the session and was so in tuned with Sabrina's behavior. As long as Cat pointed and bashed Sabrina, it allowed her to escape from dealing with the real issue. Cat had to self reflect and think about what caused her to start caring about what others thought of her. What pain and hurt was she masking?

198

When it came back that Sabrina had sex with three different guys in the same night, Cat was concerned about her being pregnant and not knowing who the father was. That brought up Cat's own embarrassment. Cat was embarrassed about being pregnant and not knowing if it was Bobby's baby or her uncle's. She didn't want anyone to ever find out about those skeletons that she hoped stayed in the closet. Cat never even told Samantha and Sabrina. That was a skeleton that she was taking to her grave. Sabrina's situation made Cat face her own feelings that were stirring up inside of her. Cat suppressed them back down. Pretending that they did not exist, she bottled them up and put the cap on. Cat had it in her mind that for the next two weeks she was going to make an excuse for why she couldn't go to her therapy sessions. Cat wanted to ensure that Mrs. Mayo forgot about their last conversation because that was a question that she did not want to answer.

When Cat arrived home, Bobby's dad was at the front door knocking. Connie parked and they got out of the car. Connie greeted Bobby's dad and Cat greeted him with a hug. Connie invited him in but he declined, saying that he was already running late for a meeting.

"I wanted to catch you before I go out of town because I will be overseas for some time and I wanted to give you this blank check for your college tuition. It would be nice to get a text or call sometimes Cat," he said.

Cat looked at the check. She wanted to refuse it but did not want to be seen as being ungrateful, so she took the check anyway, and thanked him. Bobby's dad rushed off and sped away. Cat went in her room and set the check on her dresser. She stared at it for a brief second and contemplated if she should use it.

Cat called Samantha and spent the remainder of the night talking to her about college. Samantha brought up valid points of living on campus and having the full college experience. It made Cat think about changing her schools. The enrollment deadline had passed when she looked online while she talked to Samantha over the phone. Cat knew that Connie was not going to agree to her living in the dorms at Cal State San Bernardino because of all the killings on the news. The most recent killing was a man and his son who had been standing in front of a liquor store. Cat wanted the full college experience, not just going to class and then going home. Cat had a lot of things to think about, one of them being how she was going to finagle her way into living in the dorms.

It was a week before graduation. Connie ordered Cat's cap and gown. Cat was excited about walking across that stage. They had so many senior excursions and Cat was caught up in all the fun. Samantha was back at home with her mom and ready to go off to Harvard. The chatter at school about Samantha had subsided once Kyla was released from the hospital and was back at school. Most of the kids were surprised that Kyla had no ill feelings toward Samantha or her mother. Ultimately, Kyla took responsibility for her actions.

While at lunch, Kyla and Samantha discussed what happened. "Kyla, I am so sorry for what happened to you."

"No, Samantha, it was my own fault. I'm seventeen and old enough to know right from wrong, regardless of whether or not your mother provided the alcohol. I'm not saying your mother was not wrong for allowing me to drink in her house, because she was, but I knew what I was doing. My mom wanted to go after your mom and make sure she never saw the light of day again, but I didn't think that was right. My mom has known that I drink for some time now. I was pissed with Brenda. That little cunt is always drunk and went around bashing you, from what I heard, and I didn't like that either. We are friends Samantha, and I believe in loyalty. You do not bail on your friends when everything goes south. We knew what we were doing, so why would I put the blame all on you? That wasn't right. I told my mom that your mom was in jail and you were in a group home. My mom is still pressing charges so we are not on good terms right now," Kyla rambled on.

Samantha cut her off, "It's all good. Money talks, and my dad was able to pay a high scale attorney to get the charges dropped. So it worked out after all.

Cat sat and listened to their conversation as they went back and forth talking about everything that had transpired. Cat concluded that this must have been their first time talking since the incident because they spent the entire lunch talking about it. Cat wondered what lesson Samantha's mom was learning if she could just buy her way out of consequences. And what was that teaching Samantha?

It was graduation day and Cat was nervous, but excited at the same time. She anticipated walking across the stage and could not wait to throw her cap high into the air. Cat was all dressed up and headed over to the school with her family. Family members that she didn't even know existed were calling

Connie's cellphone to get directions to the graduation.

Cat arrived an hour before the ceremony started and lined up with her fellow classmates. An hour later the music started and Cat got excited all over again. She walked in with her head held high. Regardless of whether or not anyone else acknowledged her accomplishments, she did. Cat felt like through everything she was faced with since moving to California, she had become a conqueror and not a victim, and receiving that diploma was proof of it. She did not let her circumstances hinder her, and she was very proud that day. She sat through the Valedictorian speech, among many others, and then it was finally time to announce the graduates of the year 2016. Cat stood with pride and tossed her cap high in the air.

Cat and Samantha hugged and Samantha said, "We did it Cat."

They smiled and took selfies. Cat rushed to find her family because she didn't have much time before leaving on the bus to go to grad night. Connie got what seemed like a million calls but the only people there were Reggie, Trina, Sabrina, Aunt Sharon, and Grandma Pie. Cat took pictures with her family and then went to the car with Connie so she could be taken home to change her clothes and rush back to get on the bus for grad night.

Cat ran into the house to change but was greeted by a house full of family with food, balloons, and gifts. They jumped out of everywhere and yelled, "Surprise!"

Cat was definitely surprised. She grabbed her heart and froze. Cat was happy that everyone made a point to surprise her and cook dinner. She went around the house hugging and thanking everyone for coming and celebrating her accomplishment. Cat glanced at all the food on the counter and looked back at Sabrina and asked her to make her a plate to go. Sabrina nodded her head.

Cat dashed upstairs to change so that she could go back to the high school where the buses were waiting for her for grad night. Cat walked out the door and the whole family was in an uproar, chattering among one another asking the question, "Where is she going?"

Connie looked back at the crowd of family and said, "She has grad night."

Everyone yelled across the room for her to have fun. Connie drove back to the school and Cat ate her plate of soul food on the way.

Connie leaned over as Cat was eating and said, "I am so proud of you baby. You did it. I have watched you transition into a young woman over the years, effortlessly. Have fun and enjoy it."

Cat looked over with a mouth full of food and smiled. Connie pulled up to the school where hundreds of kids were waiting to load onto the buses. Connie waved goodbye and off Cat went to enjoy her last night of gathering with her senior class.

Chapter 16

It was time to face Mrs. Mayo during her counseling session. Cat strolled into her office, hoping that she had forgotten about their last session. Cat was confident that Mrs. Mayo would not remember what they discussed weeks prior. Cat sat in the chair waiting for Mrs. Mayo to speak before saying anything. Mrs. Mayo knew what Cat was doing.

"So do you want to answer that question today? Mrs. Mayo said.

Cat looked stunned and said, "How..."

Mrs. Mayo interrupted her before forming a complete sentence.

"After each session I write a progress note, chronicling what we discussed during our session."

Cat let the cat out of the bag. "I realized that I was so focused on Sabrina because I was embarrassed, and I was reflecting on my own situation with being pregnant and not knowing who the father was. I was embarrassed and angry about what happened to me. Sabrina having sex with three different guys in the same night made me angry because she had a choice and I was not given one. There it is, I said it."

Mrs. Mayo leaned in and placed her hand on Cat's knee and said, "I'm proud of you Cat, owning your truth is how you grow in life. It wasn't about me outing you and making you feel bad. It was about me, as a therapist, challenging you to be the best you. If you lie to yourself throughout life, you will forever live a lie, telling yourself what you want to hear and focusing on other people is only hurting you. I'm teaching you how to challenge yourself by being honest with yourself so when you are no longer in therapy you'll know how to pick up the pieces of life and properly put them in place. That's something that not even most adults know how to do. It's called preparing you for the real world, kid."

It made Cat feel good that she had told her truth and was able to express it verbally without feeling ashamed. Cat left therapy that day feeling like she could take on the world.

The talks with Samantha about college raised questions with Cat. It had been two weeks since the last day of school and Cat knew she needed to ask Connie about staying in the dorms before it was too late. Cat waited for the perfect time.

Connie was in the kitchen cooking while listening to gospel music and Cat knew she would be willing to hear what she had to say.

"Mom, I was talking to Samantha and I want the full experience of the college life."

"Okay, I'm confused on why you're saying this. College is what you make of it."

"I meant living in the dorm."

"Absolutely not. You're an adult, so ultimately you're going to do what you want. But you will not have my blessing going to Cal State San Bernardino in such a dangerous city. I just saw on the news that another child was killed, absolutely not!"

"Well what if I go to another school and stay in the dorms?"

"It's been years since I attended college but I believe registration is over for the next semester; you might have to wait Cat. However, I'm okay with you going if it's somewhere else"

Cat ran to her room and got on her laptop and started calling schools to see if it was too late to register for classes and live in the dorms. All the schools told her that she would have to register for the following semester. Samantha came over Cat's house and Cat expressed her frustrations about having to sit out a semester. Samantha and Cat both called all the schools they could think of but they all said 'no'. Samantha grabbed Cat's charger off of her dresser to charge her phone and saw a blank check that said it was for tuition. Samantha picked it up and looked at it.

"Cat, what's this?"

"Oh, it's a check that Bobby's dad gave me for my college tuition, but I'm not going to use it"

"You are such an idiot, Cat! This whole time we were calling around to see if the deadline to apply for a school has passed and you've been sitting on a blank check?"

"Okay, and?"

"What do you mean, 'and'? Cash is king. No one will tell you 'no' if you can pay for your tuition out of pocket. Do you really think those rich kids get into Ivy League schools with their grades? I mean, look at me. The only reason why I got into Harvard was because my dad paid out of pocket."

"Money does not matter. The rules are the rules Samantha. If I could just pay to get in, don't you think they would have offered that option?"

"No! They didn't tell you because you didn't ask. People with money don't ask; they tell them what they are going to do and they just do it!" Cat looked at Samantha and rolled her eyes.

"Okay, you think I'm playing. I guess I have to turn you into a believer. Let's go," Samantha said as she grabbed Cat by the arm and motioned her to the door.

Samantha ran into her house and grabbed her keys to her brand new Mercedes Benz G wagon. They hopped in and Samantha drove to the last college that she called, which was Cal State Long Beach.

Samantha pulled up into the school and parked. They walked across the campus. Cat was in awe anticipating the college life. They walked around until they found admissions. Samantha and Cat approached the receptionist and asked to speak to someone regarding attending Cal State Long Beach while residing in the dormitory. The receptionist spoke to a younger white girl that looked like she was in her late twenties. She had blonde hair and green eyes. Her name was Christian. Cat explained to her that she wanted to attend there but missed the deadline to apply for admissions.

Christian informed Cat that there was nothing that she could do, she would have to wait for the following semester to apply. Cat informed Christian that she could pay out of pocket. Christian's eyes looked amazed.

"Well if you can pay for your tuition we can work something out to get you in."

Cat pulled out the check. Christian looked at the check and smirked, and walked over to another young lady's desk and started whispering.

"What is all the chatter about?" Samantha asked cynically.

Christian walked back to the desk where Cat and Samantha were sitting and asked, "Is this your check? I'm about to report this check stolen."

Samantha snatched the check out of Christian's hand just as an older Hispanic woman walked into the room. Christian's whole demeanor changed. The older Hispanic lady asked what was going on and Samantha proceeded to tell her. The older Hispanic woman walked over to Christian and took her aside and was speaking to her.

Samantha tiptoed behind the older Hispanic lady and stood where neither of the two could see her and she overheard the Hispanic woman say, "People come in here with checks all the time. I agree that because it is blank and only has a signature and says 'for tuition', it may look suspicious. However, that is no different from a parent writing a blank check for their child because they don't know the exact cost of things. Next time, before jumping to conclusions, gather more information and see if she actually wants to attend here before saying you're going to report the check stolen. That was a discriminatory statement. I don't know if you based it on her race or what, but please do not let that happen again."

Samantha allowed Christian to see her and returned the smirk that she had given Cat earlier, and walked away. The older Hispanic woman apologized and asked Cat if she wanted to proceed with admissions.

Samantha spoke for Cat and said, "No."

Cat looked at Samantha as if she wanted to strangle her. The older Hispanic lady thanked them for considering the school and told them that if they changed their minds or had any questions to call her directly. She extended a business card to both Cat and Samantha. They thanked her and walked out of the admissions office.

Once outside, Cat asked, "What was that, Samantha? What were you thinking? I was trying to enroll and ask about living in the dorms."

"Cat, you are so naïve. This man gave you a blank check. Why are you going to a Cal State and not an Ivy League or USC? What am *I* thinking, no, what are *you* thinking?"

"I'm not trying to spend Bobby's parents' money, Samantha. I had tuition covered until you got me all hyped about 'having the whole college experience'."

"Cat, they gave it to you for a reason. If Bobby were still alive you would attend wherever he was going, right?"

"Right, but--"

"No, there are no buts. Bottom line, if Bobby were here you would allow them to pay for whatever schools you both attended together. So what is the difference? Bobby would want the best for you. He wouldn't want you to settle, so why are you settling?" Samantha asked as she threw her hands up in disbelief.

Cat stood there for a moment and said, "I don't use people, Samantha."

"Please explain to me how that is using someone when he gave it to you based on his son's wishes? Cat, sometimes God places people in our life for a reason. This was destined to happen. So take the check and write the school that you want to attend on it. If you can't get in then we'll leave it alone, and that just means you are not supposed to use the check."

Samantha stopped a student walking by and asked for a pen and then handed it to Cat.

Once in the car, Samantha asked what school she wanted to go to and Cat told her, "UCLA, that's what Bobby and I agreed on."

Samantha took off toward UCLA. They were driving and listening to Beyonce's new album, *Lemonade,* discussing whether or not the stories in her music were true. They were trying to figure out who 'Becky with the good hair' was.

Cat looked down at the check and said, "Oh shoot, Samantha, I wrote USC on the check."

Samantha exited off the freeway to go in the direction of USC.

"Well, USC it is. It wasn't meant for you to go to UCLA."

Samantha was optimistic and determined to get Cat into a school with that check with a full ride, and she was not leaving until it was done. They reached USC and Samantha and Cat strolled around campus until they located the admissions office. Samantha did all the talking for Cat. The personnel asked Cat if she wanted to see the dormitory and walked her over and showed her where she would be staying. The staff walked Cat over to registration, gave her a book of classes, and allowed her to enroll into classes classified as a full-time student. Cat was amused. The staff told Cat the cost of the four-year tuition and Cat filled out the check and handed it over. Cat filled out her paperwork and everything was complete. She had a move in date and a date for when classes started.

Samantha looked over at Cat and said, "Now that is how it is done, my friend."

On the way to the car they saw a handsome African American guy wearing a shirt that said "GrindFace". Samantha looked at Cat and said, "What is GrindFace?"

Cat looked up at his shirt as he passed by, trying to get a better look.

"I don't know. I've heard of it and have seen it on Snapchat but I'm not sure what it is."

On the way home, Cat thought about how money meant something to people. Cash was king. Cat realized that when you had money, people treated you differently. It was almost impossible to get a 'no' with money. Cat thought about how she had been at a disadvantage for so many years. She never gave much thought about it before but it was starting to sink in. She knew if she didn't have that check, her chances of getting into USC were slim to none.

She instantly texted Bobby's parents in a group text and stated, "I really appreciate how you both have been so kind to me. I just want to say thank you for providing me with a blank check for me to attend school. I will be attending USC in the fall." Cat added the cost and ended the text with heart emojis.

Cat was truly thankful. She leaned over while Samantha was driving and hugged her. Samantha swerved into the next lane.

"Cat, what are you doing?

"I'm just showing my appreciation for you pushing me to not settle."

Cat leaned back to the door and window of the passenger side of the car. She looked out the window during the ride home and thought about all the endless possibilities that could come from her attending USC.

Cat went home and told Connie about her encounters for the day. Connie was happy but did not want to appear as a charity case. Connie pushed her feelings aside. She wanted to be happy for Cat and not let her own feelings get in the way of such a huge step in Cat's life.

"Did you tell Bobby's parents 'thank you'?"

"Yeah, I did," Cat replied.

Cat looked down at her phone to see if they had responded. Both of his parents had responded.

His mom texted, "You are welcome."

His dad's message read, "Anytime kiddo. We want the best for you. Text me sometime and let me know how college life is treating you."

Cat responded, "Okay, will do."

Cat assumed that Bobby's mom's text was withdrawn as if she was not really interested in pursuing a relationship and his dad's response was more as if he wanted to remain in Cat's life. They gave her two complete different vibes. Cat would have asked his mom why she was so short in the text but she took the focus off of herself. That was one thing that Mrs. Mayo was adamant about, seeing things from the other person's perspective. Cat had to think like his mom. She put herself in her shoes and realized that it would be hard to keep in contact with a person that made you think about your deceased son. Cat packed those thoughts away about his mother. She wanted to be sensitive to her needs and not just thinking of her own, so she added a text in the group.

"BTW, I hope you both have been doing well and enjoying life."

Bobby's mom instantly responded and said, "Thank you Cat, I really appreciate you saying that. It is hard sometimes, but I'm managing."

Bobby's dad followed up with a smiley face. Cat made it a point that day that she would check on his parents from time to time. She knew how she felt when Bobby passed away so she could not even imagine how they felt. Cat wanted to spend as much time as possible with her family and friends before leaving for USC; and she did just that.

Chapter 17

The day was finally here and it was time to move into the USC dormitory. Cat packed all her clothes and was ready to go. Reggie and Trina met Cat there with a mini refrigerator, thirty-inch flat screen television, and an Apple iMac. Connie purchased the rest of Cat's things that she needed for her college dorm. Cat was excited and ready to dive into the college world headfirst. The bed next to Cat's was empty and she could only imagine what her roommate would be like. Cat kissed her family goodbye.

As soon as she came back from walking them to the car, she started to unpack. Cat was organizing everything with consideration of her roommate. She made sure that she had all of her belongings on one side of the room to ensure that her roommate had adequate space to do as she pleased. Once Cat was finished, she sat on her bed and made a few Snapchat posts, letting everyone know that she had moved into the USC dorms.

The door opened and an African-American girl walked in with her mom and dad. She was very soft spoken but she unconsciously commanded attention without speaking. Her beauty would draw anyone's attention when she walked into the room. Her parents immediately introduced themselves. Cat stood up and introduced herself and shook the girl's parents' hands.

Once the girl walked her parents back to the car and came back she said, "I apologize about that, you must think I'm rude. I was just trying to get all my stuff in the room, I didn't even think to introduce myself. My name is Michelle."

Michelle was very thin, and tall, with box braids. She looked as if she could be a model.

"My name is Cat. Do you know anyone that goes here?"

"I have a few friends but they're all males. I usually don't get along with females. Hopefully that won't be the case with you," Michelle said in an assertive tone.

Even though she had a soft voice when she spoke, it was clear she meant what she said. Michelle received a text and then asked Cat if she wanted to join her and her friends. Cat agreed to going.

Cat and Michelle were standing out front waiting for Michelle's friends to pull up. They stood there getting acquainted with one another. A 2016 7 series BMW pulled up. It had GrindFace on the back of the car.

Cat leaned over, not trying to sound foolish, and whispered to Michelle, "What is GrindFace?"

Michelle started laughing. "It's a term like game face. Instead of saying game face he made the term grind face. It means a person that is actively pursuing their goals without ceasing. He just got it in the Urban Dictionary and now he is looking into getting it into Merriam-Webster Dictionary. We call him GrindFace because not only is it his brand, he is the definition of GrindFace. He has a clothing line, media productions, photography, and branding all under the GrindFace umbrella. He is dope. You're going to like him. He comes from humble beginnings and he let that be his motivation."

Cat was now curious about this Mr. GrindFace guy. He pulled up to the curb and they both got in. Michelle got in the backseat purposely, forcing Cat to sit in the front passenger seat. Both Cat and GrindFace looked at Michelle, knowing what she was doing.

Cat said, "Hi."

He responded with, "Hey," and they drove to the local Denny's.

A group of Michelle's friends were waiting for them when they arrived. Cat felt nervous at first, but after Michelle introduced her as her roommate, they all seemed to be welcoming. One of Michelle's friends, Crystal, made the statement that Cat must have been cool because Michelle does not hang out with people when she just meets them.

Cat could tell that Crystal was a pushover and didn't think for herself. Whatever Michelle said, she agreed with it. Michelle made the statement that Denny's was the dirtiest place she had ever eaten. Crystal agreed with her even after she had just said that she loved going to Denny's. Cat saw it as Michelle trying to make Crystal look dumb in front of the group. Cat could see clearly the reason why Michelle did not get along with other females.

Michelle told her friends that Cat had a cool vibe and she could tell that they were going to get along. GrindFace kept watching Cat. Cat avoided eye contact and pretended as if she didn't notice him watching her. GrindFace was attractive to Cat. He was tall and had wavy hair and had a certain type of swag about him that was like no other. He got up and sat right next to Cat. Just as he sat down, his friend asked him what he did over the summer. He talked about his business ventures and the direction he saw himself going in. Cat was captivated. She could not take her eyes off of him. She had never heard someone so young speak of goals the way he did. He was only one year older than Cat but he spoke like a thirty- year- old man with his life all together and mapped out.

He looked over at Cat when he concluded his conversation and said, "What are your five year goals?"

Cat was caught like a deer in the headlights. She didn't know what to say. The last time she talked about goals was when she and Bobby discussed going to college. They never went into detailed conversations of five-year goals. They just knew they wanted to go to school and become something in life. Cat didn't respond because she didn't know what to say.

GrindFace leaned over and said, so no one would hear, "I can't have a girl that doesn't have goals."

Cat was embarrassed that she did not have a plan and needed to be witty and quick, so she responded with, "I cannot converse with someone by the name of GrindFace."

GrindFace laughed and said, "That was a quick clap back. I see you have a smart mouth. Well, if you wanted to know my government name then you should have asked. My name is Dimitrius Mayo. Nice to meet you," he reached out his hand as he spoke.

Cat shook his hand and tried to swiftly get up and go to the bathroom to avoid being stuck in another conversation with him. When Cat returned from the bathroom she tried to sit on the other side of the table by Michelle's friend Crystal. GrindFace got up and had everyone rearrange so he could sit next to her. Cat saw that he was a leader and his friends adapted to him without question.

He leaned over and said, "Do you want to know why I'm so successful?" Cat looked at him in silence and then he proceeded, "Because I am persistent when I know what I want. Even when it looks like it's failing and it's not going in my favor, I don't give up, and I always get the outcome that I want."

Cat learned something valuable that day. His name was not just a saying. It really had meaning and it defined who he was as a person and businessman. Cat also knew the underlining of the conversation. She knew that he was overtly telling her that he wanted her and he would get her. Cat respected his directness because she too was very direct. She also respected that he was open with his feelings without being apologetic. Most guys played games and told females what they wanted to hear, but he was a straight shooter, and Cat caught herself for the first time after Bobby's death taking a liking to another guy.

Cat talked to people from home often, especially Yessenia and Nancy. Cat was not hearing from Sabrina at all. Cat would call but would get her voicemail; and when she sent texts, Sabrina would respond and be very vague. Cat would see Sabrina on social media and she seemed to be in good spirits, so she figured, maybe Sabrina was finding herself without her. Cat and Samantha would face time for hours and discuss their college experiences; but as time went on, their face time decreased, just like the communication with Sabrina.

Samantha and Cat both loved one another. They were in two separate states and enjoying life. Cat called Samantha when she missed her. Those were usually the days that Michelle got on her nerves and it made her reflect on her relationship with Samantha and how much she appreciated her. Samantha did not have to worry about the whole roommate thing because her dad had gotten her an apartment near campus. During a phone call, Samantha suggested that Cat reach out to Bobby's parents and ask them for additional funds to get an apartment. Cat declined. She did not want to ask them for anything else. Cat felt as though that was going a bit too far to continue to ask them for money after they had paid for her college tuition, which wasn't cheap.

Cat said to Samantha, "Because you have everything at your disposal, I don't think you consider other people and the cost of things."

"What do you mean, Cat?"

"I just feel like your parents throw money at problems instead of dealing with them, which has made you have this mentality of entitlement, and before you cut me off, let me give you an example. I went to your house after the whole Kayla thing and spoke to your mom. Your mom would not take responsibility for the part she played. I feel like that's your family's reality. You just throw money at it and everything will be okay. Asking Bobby's parents for money every time I have a problem is not okay. You don't just call people when you need something. I mean, I do text them from time to time, but they have already done enough. They are not obligated to give me money. So what they have given me, I appreciate. I am not going to keep asking them for money."

"Well that is the difference between you and I because if I see an opportunity, I'm taking it," Samantha said as they both started laughing.

"Bye Ms. Opportunist, I have to go," Cat giggled and then hung up the phone.

A month had passed and Cat would see GrindFace around campus and they would speak briefly, but Cat always made up an excuse to have to leave. Cat was not sure about dating even though she really liked GrindFace. She did not want to deal with all the emotions that kept trying to arise regarding Bobby. Cat felt guilty when thinking about moving on. She was no longer seeing Mrs. Mayo and had no one to process her feelings with, so she wanted to avoid the situation all together.

Cat was seeing more and more why Michelle did not get along with other females. Every time Cat expressed to Michelle that there was something that she was doing in the dorm that she did not like, Michelle would say Cat was just jealous of her. It was like that was the only thing that Michelle knew how to say, instead of acknowledging the issue. Cat could tell that Michelle's past friendship mishaps were primarily based on Michelle not being honest with herself.

Cat liked to stay on campus on the weekends. She was studying for an exam. Michelle came in with Crystal, loud and obnoxious. It appeared as though they were getting ready for a party. Cat asked very politely if Michelle could lower her voice and get dressed quietly. Michelle looked at Crystal and continued talking to her as if Cat was not sitting there.

"Females always get jealous when you're pretty. I don't understand why females can't just compliment one another. I mean, it's not my fault that my momma blessed me with good genes."

Cat had had enough. She was not going to let this one go this time. Cat stood up and got in Michelle's face and said, "Look at me. Jealous of what? You are cute, but so am I, in case you haven't noticed. You're used to your little flunkies following you around and kissing your butt, but that's not me. I don't follow the trend, I am the trend. Better yet, I am a classic. Trends come and go just like you. Your friends do what you say and how you tell them to do it. I am not your little puppet and you will respect me whether you like it or not.

"I tried to play nice but what I won't do, is let you walk all over me. You're insecure and intimidated by other pretty girls--especially the ones that have a voice. You don't like people around you that actually have a brain because you don't want to be told the truth. Well here it is; the truth. You don't have friends because you are selfish. You only think about yourself, and anytime someone goes against what you want them to do or tell you the truth, all of a sudden, they are jealous of you.

"Jealousy is an overused word that you have played out and obviously don't know the meaning of. The reality is, you don't have friends because of you. If you don't get along with most females, they are not the problem, you are. You are the common denominator in different situations with different people. Now that is some reality for you. The only reason why Crystal is your friend is because she has low self-esteem and she's a follower. No leader will ever be your friend!"

Crystal put her head down in embarrassment. Michelle always looked for Crystal to defend her and validate her position, but this time, Crystal did not defend Michelle even though Michelle was glaring at her, but said, "What, I mean she is telling the truth."

For the first time Crystal stood up to Michelle.

Michelle stormed out the room yelling, "Basic jealous whores!"

That was the last time Cat saw Michelle, besides the day she arrived with some USC staff to get her belongings, claiming that she did not feel safe sharing a room with Cat. Cat couldn't care less. She just wanted Michelle out of her room and out of her life. Rumors had quickly spread around the campus that Michelle changed rooms because Cat was jealous of her. Michelle created a rumor that Cat wanted to date GrindFace but he liked her. Cat thought the whole gimmick was comical. Anyone who had been around knew who GrindFace had his eye on. Cat dismissed the rumors and when people asked, she referred them back to Michelle.

Cat would say when discussing Michelle, "Unlike Michelle, 'when she goes low, I go high', like the "real" Michelle." Everyone would laugh knowing that Cat was quoting Michelle Obama in a famous speech. They also knew that Cat meant that she was not going to reach down to Michelle's level and defend the lie. This made people take to Cat because they saw she was a person with integrity.

Michelle really cleared the rumor up when she tried to get GrindFace to go along with her story in front of a group of people. Michelle figured that because he was her friend, he would defend her and make Cat look bad.

Michelle started off by saying, "I guess Cat has an issue with me because you were feeling me and now she wants to date you."

GrindFace did not appreciate how Michelle was trying to twist a situation to her benefit, especially when she was leaving out factual details.

GrindFace responded, "Michelle, I approached you back in high school before I got to know the real you. After talking for a day, it was I that told you that I was no longer interested."

He told Michelle the truth about herself, which ultimately left her embarrassed in front of a group of people that she was trying to win over— people that she didn't even know.

Michelle walked over to have a sidebar conversation with GrindFace and said, "Why would you try to blast me like that in front of everybody for a female you barely even know?"

"You already know that I don't do the little kid games. So for you to try to make it seem like I wanted you and you dissed me, was not going to fly. Why are you so concerned about a female that is not concerned about you?"

"She is so jealous of me."

"That is all you ever say. Find a new line. Cat doesn't even mention you. I've been around when people have asked her about you and she always refers them back to you," GrindFace responded.

"That's not what I heard."

GrindFace looked at Michelle in a way that was very dismissive and walked away. He did not want to entertain the conversation further.

Chapter 18

Cat needed to get out after a long night of studying. She heard about a frat party and decided that she would go. Cat got dressed really cute. She put on some ripped jeans, a white halter-top, and white sneakers.

The party was packed, with barely any room to walk around. Cat didn't see anyone familiar, but it didn't matter. She loved to dance, so she went straight to the dance floor. Cat started out dancing alone. People soon started to gather around her and record her dancing. Cat had become the life of the party. A Hispanic guy started dancing with Cat and he danced really well. Cat loved a good dancer.

After five songs Cat wanted something to drink. She saw alcohol everywhere. She noticed a bowl of punch and thought about getting some but then decided not to, thinking that the punch may have alcohol in it. While Cat was looking for some type of water, trying to play it safe, she saw Michelle. Michelle tried to avoid her. Michelle saw Cat while she was dancing but pretended as if she hadn't seen her. GrindFace came from behind, trying to sneak up and scare Cat, but the annoyed look on Michelle's face gave it away. Cat turned around and saw that it was GrindFace. She then realized why Michelle looked so annoyed. Cat let that thought enter into her mind and leave before it settled. She asked GrindFace if he had any water.

He laughed, "Oh, you're not a drinker."

"What's so funny?"

"Nothing; that's good that you don't drink. But let me tell you that getting a water bottle is not safe either. People put alcohol in water bottles to disguise it as water. The safest thing when coming to a party is to bring your own drinks."

He led her to his car and grabbed a bottle of water and handed it to her. Cat looked at the water and opened it and sniffed the top of the bottle to make sure it wasn't alcohol.

GrindFace laughed and said, "Do you really think I would do that to you? I am not that type of guy. I'm actually offended."

Cat took a sip to make sure it was water before gulping. Once she confirmed it was water, she drank the entire bottle within a matter of seconds.

"You must have been real thirsty," GrindFace said jokingly.

Cat laughed and headed back toward the party. She went right back to the dance floor with GrindFace following behind her. GrindFace was not a good dancer, but he knew if he wanted to get her, he had to indulge in the things she liked; and by the third song, he could tell that she loved to dance. They danced the night away.

After the party GrindFace drove Cat to her dorm. He thought he would lean in for a kiss but Cat totally curbed him without hesitation. He saw that she was not the typical girl and it would take more than a nice car to intrigue her, unlike most other girls.

Cat was in her dorm one Wednesday afternoon when she overheard some students talking about a girl that attended Harvard who had killed someone while driving intoxicated. Cat instantly picked up her phone and called Samantha. She started speaking without saying hello.

"Hey Samantha, do you know the girl that who goes to your school that was driving drunk and killed someone?

"You are speaking to her."

"OMG, what happened Sam?"

"Dang, you want all the details huh," Samantha said jokingly.

Cat was confused. Why was Samantha so relaxed given the circumstances at hand?

Samantha continued, "One night after a frat party, I was drinking and hit a man. I feel bad because he was a husband and a father of three. My Dad bailed me out. He was mad, saying I'm just like my mother and that's why he left her. He pissed me off! I only had a few drinks. It wasn't like I was intentionally going out trying to kill someone. He should be more concerned about getting me a good lawyer instead of giving me a lecture. Hopefully, the judge allows me to just do counseling. I'm thinking about claiming affluenza like that one boy did a few years ago."

Samantha went on and on about how her dad was being over the top. Cat listened to her friend and provided an ear. However, Cat was burning inside. She wanted to curse Samantha out. Cat remembered the case of the boy that claimed affluenza and she was upset that he didn't serve any jail time. Cat viewed Samantha as a spoiled brat who was out of touch with reality.

Cat could not be silent any longer; she had to say something.

"This is the very thing that I was telling you about a while ago. You just think when a problem occurs you can throw money at it and it will go away.

A wife and children have lost their husband and father and the only thing you can think about is your defense for your case, and that your dad is being dramatic. Those people's lives are forever changed. Did you even try to reach out to his loved ones and apologize or offer some type of comfort?"

Cat could not finish her sentence because as she was talking, her phone rung. It was Connie. Cat realized that Samantha had hung up in her face. If it were anyone else Cat would have thought the call had dropped, but she knew Samantha was just like her mother in that they were okay as long as the mirror wasn't put in their face. Cat told Connie that she would call her back. She then dialed Samantha's number to find that the phone rung twice and then she was sent to voicemail.

Cat left a message that stated, "Samantha, I love you. We have always been able to tell the truth when speaking to each other and that should not change because of the circumstances. I hope that when you're no longer upset you will call me back. I'm here if you need to talk." Cat ended the call.

Samantha responded via text, " I'm good."

Cat felt like their friendship was shattered with those words. Samantha had always been a straight shooter, but Cat realized that she had never challenged Samantha before in the way she had that day. Cat was disappointed in Samantha's response. She consciously told herself that she would not call Samantha again, and if Samantha wanted to talk that she would be open to speaking. Cat felt disrespected, just as she did the day when she was conversing with Samantha's mother. After an hour of lying in bed, Cat realized that she told Connie that she would call her back.

Cat returned Connie's call, "Hey mom."

Connie sounded emotional and then jumped right into what she had to say, "I'm going to be a grandmother, thanks for telling me."

Cat was confused at first, then Connie's words sank in like a mountain lion's claws. The pain of her words was too hurtful to even respond at first. Cat was hurt because Sabrina did not tell her and she was upset that her baby sister would be a teenage mother just like Connie.

"What?" was all Cat could muster up to say.

"Why do people say 'what' when they know that they heard you? You heard what I said."

Cat paused and then said, "Mom, I don't know what to say."

You sound shocked, so I'm assuming you did 't know. I thought Sabrina told you."

"No, I didn't know."

Connie went on for thirty minutes preaching that she did not want her children to follow in her footsteps. Cat let her mom vent and listened before speaking.

Cat finally cut Connie off and stated, "Mom, you cannot be mad at Sabrina for doing something what you modeled for her."

Connie paused for a few seconds and said, "You're right Cat, and I apologize for not showing you both how to be respectable young ladies." Connie immediately ended the call.

Cat could tell that Connie was reflecting on what Cat told her. Mrs. Mayo had taught Cat how to stand on the truth while also providing it. Cat felt as though she was doing her mom a disservice to be dishonest, and being silent was equivalent to being dishonest in Cat's mind. Cat had learned a lot from Mrs. Mayo and she wanted to extend that knowledge to her own family and especially to herself. Cat was not going to reach out to Sabrina and tell her that she knew about the pregnancy. Cat knew when Sabrina was ready to talk about it, she would call her.

A few days had passed since the phone conversation and Cat still had not heard from Sabrina. Cat saw a chubby Hispanic girl with long, black hair moving boxes into her room. Beside her was a USC dorm staff member. As Cat walked up, the staff member informed her that she had a new roommate.

Cat introduced herself, "Hi, my name is Cat."

The girl put her boxes down and responded, "Hi, my name is Estella."

They shook hands and Cat grabbed a few boxes and helped her move them into the room. Cat rearranged her things so that Estella could have adequate space. Cat had gotten used to not having a roommate. The staff had informed her that she may possibly be getting a roommate, but Cat held on to the word 'possibly'. Estella seemed cool, very different from Michelle. In fact, Estella was quite the opposite. She was not girly at all. She did not wear make-up, although, she didn't really need it because she was a beautiful girl. Estella was not really into fashion and wore oversized clothes. Estella and Cat seemed to click. They were polar opposites but Cat loved that she was so much different then she was. Cat felt that there was much that could be learned and she was open to learning from Estella. Mrs. Mayo taught Cat that most people run away from people

230

that are much different from them, which prevents them from learning from others' diversity, cultures, and experiences. Cat loved the uniqueness of others because it made her step out of her comfort zone and it challenged her to think.

Cat went to grab something to eat and ran into GrindFace. Every time she saw him he had GrindFace on his shirt. Sometimes it was on his pants, but everything else had GrindFace on it—even his backpack. He offered to pay for her food, but she informed him that she had money on her account. Cat walked outside and sat in the grass and he followed behind her.

Cat looked at him and asked, "Why do you have your name all over your stuff?"

He looked down at his GrindFace logo on his shirt and said, "Because I know the power in branding. As people we are a brand and everywhere we go someone is watching. It's marketing and promotion. The fact that you knew GrindFace before you knew me says a lot."

Cat looked at him, confused. He laughed and proceeded, "I'm a business man, and because of that, I think business. Business doesn't stop because you go to sleep or decide that you don't want to work today. So everywhere I go—on my car, and on my clothes, when you see GrindFace, I am handling business because I am promoting. The key thing that most people forget is that we see brands all day long on billboards, clothing, stores, and cars, among may other places and things. We promote other peoples' businesses for free. I would be a fool not to promote my own. Think about Dubai. Most people never thought to go there until Dubai was being seen everywhere on Snapchat, Instagram, Facebook, and other social media platforms. So what people were unconsciously doing was promoting Dubai as a vacation spot for free. Now everyone wants to go there. The way you present yourself matters. It can help you or work against you."

It was like a light turned on in Cat's mind. She started to see him not only as a businessman, but a smart businessman.

"What made you be so driven? You are nineteen and already have so much figured out."

"I watched how my mom struggled. She was with a man throughout my childhood, but he controlled her. She was on government assistance and he worked. Even though he had adequate funds from his job, he controlled her money too because it was *his* money. I remember being in high school and wanting to play football, but couldn't, because she didn't have money to buy me some cleats. See, I wasn't his biological son, so the desire to provide for me was not a priority. So to make a long story short, I never played football. Being deprived growing up made me realize that I never wanted to be in a position to not follow a dream because I didn't have the money or resources that I need to accomplish a goal. It also made me have the mindset to not be so dependent that I am looking for someone else to provide something for me that I can provide for myself. So instead of looking for opportunities, I create them."

Cat was intrigued. He went on about his dreams, his goals, and his life story, and Cat could relate. The only difference was, she had not taken his stance on how to accomplish things. Cat felt like she

232

was in an advanced business class when speaking to him.

"So let me ask you something. What are your goals?" GrindFace asked.

"I don't know. I know I want to help people and possibly be a therapist, but I am still trying to figure it out."

"Well let me tell you this, my girl's goals have to be equivalent to mine. I don't date girls that don't have goals and a grindface mindset," GrindFace said while chuckling.

Cat was flattered and entertained at the same time. "So what are you saying, I'm your girl?" Cat asked as she blushed.

"You're only asking because you want me to say it. Yes, it's official, you're my girl."

Cat walked away from that conversation with not only a new mindset but with a boyfriend for the first time in a year. His witty conversation had finally won her over.

Cat and GrindFace had been dating for a month, when GrindFace texted Cat and asked her if she wanted to go out for a bite to eat. It was almost midnight and only one thing went through Cat's mind. She hesitated before responding. She was going to act like she didn't see the text, but she knew that it said 'read' because she opened the message. Cat was not ready to have sex with GrindFace. It was late at night and she knew that could be the only reason that he would be texting her and saying he wanted to go grab a bite to eat. Cat sat there forming her thoughts of what to say. Her phone went off again and Cat looked at it instantly.

GrindFace must have known what she was thinking because he texted, "No, I don't want to have sex. It's late. I can't sleep, and I just want to see you."

Cat was relieved. She was so happy to see that text. She responded and told him that she would go with him. She threw on some sweats and a t-shirt, but did her hair and put on some pink lipstick to make sure that she looked cute. He texted her and said he was outside. Cat went and got in the car.

On the drive to get something to eat, GrindFace put his hand on Cat's thigh as he was driving just like Bobby used to do. GrindFace looked over at her thinking that she would remove his hand from her thigh but she didn't. It was as if she had become comfortable when he put his hand on her thigh. The truth was, Cat did feel comfortable because it reminded her of how Bobby used to treat her during their rides in the car. GrindFace turned on the radio and "Cater 2 U" by Destiny's Child came on. He looked at Cat the same way Bobby did the first day she met him when he gave her a ride home. Cat instantly started crying. All of her memories of Bobby hit her all at once. GrindFace pulled the car over and parked in a store parking lot. He was puzzled. He didn't know what to think.

"Cat what's wrong?" he asked her.

Cat cried uncontrollably. She wanted to talk but could not calm herself down to gather her thoughts to speak. GrindFace went to the passenger side and opened the door. He grabbed Cat and held her in his arms and let her cry on his shoulders. He was unsure of what was wrong with her, but he wanted to be patient because he could see the hurt in her eyes.

Cat was upset that she didn't move his hand. She felt guilty. She wanted the love that she once shared with Bobby. Cat was furious. She cried, and in her mind, questioned God about why he took Bobby from her. Then she started to think about Ray. Cat's emotions were all over the place. GrindFace rubbed the tears off of her cheeks and Cat thought about Ray and started punching GrindFace in the face.

She was taking her built up anger out on him. Cat started yelling, "Why were you rubbing my legs?! You called me this late to have sex and if I didn't want to do it then what were you going to do GrindFace?" Cat said as she continued screaming and punching. He managed to restrain her and continued to wipe the tears off of her cheeks.

After ten minutes, Cat finally calmed down. Grindface waited for Cat to speak. He did not want her to feel like he was being pushy. He rubbed her back and continued to hold her. Her body came to a complete stop. He placed each hand on the side of her head lifting it up so that she could look directly in his eyes.

He said in a soft tone, "What is wrong?"

He knew by the way she was acting that it had to be something traumatic. Cat looked in his eyes, not wanting to tell the truth. She looked away. It was obvious that she was trying to avoid answering the question.

"Cat, the only way we will have a solid relationship is by being honest with each other."

He knew it didn't have anything to do with him, but he knew whatever it was, it was very deep and heartfelt. Cat took two steps back and sat on a nearby bus stop bench. He followed behind her and sat down on the opposite side of her so that they were face to face.

"You putting your hand on me and playing that song reminded me of the first guy that I was in love with. All these feelings and memories came rushing back."

GrindFace was upset, and his facial expression displayed it. "Do you still have feelings for bro?"

"He's dead," Cat said as a tear ran down her cheek and she put her head down.

GrindFace was at ease, knowing that she was not torn between him and another guy. He instantly became sensitive and empathetic.

"Was he your first?" he questioned. He did not have to go into detail. Cat knew that he was asking if Bobby was the first guy that she had sex with.

"Yes."

"How did he die?" GrindFace was curious and while he didn't want to interrogate her, he wanted the details of their relationship.

"We were talking about me being pregnant and I was upset because I didn't know who the father was," Cat said as he cut her off.

"What?"

"No, it wasn't like that." Cat knew how she was explaining it sounded completely wrong. She had to clarify so that he could have a better understanding. Cat wanted to put it all on the table moving forward without any secrets.

"I was raped by my dad's brother shortly after having sex for the first time with my boyfriend, and I didn't know who the father was. He wanted me to

236

take a pregnancy test and once I saw the results, I freaked out. He rushed over to console me and got into a car accident and died. I have not dated since then and there are things that you do that remind me of him."

He started to feel bad about his reaction. He got up from where he was sitting and sat next to her and said, "As long as I remind you of him in a good way then we're good. But I'm here now, and I'm not going anywhere," he said as he wrapped his arms around her.

They sat and talked for hours. For the first time, Cat completely opened up to someone besides Mrs. Mayo. GrindFace felt connected with her and even though he didn't tell her, he actually respected the love that she had for Bobby. He saw her characteristics of commitment and loyalty.

Chapter 19

Cat was in class when her phone rang. Cat grabbed her phone and tried to put it on silent before it rang again. Too embarrassed to look at the call, she put it back in her pocket after putting it on silent. After class, Cat saw that she had a missed call from Sabrina.

Cat returned Sabrina's call instantly. "Hello, baby girl."

"Hey Cat, I need to talk to you."

Cat waited for her to say what she wanted. Sabrina said, "Hello?" trying to see if Cat was still on the phone.

"I'm here," Cat responded.

"I'm pregnant, and before you say anything, let me finish. Remember the night that I slept with Rakheem and his friends? Well, that was the only time I had sex. I don't know who the father is and I didn't want to say anything because I'm embarrassed."

"Don't be. I was too ashamed about being pregnant and didn't know who the father was. I understand how you feel Baby Girl."

"What?!"

"Yeah, I didn't tell anyone but Mom, my dad, Bobby's parents, and my therapist. The night that Bobby got into the car accident, he was rushing over to me because I was upset about not knowing if he or The Molester was the father. After Bobby passed away, I decided to have an abortion. I didn't tell you because I was embarrassed, so I understand your reasoning for not telling me."

"Wow, Cat I wish you would have told me. I would have gone with you to the abortion clinic."

"Its okay. I was too ashamed to even talk about it. Have you told Rakheem?"

"No, mom did. She called his mom."

"What about the other two guys?"

"I didn't mention the other boys to mom. I wasn't thinking that she was going to contact Rakheem's mom. It just so happens that his mom is Grandma Pie's neighbor. I was too embarrassed to tell mom. Rakheem didn't say anything bad though when we were talking to his mom."

"Well what did he say?"

"He just sat there; and at school the next day he said that he talked to his mom about it and she told him to step to the plate."

Cat wanted answers. She was questioning Sabrina as if she was in an interrogation room, "What does that mean, 'step to the plate'?

"I told him I was uncomfortable with telling the other boys. He said that he would do a DNA test and if it's his then he will not mention it to his friends. He also said if it's not his baby then it's up to me to tell his friends on my own. I thought that he was going to bash me but he didn't. I was shocked. . . I have to go. I will call you later."

Sabrina ended the call with Cat still wondering what Rakheem told Sabrina. Cat messaged Rakheem on Twitter and asked for his number. She found his page after searching through his friends that followed him. To Cat's surprise, he responded right away. Most people waited to respond even if they saw the message, as if they were wanting to seem like they were busy. Cat thought it was foolish because most of her peers kept their phones in their hand, so she did not understand the point of the facade.

Cat called Rakheem and when he answered, she jumped right in without hesitation, "Are you telling my sister that you are not going to tell anyone but really plan on making her look like a ho?"

Rakheem responded swiftly, "Well, actually I wouldn't be making her look like anything because that is what she is. Okay, well let me change that. She is not a ho, she exhibited the characteristics of a ho that night."

Cat was pissed! "So then why make her feel like you are going to be there when you really feel like she's a ho? I don't agree with what she did, but don't make her look stupid, Rakheem," Cat said in an assertive tone.

"I'm not. She may be my child's mom and I wouldn't even refer to her as my baby's momma. To be real with you Cat, I had a conversation with my mom, whom you remind me of, but anyways, she made me rethink the whole situation. I had to see the part that I played in the situation. No, I didn't tell her to sleep with my friends, but I feel like me belittling black girls played a part in Sabrina's demise. I think Sabrina was so excited that someone finally took notice of her that she went about the attention the wrong way. I feel bad about that. It took me talking to my mom to get it. She asked me how I would feel if that was my baby. She told me to imagine if it was a girl, and she felt like she was not good enough because she saw her father belittling girls that looked like her.

"I told my mom that she would feel bad about herself. My mom then said, 'Well, that's how I feel every time I hear my own son belittle females that look like me.' I will admit, when I was saying those things in the past, I didn't think about how it affected my mother and my future daughter. My mom made me understand Sabrina's hurt. So when I told your sister that I would step up to the plate, I meant if the baby is mine. I will not tell anyone that she is pregnant unless she wants me to."

Cat was relieved that Rakheem was genuine. Cat thanked Rakheem for being understanding and ended the call. Cat prayed that the baby would be Rakheem's and that Sabrina would learn from this experience; Cat did not want Sabrina to carry the burden of the embarrassment.

As Cat stood in the hallway about to go back into her classroom, she noticed a rally going on. She walked toward the rally and saw students protesting about human trafficking. Cat had heard about it before, but never knew what it was. She thought it was about foreigners kidnapping kids in other countries and selling them for sex. As Cat approached the crowd, she realized that they were protesting for children right here in the states. Cat was baffled. She had no idea that people were selling kids for sex in the United States. This type of thing just doesn't happen here, Cat thought. Cat was engaged and stayed to hear what the speaker had to say.

There was a person behind Cat talking to her friends and Cat overheard her say, "They are not selling drugs anymore; the new come up is selling these kids."

Cat became furious the more she listened in on the speech. Cat had to talk about it. She was too angry to go back to class. She went into the classroom to get her backpack and went straight to her dorm.

Estella was sitting on her bed reading a book. Cat barged through the door ranting and raving about human trafficking and how they should send the pimps to jail for life. She was enraged. Estella caught bits and pieces of Cat's rant. Estella heard enough to sum up what she was talking about. She told Cat to calm down and explained to her that there are many injustices in the world that need to be addressed. Estella quickly shifted the topic of conversation to the LGBT community.

Estella said, "You are ranting and raving about these kids, but what about us lesbians, the LGBT community. What about us Cat? We get targeted for hate crimes, killed, and beaten. Look at the last incident in Miami at the night club."

Cat was trying to figure out the correlation between human trafficking and the LGBT community. Cat went along with Estella because she realized that this was Estella's way of coming out of the closet and telling Cat in a passive way that she was a lesbian; not that Cat cared one way or the other. Cat listened as Estella went on and on regarding the injustices. The conversation took a quick turn when Estella asked Cat, "What do you think about the LGBT community?"

"I mean, to each their own but I don't agree with it. I mean, I wouldn't do it, it goes against my beliefs of what God says according to his word."

"So you're a homophobe?"

"What?"

"You're against the LGBT community. Why do people use God as an excuse? I didn't ask to be like this, I was born this way. I get sick of people saying what the bible says. Do you follow everything in the bible?"

"No, but I try to do what's right. I am going to end this conversation Estella because I don't want to argue."

"Why, I'm not arguing, I'm just having a conversation."

"Because when you said you were a lesbian, I respected your beliefs. I did not question you or ask you about your moral compass. You asked me how I felt about the LGBT community and I gave you my honest answer. But because my beliefs don't align with yours, I'm a homophobe, and I get questioned about my moral compass. I am so tired of the LGBT community throwing their beliefs in everyone's face and expecting them to be okay with it. But the moment we don't agree, our beliefs are not valued with the same standard. I don't care if you're a lesbian; that's your choice. But I don't have to agree with it because that is my choice. If you want respect then you have to give it. You can't force guilt upon people because they do not view homosexuality the way you do. As soon as I answered your question, you became defensive and started bashing me."

"You are the first person that has brought this to my attention, and you're right. Sometimes we do tend to force our beliefs on others without considering theirs. We had to fight so long to get this far, and when people don't agree, I automatically feel as though they're against the LGBT community."

"I am not in agreement with the LGBT community but I respect their beliefs. Now if I had to vote on something for LGBT's, I would vote against it. But does that mean I'm against you as a person?

No, it doesn't. It's equivalent to having a friend that drinks. I don't like drinking and I don't drink, but am I not going to be friends with that person because I don't agree with what they do? No. However, if I had to vote on a law that banned drinking, would I? Yes, absolutely. All I'm saying is, respect my beliefs the way you want me to respect yours, without condemning me and trying to force guilt on me, because it is totally unnecessary"

Estella hugged Cat and thanked her for being so straight forward and taking the time to explain, instead of instantly getting mad and allowing the conversation to escalate.

Cat and Estella had learned to respect one another's beliefs and were getting along just fine. Cat and GrindFace were an item and it was known around campus.

Cat's college life was great. She was establishing a healthy respectful relationship with Estella and experiencing life with a different lens. Cat could only think about how Bobby and Reggie taught her what love looked like when a man really loved and valued a woman. Bobby was attentive to Cat down to the last day of his life. He showed Cat what it looked like when a guy really cared. Reggie showed Cat that when you loved someone, you rescue him or her when they are in harm's way, even if it means it will cause disruption in your own home. Cat pondered on her relationships with Bobby and Reggie. The very things that made her love Bobby and her dad were the same characteristics that GrindFace had; he just added more. He challenged Cat in ways no one ever had. Mrs. Mayo challenged Cat to reflect on her actions and thought process to produce the healthiest outcome, but GrindFace challenged Cat to dream. He taught her not to just dream, but to take action to make those dreams a reality. In all the months that she was dating him, he never mentioned sex. Cat had come to terms with the idea that Bobby had come into her life to teach her what loved looked like. Had she not dated a person like him, her view of a boyfriend would have been distorted. Her idea of love would have been based on the relationships she had seen Connie engage in.

Chapter 20

It was the month of December and Cat was home for the holidays. Sabrina was growing by the month and she could no longer hide her pregnancy. She was now seven months pregnant. Connie took her out of school and placed her on independent studies. Cat was excited to see Sabrina, Nancy, and Yessenia. She was still upset with Samantha, and was not looking forward to seeing her since Samantha had never called back and apologized. It had been months since Cat had heard from Samantha. Cat spent most of her time rubbing on Sabrina's belly and taking pictures with her stomach. Cat was excited to be an auntie and kept referring to Sabrina's unborn child as "our baby." Sabrina was happy that Cat was home. Cat was happy to see her siblings. She really missed them. She read the younger kids stories and slept with them in their room, trying to enjoy the moments of being at home. Cat did not go to school far away but since she did not go home on the weekends, she had been away from her family for several months.

Cat was playing out in the front yard with her little brothers. They were playing catch. Samantha saw Cat at home and decided to go over and speak to her.

"Hey Cat."

Cat looked over and saw Samantha standing in her driveway. Samantha walked over to Cat. Cat was still annoyed with Samantha for hanging up in her face and being disrespectful. Samantha knew that Cat was upset with her but she was not going to let that stop her from speaking to her. Samantha walked over to Cat's yard and stood directly in front of her and apologized for her behavior. Cat rolled her eyes, dismissing what Samantha said. Samantha grabbed Cat and hugged her. Cat did not reciprocate the hug. Cat's hands were dangling on the side of her body while her chest was touching Samantha's chest.

Samantha wrapped her arms around Cat and said, "Stop flexing, you know you missed me."

"So what, that's not the point. You hurt my feelings. I was being honest with you and for you to hang up in my face and not call back was wrong Sam."

"I admit it. I was wrong. I just did not want to hear what you were saying at the time. I thought about what you said after I got off the phone. Well not exactly right after, but a month later after," Samantha said as she laughed.

"It's not funny Samantha."

"I know, but I missed you friend, and I just don't want you to be mad at me."

"So what happened; did you just pay your way out of jail?" Cat said sarcastically.

"You have definitely been playing too much monopoly. 'Pay your way out of jail'. Cat, really. But to answer your question, I was convicted with a DUI and I am on probation for six months."

"That's it?!"

"What do you mean, 'that's it'; wow, really Cat? Are you my friend or one of his family members advocating for him?"

"I am happy that you didn't get life but you took someone's life Samantha, and the sad thing about it is, I don't think you learned your lesson. I think you will be out drunk again sometime next year, and I'm pretty sure it will be on New Year's. I would have thought you learned from your mom and the situation with Kayla. But no, I guess it's as the saying goes, 'like mother, like daughter'."

"You know what? Screw you, Cat. You're right, 'like mother, like daughter'. So I guess you have probably had sex with the whole college campus by now!" Samantha said as she walked away, furious.

Cat could not let her throw that dig and get away with it, so she responded with, "Nope, I have class—unlike you."

Samantha did not turn around and respond. She walked into her house and slammed the door behind her.

Later that day, Nancy and Yessenia came over. They asked Cat about college. They were intrigued about the college life. Cat told them about the wild party she attended and how she was thirsty and realized it wasn't safe to get something to drink at the party. She told them how GrindFace took her to his car and gave her something to drink.

Nancy stopped Cat and asked, "You know GrindFace?"

"That's my boyfriend, why? Do you know him?"

Yessenia and Sabrina jumped up and said at the same time, "Boyfriend?"

Cat started laughing. "Yes, my boyfriend."

Nancy answered Cat's question by saying, "Everyone wears GrindFace t-shirts now, but I never knew what it was."

"Yeah, that's his clothing line."

Sabrina and Yessenia did not care about his business or any other thing; they just wanted her to elaborate about him. "Details about your boyfriend please," they said in unison.

"You'll meet him on Christmas. He's coming over."

"Aw snap," Yessenia said, as they all start giggling.

"Where is Samantha? I saw you outside talking to her earlier," Sabrina asked.

"Can we have a moment of truth?" Nancy asked. Cat did not answer Sabrina's question before Nancy continued, "I never liked her. I played nice because of you, Cat but I really don't see what you two have in common. She is a drunk and you're not. Yeah, she comes from money, but she carries herself like white trash with no class."

Cat cut Nancy off, "That's my friend and you should know by now, I don't talk about people I break bread with. If you have a problem, that's between you two. Besides, I don't know what the issue is between you guys and I really don't care. Samantha does not discuss you, so don't discuss her to me."

Cat was serious about being a true friend. She did not believe in talking behind peoples' backs. If she had an issue, she would address that person. Cat felt like Nancy was trying to get Cat to gossip about Samantha's DUI charge, and she was not going to. Even though Cat was mad at Samantha, she was not going to make her best friend look bad, regardless of their issues.

Sabrina chimed in, "Well Cat cover your ears because I want to know, why don't you guys get along?"

"I think she thinks I started a rumor about her that a boy really started."

"Is that what all the drama was over, a rumor? Both of y'all need to get your life!"

Cat rolled her eyes, annoyed by the fact that the whole time they were at each other's throats was all over a measly rumor.

Later that night, Trina came to pick up Yessenia. Cat gathered a day's worth of clothing to spend the night. When they arrived at the house, Trina told Yessenia to go inside. She asked Cat to stay behind so she could talk to her. Cat was not sure what Trina wanted and was hoping it wasn't Trina reverting back to her old, immature self with something up her sleeve.

Trina turned to Cat and said, "I'm sorry Cat. I never meant to make you feel like you were not a part of this family. When I saw you for the first time at your grandmother's house, it brought up a lot of past hurt. Then, when you moved in with us, I saw you as the betrayal from both your mom and dad. It was never really about you; and I'm sorry. You were an innocent child in this entire equation. You did not ask to be involved in this. I had to realize that I was still hurt and dealing with things that I didn't know I was still angry about. After looking at your mom and dad, I had to look at myself. I was mad at me for not loving myself enough for leaving your dad. That's why I was so resentful and bitter, and I took it out on you and your mom.

"Your dad and I are in a different place now and have dealt with our issues. However, I realize that I was not setting a good example for you or Yessenia. The kids never knew that you existed. Yessenia knew you were her cousin, but she never knew that you were her sister too. That was hurtful to her. I think

250

the most hurtful part was Reggie having kids by two cousins. After talking to Yessenia, she was more embarrassed than anything because at school people knew you guys as cousins, and then she had to explain how you were sisters. I can understand how that can be embarrassing. I also understand how that could be embarrassing as a daughter looking at your mom. I looked down on your mom for many years, but then I had to realize that I was no different. I stayed with a man that had sex with my cousin. I had a baby a year later to prove to her that he loved *me*. But the fact was that he didn't love either of us. He only loved himself and was treating us how we allowed him to treat us. Now, as a mother, I know how deeply hurt I would be if a man ever did that to any of you guys. Cat, from this day forward, I vow to be an example for you because I do not want you to ever think it's okay for a man to mistreat you."

Cat didn't know what to say and Trina could tell that Cat was caught off guard. Trina hugged Cat and kissed her on the cheek. They got out of the car. Cat never mentioned the conversation to anyone, but Trina's words meant a lot. Cat thought about her relationships with the different males in her life. She knew she didn't want to be a single mother, and she definitely didn't want to have a baby by a man that had sexual relations with a family member. Trina may have thought that Cat was not listening, but Cat realized and learned a whole lot that day from Trina and Connie's experience.

Cat wanted to see Mrs. Mayo after her conversation with Trina. Three days later Cat contacted Mrs. Mayo's office to schedule an appointment. Cat was hoping that she had not left for the holidays, and she hadn't. Her receptionist scheduled Cat for the following day. The next day, Cat went to Mrs. Mayo's private practice and waited in the sitting room, anticipating learning something new about herself. Mrs. Mayo opened the door and greeted Cat with a bright smile. Cat had really missed her. She gave her a hug before she walked in because just going straight to the chair would not suffice in that moment. Cat was like a person that hadn't had a Thanksgiving meal in years and was ready to eat. She told Mrs. Mayo what Trina told her, and her feelings about what she said. Mrs. Mayo always made Cat dig deep and this was a session that Cat either had to put up or shut up.

Mrs. Mayo firmly grabbed Cat's hand and said, "What do you decide today? Do you decide to leave here as a victim, or a conqueror? Trina chose to be a conqueror. Her past hurt bound her and kept her in an emotional state where she remained a victim, lashing out at everyone that she felt wronged her. Trina's hurt was interfering in her relationship with both you and Yessenia."

Cat was confused. She saw the way Trina allowed the relationship to effect Cat, but not Yessenia. She was not seeing the connection between the two.

Cat interrupted Mrs. Mayo and asked, "How did it effect Trina and Yessenia's relationship?"

Mrs. Mayo sat up in her chair as if she was about to go real deep by revealing some unanswered mystery. She cleared her throat and stated, "Had Trina told Yessenia about you long before she met you, it would have reduced the resentment toward you, and most importantly, her mother. See, when we

252

hold on to things, it only hurts us in the long run. We torture ourselves by carrying years of pain and guilt, among many other things, when we hold on to things that could have been dealt with years ago. Talking about the truth allows you to be free from the shame and guilt. Trina thought by keeping you a secret she was protecting Yessenia and protecting her character. However, look how that turned out.

"So I'm asking you, are you going to leave today being the victim or the conqueror? You can decide to let your experience push you to help others, or let your experience make you bitter, and hurt yourself and others. I don't know if you are dating, but if you do not mourn Bobby and forgive Ray and move on, you will never be able to have a healthy relationship with any man in your future. I want you to understand, it is not about Ray raping you, but it is about you and how you let that experience define who you are and what you become."

Cat felt like she won the lottery. Mrs. Mayo was dropping gems and Cat needed to catch them. She was telling Cat what she needed to hear and not what she wanted to hear. Cat had thought about the day she was in the car with GrindFace and how she allowed her emotions regarding Ray and Bobby to get the best of her. Cat did not ever want to be that person again. She was thankful that GrindFace was not scared off and just continued to be patient with her.

Cat had to ask the question, "How would I know if I am the conqueror or the victim?"

"When you no longer allow old triggers that bring forth certain actions and emotions to effect you; that's when you will become a conqueror."

She knew that if she did not become the conqueror then her past experiences would sabotage her relationship with GrindFace. Cat stood up and just before walking out of the office, she said, "I decide to be the conqueror."

Mrs. Mayo smiled and Cat left her office that day knowing that she would never return. She had learned enough to put her talk into action.

Cat went home that day to join Sabrina and Connie watching the news about a police officer killing an unarmed teenaged African American male. Connie and Sabrina were ranting and raving about the injustices in the United States. Cat stood in front of the television and said, "Are you guys going to be the victim or the conqueror?"

Connie and Sabrina looked at Cat as if she was crazy. Connie asked, "What?"

Cat said, "You heard me. Are you going to be the victim or the conqueror? Are you going to sit and complain about the situation or are you going to get up and take action and do something about it? Mom, we have been living here for two years now. Have you been active in our city—going to the city meetings and expressing your concerns?"

"That is not the point. What they're doing is wrong."

"But that is the point, mom. If you're not a part of the solution, then you are a part of the problem. You have sons, and if you want to see something done for their sakes, then you need to step up and act. Are you going to be a conqueror or a victim? Victims cry, complain, and seek sympathy, but conquerors get up and do something about it to help themselves and others suffering with the same hurt."

Cat was passionate about what she was saying and felt as if she was giving a motivational speech. Sabrina and Connie looked at Cat in awe. Connie was shocked, but proud at the same time. She was watching her daughter transition from a victim to a conqueror. There had been sleepless nights for Connie because she was concerned about Cat's outcome after the rape and losing Bobby. However, in that moment, Connie was happy that she made the decision to get Cat into counseling. She could see it was benefitting her. Connie watched her go on and on and thought about getting counseling herself. She wanted to be the conqueror that Cat talked so passionately about.

Christmas Day was finally here and Cat had stayed up the night before helping Connie wrap all the gifts for her siblings. All the kids were up at the crack of dawn, but Cat was still in bed. Cat didn't really care about Christmas anymore. She only cared about seeing her siblings with a smile on their face. It was noon and Cat was just getting up. She stumbled downstairs with her pajamas on and her hair all over her head. Her feet touched the last stair at the bottom of the staircase, and she looked up to see GrindFace standing next to the Christmas tree with a bow tied around his neck. Cat smiled. She could not stop cheesing. He gave Cat a big hug and said jokingly, "If I had to stand here any longer I was coming to your room and breaking the door down."

She was trying not to breathe, hoping that he didn't smell her dragon breath. He kissed her on the forehead. Cat squirmed. She wanted to slap him and wash her face. She felt herself hyperventilating. Cat didn't move; she stood in one spot.

Cat told herself, "This is not Bobby or Ray, this is GrindFace." In her head, Cat continued to talk herself through what she was feeling, until she was no longer hyperventilating, or wanting to wash her face. A sense of peace came over her, and for the first time since the rape, she felt okay with being kissed on the forehead. She got on her tippy toes and kissed him back on his forehead. Cat had passed her test of not letting that old trigger get the best of her. Cat hugged GrindFace and did not want to let him go.

He felt a different connection between them that day. He did not know what happened, but he could tell that Cat had turned over a new leaf. Cat did not have to say she changed; it was apparent to those that were around her. Cat was cold and withdrawn before, but now he could see that she was actually an affectionate person. In his mind, he attributed this to being persistent and breaking down her defenses.

There was a knock on the door and Cat opened it-still looking disheveled. Rakheem had never seen Cat not put together, so he thought it was comical. He could tell by the look on her face that she was embarrassed. Cat was not expecting Rakheem to be at the door. She called for Sabrina and moved to the side so that he and his mother could come in. His mother had a basket full of gifts for both Sabrina and the baby. Cat tried to introduce Sabrina to GrindFace but saw by the way they were interacting, that they had already met.

Cat said, "Dang, how long were you here before I came downstairs?"

"Long enough to meet your family."

GrindFace named all of her siblings including, Yessenia. Cat was impressed that he took the time to interact with her family and to get to know a little bit about them. It showed her what type of person he was and that he was not just interested in her, but everything about her. Sabrina opened up her gifts. Cat sat down and watched her open up her gifts while Rakheem and GrindFace talked about college and goals. Cat overheard GrindFace telling Rakheem that he had to step up to the plate and be a man, even though he was in high school. Rakheem said that he was. Cat motioned for GrindFace to follow her into the kitchen so that she could have a private conversation with him.

Cat told him, "You need to tell him that he needs to be involved whether it's his baby or not."

"Wow, *if* it's his baby? Cat, you have to learn to allow people to handle their own problems. I understand that's your little sister, but she has to figure it out. You can't help everyone all the time. I can already tell that you want to fix it. Her not knowing who her child's father is is based on a decision that she made, and you cannot change that," He said in a stern tone.

Cat was hoping that Rakheem stepped up to the plate. She was unsure if he was the father and she did not want Sabrina to be a single mother whose child's father was not active in their life. Cat took her sister's affairs personal, as if they were her own.

Samantha barged in the door crying. She hugged Cat and apologized for the second time. Cat could tell that something was really bothering Samantha. Cat felt as though Samantha was out of touch with reality and did not have consideration for others, yet, Cat could not blame her because that is how her mother was, and Samantha was only doing what she had been taught from the time she was a little girl.

GrindFace excused himself and went back into the living room and continued his conversation with Rakheem, as Sabrina and his mom talked about baby names.

Cat stated, "Samantha, I too apologize, because you needed a friend, and not a mother. I should have listened without being so critical."

Samantha needed to hear the truth, but Cat realized that if Samantha was not open to hear it then she could not force-feed it to her. Cat valued her friendship more than her desire to get Samantha to see her character. Besides, GrindFace was right; it was not her job to try to fix everyone and ultimately, Cat was trying to fix Samantha by pointing out that she was broken. Cat came to the conclusion that she could not help someone that did not want to be helped. Samantha had to come to terms with what she did and change her decisions and her behavior on her own.

Cat made Samantha a plate of food as a peace offering. Samantha loved Connie's cooking, especially when she used Arturo and Anise seasoning. Samantha sat at the table and ate her food as she watched Cat's younger siblings play Monopoly. Samantha giggled as she was eating.

"What's so funny?" Cat asked.

"That is literally all you guys play--Monopoly."

They both started laughing. Cat reflected on Samantha's comment when they had an argument in the front yard. Connie never had much before moving to California, so when they spent time together it was over food and a game of Monopoly.

Samantha took a bottle of Vodka out of her purse and put it in her punch. Cat looked at Samantha, wondering if that would be the last time she saw her. She took a few pictures with Samantha and told her that she loved her. Cat knew that Samantha would get wasted on New Year's and she thought about her doing something stupid that she couldn't come back from. As hard as it was watching her best friend continue down the road of destruction, she had to swallow her words, suck it up, and shut up. Samantha wanted to be lied to and wanted Cat to overlook the fact that she was an alcoholic. Cat could not overlook it and would not justify it and pretend that Samantha did not drink too much. Therefore, Cat did not say anything at all. She let her be.

Cat went back into the living room and left Samantha there at the table. She knew it wouldn't be long before she had to walk her next door because she was wasted. Rakheem could tell that something was bothering Cat. He asked her what was wrong. Cat lied and said it was nothing. Cat was bothered by Samantha's choices but she knew that she could not allow that to consume her. She stopped thinking about Samantha and became present in the living room.

Cat jumped right into Rakheem's mom and Sabrina's conversation about baby names. Cat suggested that they name the baby after her, and Rakheem instantly gave Cat his undivided attention.

"No one is naming their baby after you."

"Why not?"

"Because it's my baby and I said we're not," Rakheem said as he laughed. Sabrina started smiling.

Cat and Rakheem were playing, but Sabrina enjoyed the fact that he was speaking about the baby as if it was his own. She had never heard him do that before. He made comments about stepping up but actually identifying himself as the father was a different story. They all got in on the fun. GrindFace and Rakheem's mom started to suggest baby names and Rakheem turned every one down.

"I already know what I'm going to name our son."

Rakheem's mother stopped laughing and said, "What are you going to name him, Rakheem?"

"Well, if it's a boy, of course he will be named after me, and if it's a girl, then Sabrina can name her."

His mom smiled. She too caught on to him attaching himself to the baby. GrindFace got in on the conversation, referring to the baby as his nephew. Cat loved the dynamics of everyone and was hoping that it all turned out in her family's favor. She hoped that Sabrina's baby would be Rakheem's and that GrindFace would be around long enough to be an uncle. Cat was shaken from her hopes for the future when Jeremiah came and informed her that Samantha was in the family room acting weird.

Cat got up and said, "That's my cue," and walked off.

Cat went into the family room where Samantha was stumbling and her words were slurred. Cat grabbed Samantha's arm and she slouched over. Cat let her lean on her as she escorted her home. Cat knocked on the door and Samantha's mom answered it. She was just as drunk as Samantha. Cat knew that her mom wouldn't be able to take care of her, so Cat walked her upstairs to her room, put her in her bed, and told her mom to keep an eye on her. Samantha's mom nodded her head and put her hand up as if to say, 'okay, now you can go,' but she was so drunk her gesture looked like a waving advertisement. Cat didn't even bother asking her what she meant. She walked out the door and made sure it was locked before she closed it behind her.

Sabrina was standing outside waiting on Cat so she could talk to her. "What's up Sabrina?" Cat asked, knowing that she wanted to tell her something.

Sabrina walked up to Cat and started whispering, "Ay, did you hear Rakheem?"

"Yeah."

"What do you think?"

"I think he's warming up to the idea of being a father, but I don't want you to focus on him. You do what you have to do whether he is there or not. Don't listen to what people say, but take heed to what they do. Action speaks louder than words. You are letting your feelings get caught up in hoping that he wants to be a father, but that shouldn't be your focus. I don't want you to get happy thinking he is going to be there, and he doesn't step up to the plate. Yes, I would love for him to be an active father and I'm praying that the baby is actually his, but if not, you make sure that you be the best mother you can be, regardless of the position he decides to take."

Cat didn't want to rain on Sabrina's parade, but she wanted her to be open to the possibilities of what could happen, instead of relying on what Rakheem was saying, only to be hurt in the end. Cat wanted to talk to Rakheem to see where his head was, but knew GrindFace was right; that she needed to mind her own business. Sabrina looked at Cat in despair. She knew Cat was right and did not want to be disappointed in the end.

As Cat and Sabrina walked back into the house, Rakheem and GrindFace were having a conversation about men being active fathers. Rakheem's mom was going on a tangent. It was obvious that she was passionate about the topic.

She said, "I am so tired of boys having kids and not wanting to take on the responsibility of helping raise them. I don't even refer to the adults that call themselves men because a man is a father, but a person that doesn't take care of his responsibilities, is a boy. Rakheem, I can't tell you how to be a father, but what I will tell you, is that you're going to be an active father, or you won't be living under my roof."

At that point Connie walked into the living room to see what all the commotion was about. She saw that they were having a deep conversation and decided to accompany them. Rakheem's mom continued talking about a man versus a boy. Rakheem looked as though he had heard her speech many times before. He didn't appear to be annoyed, but he didn't appear to be interested either. Cat thought that Rakheem's mom was doing the right thing by Sabrina, but the more she spoke, the clearer it became. His mom was using Rakheem as an escape because of what happened to her. She talked about Rakheem's dad leaving her when she was a senior in high school and how he did not help raise him. His mom was still hurting from her past and she was making Rakheem pay for his dad's mistake. It was good that she wanted him to step up, but she was going about it the wrong way. She was forcing it on him, instead of encouraging him to make a healthy decision.

Connie placed her hand on Rakheem's mom's shoulder and said, "It's okay, Rakheem is not his father, and you are not Sabrina."

His mom broke down crying. It bothered Rakheem to see his mom hurt the way she did. GrindFace said to Rakheem, "Come on man, let's let the ladies talk."

They walked out of the living room. Cat looked at Sabrina, motioning her to leave as well. Cat felt like that was a moment for two grown women that had experienced being single mothers to process their hurt and feelings amongst each other. Cat and Sabrina joined GrindFace and Rakheem in the family room. They all sat at the table and the real conversation started. Usually Cat would lead the conversation and get to the bottom of things, but this time, she let the parties involved discuss their issues.

Sabrina looked across the table at Rakheem and asked, "If the baby is not yours, are you still going to claim the baby?"

Rakheem sat straight up as if he was on trial. Rakheem was conflicted. He did not want to take care of a child that wasn't his, but he saw the hurt that his mom went through. He felt forced to make a decision whether he agreed with it or not.

"I don't know Sabrina; and to tell you that I would, would be a lie. I really can't say. I don't know how I will feel until the test results are finalized. Everyone is already looking at me crazy knowing that you're pregnant and I'm not bashing you with my bros"

Cat respected his honesty, but Sabrina really didn't want to hear the truth. She would have preferred him to have given her the lie because it made her feel better. It allowed her to escape reality and not have to deal with the situation at hand.

GrindFace got up from the table while looking at Cat, cueing her to go with him. They walked outside. By this time it was night. Cat thought he was leaving. Cat wanted to hear Rakheem's and Sabrina's conversation. She thought by her being present she could still help while being silent and observing.

GrindFace knew what she was doing and he said, "Cat, you have to learn to let people figure it out."

"What are you talking about?" Cat said, appearing to be oblivious.

"You know what I'm talking about. You wanted to sit there and listen to their conversation, and for what? So you can give Sabrina pointers later? What is she going to do when you're not around? Let her figure it out."

Cat laughed and said, "You know me way too well."

"I'm supposed to," Grindface said as he pulled Cat close to him and kissed her.

This was the first time they shared an intimate kiss. They usually kissed on the cheek. Tongue had never been introduced until that day. Cat didn't know how to feel at first. Then as the kissing continued, she was relaxed. She had gotten too relaxed. They started groping one another and GrindFace stepped back. Cat was puzzled. She didn't understand why he was backing up.

GrindFace caught her facial expression and asked, "Do you plan on having sex?"

"No," she said, almost as if she was saying with her facial expression, 'duh, do you really think I would have sex out here?'

"Well, then stop saying you want to have sex with your actions."

Cat hadn't thought of it like that, but she knew he was right. She did not intend on having sex, but her actions were saying the opposite of what she wanted to do. For the first time, she saw a man that actually had self-control. As gentle as Bobby was, when it came to sex, he let his desires overtake him, and Ray had no control at all. Cat made the conscious decision that day that she would not interact with GrindFace in that manner unless she knew beforehand that she wanted to take it to the next level and have sex.

GrindFace was turned on by the fact that Cat was not like most girls. He could have sex with them only knowing them for a very short time. Cat was the opposite. She was not open to having sex just because a man wanted her to, like other females. Everything about her displayed respect. From the way she carried herself even down to the way she dressed and spoke. That was what he looked at when considering dating. Not to say that he wouldn't just have sex with any random girl because he would, but it would never be a girl that he would take home to meet his mother. After spending time with Cat's family, he knew it was time for her to be introduced to his mom as his girlfriend. Before leaving, he told Cat, "I want you to meet my mom."

"I was wondering when that would happen since you met mine."

With a serious face, GrindFace said, "Well, to be honest, everything about you is cool, but after tonight I definitely know that I want you to meet my mom."

"What changed tonight that you did not see before?"

"I always felt like you had respect for yourself, but the night at the bus top when you went crazy on me..." he laughed before continuing, "I thought you were only not having sex because you were raped, but after tonight, I see that it's not something that you're willing to do so easily, and that it has nothing to do with what happened to you. Most girls would have been in my car having sex shortly after a kiss like that, but I could tell that you were kissing me but it was not saying, 'let's have sex.' I like that about you. You are not willing to compromise who you are to get a man. You wouldn't even give me the time of day at first. Heck, you wouldn't even kiss me on the lips for months. I'm like, 'if she wouldn't kiss me; I know she is not about to have sex with me after a tongue kiss.'

"I have had sex with many females just on account of them knowing that I was GrindFace. They were thinking that I would make them my girl. One thing I can't stand is a woman with no respect or class, and no goals; but confidence drives me crazy. Yeah, I love confidence. When we met and you had a quick comeback about my name, I was like, 'yeah that's me'."

"Okay, so when do I meet her?"

"Dang, you just jump to it. You didn't even comment on anything I had to say. I want to take you over there tomorrow."

"Well there wasn't much to say. All you did was confirm who I was, and how I carry myself— both things I already knew. Besides, no dude that is not really into someone spends the entire holiday with them and their family. So I knew meeting moms was the next step." Cat said jokingly.

"Oh, there's that confidence that I love. I'll see you tomorrow pumpkin," GrindFace said as he got into his car and drove off.

Cat went back into the house and called it a night.

Chapter 21

The next day, Cat woke up at 9 am because GrindFace didn't tell her a specific time, and she wanted to be ready, and of course, cute. There was a knock on the door an hour later and it was him. They left to his mother's house. It took them an hour to get to Victorville. Cat got out of the car. She was nervous, not knowing what to expect, and the dozens of cars outside of his mother's house did not make it any better. It looked like he had a big family—much bigger than hers based on the number of cars parked out front.

They went in and Cat walked closely behind him. There were people everywhere. They were similar to Cat's family. People were playing Spades. In another part of the house others were playing dominoes. Kids were running around. People were sitting around talking, but when they walked in it was like a celebrity had stepped into the building. Everyone was trying to give him a hug—even the little kids. Cat found it amusing that some family members called him Dimitrius but many others called him GrindFace. People were looking at her as if they were waiting for him to introduce her.

After he finished up with his hugs he pulled Cat beside him and said, "This is my girl, Cat."

They swarmed in and started to introduce themselves and greeted her with hugs. Cat did not know why they were all telling her their relation and name because it was impossible for her to remember all of them. There was one particular person that stood out to her because she did not look happy to see Cat, nor was she trying to introduce herself.

Once they made it into the kitchen and GrindFace started making their plates, she pulled him close and whispered, "Who is that girl with pink hair; the one with the blue on?"

GrindFace scanned the room to see who Cat was referring to. The girl followed them into the family room next to the kitchen and sat on the couch. His eyes locked in on the girl and she was staring right at both him and Cat.

Cat whispered, "Her, the one that keeps staring at us."

GrindFace appeared to be irritated once he recognized the mystery girl and said, "That's my ex. I don't know why she's here. Well, she's not really my ex. She's my cousin's friend, who I use to have sex with occasionally. Don't trip, hold on."

He walked away to the other side of the room to another girl. They talked for a few minutes and he made his way back to Cat. Shortly after speaking to the girl, the mystery girl got up and left out of the family room.

Cat asked who the other girl was that he was speaking to, and he said, "My cousin; I told her to tell her friend to leave. I don't even know why she was here."

His cousin walked up to Cat and apologized. Cat was impressed by his actions. He didn't want Cat to feel uncomfortable, so he handled the situation so she wouldn't be. Cat couldn't care less about the mystery girl being there. As long as she did not say anything to her, she was fine.

Finally, the woman of the house came downstairs and hugged GrindFace as if she had just given birth to him. She kissed him a dozen times. She was happy to see her son. Like Cat, GrindFace also stayed on campus on the weekends and only went home on the holidays. He introduced Cat to his mom and she embraced Cat with a tight squeeze. Cat thought that she was going to pass out. If she didn't think his mom would like her, the hug confirmed that it was genuine.

She told Cat to call her "Ms. Jay," so Cat did. Cat played Spades with his mom and aunts and fit right in because they were so much like her own family. His Aunt Ann was getting mad at Cat because she kept under bidding. Cat was playing for fun, but she quickly saw that they were very competitive. His other aunt, Jane, was a cheater, and got butt hurt when they would call her out on it. Cat started to bid appropriately to get in his aunt's good graces. They started winning and oh, did his aunt take to Cat after that. They bragged about Cat's skills and made her an official member of the family. They laughed and had a great time throughout the day.

Hours after being there, GrindFace took Cat up to his room. He laid down on his bed and put on *Power*. Now Cat was already in love but the fact that he was a *Power* and movie lover too was the icing on the cake. Cat could watch movies and Netflix for hours. She cuddled up next to him.

After the movie they watched episode after episode of *Power*. He was catching up because he had missed the last season. Cat was really into the show. She noticed that it had excessive and explicit sex scenes. She wanted to see how he would respond to watching soft porn while watching the show; but he didn't respond to it at all. She kept scooting her butt back during the sex scenes to see if his penis would rise, and it didn't. It was apparent that he was interested in the show and not the sex.

He noticed what Cat was doing and said, "No, I am not getting turned on by the show. Besides, I'm not attracted to Hispanic women, so you can stop putting your butt on me to check."

Cat started laughing because he was so in tuned with her body language. Either he was very analytical like Cat and observed everything, or he really knew her well. Either way, Cat was pleased. Cat laughed because she knew she was busted. She did not have a comeback because he called her out and she wasn't going to lie about what she was doing. They fell asleep watching *Power*.

Cat woke up to a phone call from Connie telling her that Sabrina was going into premature labor and the doctors were conducting an emergency cesarean section. GrindFace woke up after hearing the panic in Cat's voice. He sat straight up in the bed, with his back leaning on the wall. He waited for Cat to end the call as he listened to what she was saying to her mom. Based on what Cat was saying, he knew that something was wrong with Sabrina and her unborn child. Cat ended the call and told GrindFace that she had to leave. He got up and put his shoes on, and started to walk into the living room. Cat followed behind him. It was midnight and most of his family had left, but there were family members still there. They were playing games and sitting around talking and laughing. Cat was trying to tell everyone 'bye' to not seem rude. GrindFace grabbed her hand and rushed her out the door.

Once in the car he said, "You didn't have to say 'bye'; you will see them again; they understand. Where are we going?"

"Kaiser; in Ontario—off of the 60 freeway."

He started to speed down the streets and Cat got nervous. She thought about Bobby and the night of his fatal car accident. Cat gripped the side of the door. "Please slow down," she begged.

He could see that she was terrified. He slowed down and drove according to the speed limit. He remembered Cat telling him about the way her ex-boyfriend died and he tried soothing her by running his hand over her head and the back of her neck. Cat calmed down right away.

"I just hope she doesn't lose the baby. I hope Rakheem is there and does what he said he was going to do," Cat said to GrindFace. He let her talk out of her frustration and he actively listened to her. It took them an hour to get to the hospital.

As they pulled up, Cat saw her mom's car. Cat was hesitant to walk in at first because she didn't want to hear any bad news. Cat and GrindFace went into the hospital and asked if they could see Sabrina. The receptionist sent them to the maternity ward. Cat walked into the room and found Sabrina crying and asking the nurses if her baby was going to be okay. She had already had the surgery and the baby was in the intensive care unit by the time Cat arrived. Cat hugged Sabrina and told her that it would be okay. Cat asked Connie if she had notified Rakheem. Connie did not want Sabrina to get upset so she nodded, yes, so Sabrina would not know her response. Cat caught on to what her mom was doing, and was furious that he was not at the hospital. She went for her phone to start texting him and GrindFace grabbed her phone—basically, telling her to let Sabrina handle her own affairs.

Two hours had passed and Rakheem was still not at the hospital, and by this time, even Sabrina noticed it. She called him on speakerphone and asked if he was coming to the hospital.

He said, "I don't want to get attached to the baby until I know that it's mine. After the DNA test is done, and I know if it's mine, then I will see the baby. I just don't want to get attached then it not be my baby."

Sabrina put her head down and asked, "Are you at least going to come and sign the birth certificate?"

"No, I have to go." he said, and hung up the phone.

Connie and Cat hurt for Sabrina; they felt her pain and disappointment. Cat could not miss the opportunity to be honest with her sister, just as she did with Samantha.

Cat sat on Sabrina's hospital bed and said, "Sabrina you have to be honest with yourself. As bad as it hurts, you put yourself in this position. You cannot be mad at Rakheem for not wanting to get attached to a baby that might not be his. You created this situation, and now you want him to fall in line with your request. That is not realistic, Sabrina. I'm going to be honest, at first, I was mad too, but I had to be real with myself. If I were in his position, I would feel the same way. I can't be a hypocrite because you're my sister. I think for him to continue to treat you with respect says a lot about his character. Most guys would have gone around saying that the baby isn't theirs and he hasn't said anything. He wants to wait for the results to see how he wants to move forward."

Sabrina lifted her head and looked at Cat and said, "Everything that you're saying is true, but that doesn't change the fact that it still hurts."

"Yeah, it hurts; but it hurts because you put yourself in a position to be hurt. Learn from this and make sure that this is something you will never do again. Because you never saw the beauty in you, you let others define it for you—even if it meant your beauty and worth were defined by sex. You not knowing your worth and believing that you were good enough made you settle, and this is the result of settling and allowing yourself to be used for temporary gratification. Now, I have to ask, was it worth it?"

Sabrina looked at Cat and rolled her eyes and said, "Yeah it was worth it, really Cat. I get it. I made a dumb decision out of my own insecurities. I get it."

"As long as you get it to prevent it from happening again, I'm okay with getting on your nerves," Cat said as she kissed Sabrina on the head.

Cat looked over at Connie and asked if she was staying the night with Sabrina. Connie said, "Yes. Grandma Pie is at the house with the kids so I don't need you to go home."

Cat and GrindFace hugged both Sabrina and Connie and said goodbye. When they were on their way back to the car, GrindFace asked Cat if she wanted him to drop her off at her house, and she said, "No."

"Okay, well where do you want to go?" He asked. "I don't know; surprise me," Cat said as she continued walking toward the car.

They got into the car and GrindFace drove in the opposite direction of his house, so it was obvious they were not going back there. As they got closer to her house and the school, he took a different freeway. She learned that night that he was spontaneous—another characteristic that she loved. Cat asked for a surprise so he was giving her what she asked for. He stopped at a twenty-four hour Wal-Mart and told her to stay in the car. When he came out of the store he put the bags in the trunk. Cat tried to be nosey to see what he had but she couldn't see from the passenger seat. He got back into the car and drove along the streets. By this time it was 3am. They arrived at the beach. He popped the trunk and got the bags out. Cat stayed in the car. She didn't like the fact that he didn't open her car door. So she thought to herself, 'do I just get out or stay in the car so he can come and open my door?' Cat decided on staying in the car and letting him open her door. She wanted to make her expectations known without settling. She did not want him to get accustomed to not opening her door.

GrindFace looked at her, waiting for her to get out the car. He figured she was trying to do something before she got out. He walked ahead. Cat called out his name. He turned around and stood there waiting for her to speak.

"Are you going to open my door?"

He went back to the car and said, "All the times you rode in my car, why are you asking for me to open your door today?"

"Because after talking to Sabrina, I realized that I too, was settling. This is something that I'm accustomed to and I should have told you. But now I'm telling you what my expectations are so that you will know."

Cat rolled her window up and GrindFace opened her door with one hand, and the bags in the other, and said, "Okay, since we are making our expectations known; I like a woman that helps her man and is a team player. Can you help me carry some of the bags?" Cat laughed and grabbed the bags as she peeked in and saw a blanket.

They walked closer to the water and he sat the bags down and grabbed out a tent. He handed Cat a flashlight to hold so that he could set up the tent. Once he was finished, he laid a blanket and pillows down inside. He had drinks and snacks that he put in the tent as well. Once that was done, they both climbed in and laid on their backs, side by side. He talked about his dreams and aspirations, of what he wanted to be, and where he saw himself ten years from now. Cat listened in awe, wanting to be present in the moment and mentally noting every word that came out of his mouth. He turned over on his side and asked Cat where she saw herself in ten years.

Cat turned on her side facing him and said, "With you." They both laughed and GrindFace said, "Besides that. What do you envision?" "I see myself married with kids. I really want to be different from what my mom has shown me. I don't want to be another statistic. That's why I don't want to have sex until I am totally secure in my relationship, but most importantly, secure within myself. I want to be a therapist and have my own private practice, like Mrs.

Mayo. I mean, the possibilities are limitless," Cat answered.

As the night went on, they talked about cycles and how they wanted to break them, which brought them to discussing Sabrina.

"I like how you handled that situation with Sabrina by telling her the truth. If I were Rakheem, I would feel the same way. That's what I meant when I was saying that you stand apart from other females because of the way you carry yourself. Men treat women how they silently ask to be treated. If a girl behaves like a ho' then I will treat her like a ho'. You can't meet me and within a week, I hit it, and now you're asking me to open your door and to meet my family. I mean, it just doesn't work like that. Females get mad and say that 'all men are dogs,' but we treat them according to the manual they give us. I knew right off the bat that I couldn't just tell you whatever and the panties were coming off, which made me want to pursue you because you actually interested me outside of looks and sex. You are the first girl I let meet moms, and it's funny, because she told me when you were playing Spades that you must be my wife because I've never brought a girl home.

"When I think of marriage, I think of marrying a woman that can teach my daughters what a woman looks like. I was telling Rakheem that moving forward, he needs to strap up or don't have sex at all, because a temporary situation can lead to a lifetime of problems. I think Sabrina is a good girl that got caught up in the moment, so I feel bad for her. But like you said, she put herself in that situation. Even if we don't work out Cat, don't ever let a dude come into your life and give you the bare minimum, because I would be so disappointed."

Cat started laughing and he abruptly interrupted her laugh and said, "You were supposed to say that we're not going to ever break up."

"Naw bro, that's what you wanted me to say," Cat said, as they both laughed.

The next week they were back at school. Cat had been thinking about her life because she had to do a presentation for her English class. The assignment was to write a paper about what they had learned throughout their life. Cat was nervous because over the past weeks she had watched her classmates give their presentations, and they were basic and boring. All the things she thought about presenting would expose who she was and what she had been through. She didn't want to completely share her story, but she wanted to make an impact. She had talked to both Connie and GrindFace about being exposed and telling her truth in front of a room full of strangers. Connie was apprehensive and GrindFace told Cat to go for it. He always encouraged her to step out of the box, but Cat was still unsure about the assignment, so she reached out to the one person that she knew would give her healthy advice.

Cat called Mrs. Mayo. She was not available and would be on vacation for the next two weeks, but Cat's presentation was due the following Monday. Cat was fearful of not only getting a bad grade, but also not knowing what to talk about. She got up and stood in the mirror.

Cat opened her mouth and started speaking. She told a story as if she was speaking about another person.

"There was a little girl that watched her mother go through men like they were candy. She was embarrassed and ashamed to call that woman her mother in the presence of other people. At the age of eight, that same little girl walked in on her mother having sex with the neighbor's husband. The little girl thought sex and scheming was the way to a man's heart. By the time she was ten, she witnessed women come to her house day after day, to fight the woman that she was ashamed to publicly call momma. At the age of eleven, the little girl had been sent to school with bruises so often that the school could not avoid calling Child Protective Services. When they came, they were men, and she watched the lady she called momma perform oral sex right in her living room, from the entrance of her bedroom door. By the time she was twelve, she had no interest in boys, disgusted by their interactions with her mother, blaming all males for their role in her mother's behavior. By the time she was sixteen, she had already seen everything that kids her age only thought about. She had five siblings that she cared for and she was only sixteen. The little girl moved to California and a man that she called uncle, raped her. She was fatherless until a man by the name of Reggie showed up on her doorstep." Cat continued on and spoke of all the bad things that had happened to her.

GrindFace had snuck in the dorm and was standing in the doorway of Cat's room. Cat was so caught up in her speech that she didn't realize that he was standing there. Cat continued as he watched in disappointment. Cat knew she wanted to be a conqueror and thought that she was displaying that, which she was. However, she had been seeing herself through the lens of others. So when she told her story, she told it as a spectator, watching empathetically.

GrindFace interrupted her and said, "Is that all you have to talk about?"

Cat got startled and looked up at GrindFace. "What?"

"I said, is that all you have to talk about? Because the girl I know has a lot more victories than what is being told in that story. Is that the way you're going to write your story? Because I think it's missing a whole lot of stories and it needs some editing. People need to hear the downfalls as well as the victories because the Cat I know is victorious. So I am asking you, how are you going to write your story?"

Cat looked at him and then turned around and looked back at herself in the mirror. She felt her confidence grow as she said, "I am not a victim, but a conqueror; and today, I want to introduce Cat." Cat looked in the mirror, fearless and bold. She stood straight up, with her shoulders back and her projection loud and clear. She then said, "I am the conqueror because today, I have chosen to rewrite my story."

Recommended Reads

Identifying & Breaking the Cycle By: Saniyyah Mayo

Be Seen Not heard By: Dimitrius Mayo

Building Kingdom Children By: Jamondo & Lainey Leno

Father, Daddy, Dad By: Natasha Sayles

Battlefield of the Mind By: Joyce Myers